The

AMISH
CHRISTMAS
KITCHEN

The AMISH CHRISTMAS KITCHEN

KELLY LONG

JENNIFER BECKSTRAND

LISA JONES BAKER

KENSINGTON BOOKS
www.kensingtonbooks.com

KENSINGTON BOOKS are published by

Kensington Publishing Corp.
119 West 40th Street
New York, NY 10018

Compilation copyright © 2016 by Kensington Publishing Corp.
"Baking Love on Ice Mountain" © 2016 by Kelly Long
"The Christmas Bakery on Huckleberry Hill" © 2016 by Jennifer Beckstrand
"The Special Christmas Cookie" © 2016 by Lisa Jones Baker

All Kensington titles, imprints, and distributed lines are available at special quantity discounts for bulk purchases for sales promotion, premiums, fund-raising, and educational or institutional use. Special book excerpts or customized printings can also be created to fit specific needs. For details, write or phone the office of the Kensington Sales Manager: Kensington Publishing Corp., 119 West 40th Street, New York, NY 10018. Attn. Sales Department. Phone: 1-800-221-2647.

Kensington and the K logo Reg. U.S. Pat. & TM Off.

ISBN-13: 978-1-4967-0592-1
ISBN-10: 1-4967-0592-0
First Kensington Trade Paperback Edition: October 2016
First Kensington Mass Market Edition: October 2017

eISBN-13: 978-1-4967-0593-8
eISBN-10: 1-4967-0593-9
First Kensington Electronic Edition: October 2016

10 9 8 7 6 5 4 3 2 1

Printed in the United States of America

CONTENTS

BAKING LOVE ON ICE MOUNTAIN

KELLY LONG

For Joy

PROLOGUE

Early October, Ice Mountain, Pennsylvania

The ominous *crack* of the giant pine tree ricocheted through the forest and twenty-one-year-old Daniel Kauffman knew a sudden and resonating fear in his chest.

"Bad cut!" he hollered, dropping his ax and scrambling to move as fast as he could through the wet leaves underfoot. "Run!" he screamed, glancing back to see that his best friend, Seth Loftus, still hadn't moved.

The tree fell with deadly force, catching Daniel with the tips of its branches and clawing the back of his neck to stinging rawness. But then there was silence, a deafening stillness once the pine met the earth and settled. Daniel stopped running and turned, listening.

"Seth?" He started to climb over the branches. "Seth!"

He worked his way back, heedless of the dense

limbs, and found his friend lying in a widening stain of crimson against the mixed colors of the autumn leaves. Seth's lower body was trapped, and Daniel frantically began to claw at the earth, trying to dig around the huge trunk.

"Dan?"

"I'm here, Seth. Right here. I'm gonna get you out."

"*Nee* . . . please . . . *kumme* . . ."

Daniel swallowed hard as he looked up to the bloody hand raised in faint petition. He scrambled to his friend's side and bent low to cradle Seth's head.

"Let me get you out," Daniel pleaded.

"It was a widow-maker—this tree. Should have known . . ."

"Seth, please . . ." He watched Seth's blue eyes focus for a moment as he appeared to rally and reached to grasp the collar of Daniel's black coat.

"Dan, I want you to promise me something."

"*Jah,* anything."

Seth half smiled. "Clara is beautiful, inside and out."

"I know. I know." An image of Seth's wife's wide pansy eyes flashed through Daniel's mind, and he blinked away sudden tears.

"She loves baking and cooking. . . ."

Daniel choked on a sob as his friend's breathing became labored.

"You gotta take your time with Clara. She's as shy as a doe," Seth coughed. A tiny bubble of blood appeared beside his mouth.

"Don't talk, Seth. Save your strength."

"*Nee* . . . Promise . . . promise me you'll marry her,

take care of her. . . . You're the best . . . best man I know."

Daniel drew in a harsh breath.

"Promise me, Dan."

He nodded feverishly. "I promise you, Seth."

Seth's grip loosened on his coat as his broken body relaxed.

Minutes later, Daniel allowed wrenching tears to fall as he rocked his dead friend until the cold seeped through and the *nacht* drew near.

He finally walked away to get help to move the body, and he recalled the promise he'd given in desperation—a heart pledge made in a moment of panic but forged by the enduring grip of love. . . .

CHAPTER 1

Early December, Ice Mountain, Two Years Later

"You've become a recluse."

The young widow, Clara Loftus, heard the obvious concern in her older sister Sarah's words but didn't bother to disagree with the statement.

"So?" Clara shrugged her shoulders and reached into the wooden box of weekly supplies Sarah had brought from the mountain store. She looked up when Sarah caught her by the shoulders.

"Listen, Clara, I really mean it and I can't keep helping you stay holed up in this cabin forever. Seth has been gone for a long time, and he wouldn't want you to be living like this."

Clara sighed. "Sarah, I know you're the healer for the community, but I'm fine. . . ." She straightened her spine. "I have Blinks"—she gestured to the blue-eyed animal at her heels—"and it's winter. This cabin is too far up in the timberline for me to make it out a lot."

Sarah dropped her hands to her hips. "Somehow I manage to get up here every week with grocery staples, despite the distance and the snow. So you could stand to come down to the store. This is the last lot of supplies I'm bringing, Clara."

Clara knew instinctively that it hurt Sarah to be so firm. She reached out and squeezed her older sister's arms. "All right, Sarah. I'll *kumme* down if I need something."

Sarah shook her bonneted head. "But you won't admit that you need—anything. And that's what worries me."

Clara smiled, then handed her sister a small plate of cookies. "Here's some pralines I made last *nacht*. Just kiss my niece and nephew and that big, brooding husband of yours and leave the rest to me."

But when Sarah had gone and the light jingle of sleigh bells had faded into the distance of the frosty morning air, Clara sank into a kitchen chair and put her head in her hands. *If only I could truly find purpose in being part of the Ice Mountain community again. . . . Seth was always the social one, and now I—I am a recluse. . . .* She lifted her head as the goat brushed against her skirts. "But that's *gut* enough for me. . . . Right, Blinks?" she said aloud. "And I'm going to completely ignore the fact that I feel more comfortable talking to a goat than any person. . . ."

The warm glaze of sugar melted in a languorous slide down Daniel Kauffman's lean throat, and he closed his eyes to further savor the delight of the sweet.

"*Gut,* isn't it, *buwe?*" Bishop Umble asked from where he stood in the Kauffman family store.

Daniel opened his eyes and looked down into the wise *auld* face of his community's leader. "*Jah,* who made it?"

"Hmmm? *Ach,* the *gut* widow, Clara Loftus."

Daniel choked and the bishop slapped him on the back but continued talking. "*Jah.* Her sister brought a small plate of sweets down from the high timber and thought I might like a taste. I doubt there's a better baker on the mountain than Frau Loftus—but don't tell my missus that. Hmm . . . Clara has been a widow for nigh on two years now. I wonder how she's getting by without Seth?"

Daniel shrugged, feeling shaken inside. *I should have tried harder with her, kept trying. . . .* "*Take it slow . . . take it slow with Clara. . . .*" "The community sees to the care of widows and"—he began awkwardly.

"Oh, *ach,* I know that, but I'm talking about her spirit, her heart. It's bound to be lonesome up in that far cabin."

"I guess."

"*Gut* point," Bishop Umble agreed. "So you promise to return her plate to her tonight? You know women and their dishes. And you might also invite her down to a little gathering Martha and I are having in two days' time. . . . Ask her to make some more of these cookies, too." The leader cleared his throat. "Well, I appreciate it."

Daniel lifted a protesting hand. "Wait . . . what?"

"I'm going over to chat with your *fater* about some harnesses I ordered. *Danki, sohn.*"

Daniel watched helplessly as the bishop threaded his way through the busy store. He wanted to cry out to the *auld* leader to stop, that he'd made no promise. . . . *I didn't promise. . . . I never promised. . . .* But Bishop Umble had a strange way of getting around a man, and Daniel knew he'd be making the trip on up the mountain that evening, willing or not.

More than two years after her husband's death, Clara found herself grieving on the wood-pegged kitchen floor of the cabin's kitchen. She'd broken what had been Seth's favorite bowl—the heavy light blue one with the chip in the edge, the one she could still see him spooning soup or oatmeal from—a simple thing, but now shattered into small memories in the fading rays of the late afternoon sun. And she cried. She took out her hankie, blew her nose prodigiously, then looked up in surprise as a knock sounded on the cabin door.

It can't be Sarah again. . . . For a moment, she felt a clutch of fear that it might be a stranger, but then she rose to her feet in determination. *If Derr Herr wants me to be kidnapped or worse, then so be it. . . .*

She walked the few steps it took to open the door, then stepped back in sudden surprise and confusion.

Daniel Kauffman stood on her small front porch, his overly long chestnut hair tousled by the wind and his green eyes steady and penetrating as he stared down at her. *He's handsome enough to be a model,* she thought darkly, suddenly recalling an Englisch magazine she'd once hidden under her mattress during her long-ago rumspringa.

"What do you want?" she snapped, then bit her lip. *Didn't I say the same thing two years ago—has it been that long? Two years ago when he came calling with his ridiculous proposal . . .* To add to her irritation, she felt herself flush in remembrance while his eyes narrowed as if in consideration of her response. "Well?" she demanded again, resisting the urge to squint as the last of the sun's rays slipped over the mountain.

"May I *kumme* in?" he asked gently, and she felt his words held a mild rebuke at her lack of manners.

Although she had slowly ceased participating in anything much communal but church now and then since Seth had died, she still remembered the niceties. "*Nee.*"

He smiled then, a flash of white teeth in the new dusk, almost as if he'd expected her answer, and shifted his weight from one long leg to the other. He tapped his black hat against his thigh, and her gaze was irresistibly drawn to his shadowed waist for a millisecond.

She looked up, appalled at her reaction, and moved to slam the door in his face. But he shot one strong hand out and caught the wood, staying her for the moment.

"Look," she finally managed, as if she'd picked up on the conversation they'd had two years ago. "I do not want to marry you!" She stamped a small foot to punctuate her declaration.

He bent close, almost as if he was going to whisper in her ear, and she let go of the door in confusion. He ran a long finger down her hot cheek, and then, to her surprise, tapped her lightly on the nose in time to his own words. "And I—no longer want to marry you, Widow Loftus."

She felt her mouth round in surprise. "*Ach,*" she whispered. "Then, what—I mean . . ."

"Praline cookies," he announced, pulling back to turn up his collar as a brisk spray of snow blew past.

"What?"

He shrugged. "Bishop Umble requests a platter of your praline cookies, and your, er, presence, of course, at a small gathering he's having in two days' time. Though I hardly think your baking is necessary, because I make the best cookies on the mountain. But . . . the bishop seems to be laboring under some memory or another of your past attempts in the kitchen and—"

"My . . . attempts?" She felt more riled than she had in a long time, and she frowned up at him while she mentally thumbed through her recipe box. "I'll have you know that I'm an excellent baker." She sniffed. "And since when do men like you . . . I mean . . . men bake?"

He put his hat on and gave her a faint bow. "The great bakers are all men—be they Amisch or Englisch. So, are you going to make the pralines—or what?"

He sounded both doubtful and bored and she lifted her chin. "You can count on it."

"Okaay . . . Why, hello." He bent, and she watched him run the back of one strong hand over Blink's fur while the goat tried to twine itself 'round his boots. She frowned down at her mischievous companion and tried to shoo the animal back inside, but Blinks was enthralled. Only after a long, uncomfortable minute on Clara's part did Daniel rise to his full height. "I like goats," he said simply, not questioning the oddness of actually having one as a house pet.

She frowned and nodded, telling herself she wanted him gone. But then he reached a hand inside his heavy coat and drew out a circular, brown paper–wrapped object. "The true reason for my visit." He smiled. "Your cookie plate."

"Uh . . . *danki*." She clutched the parcel to her chest, then jerked it away, realizing that its warmth had come from the heat between his shirt and the black wool coat. He lifted a dark brow at her, then touched his hat and turned. She heard his clear whistle as he tucked his hands in his pockets and started to walk in the boot-printed trail she now saw in the shadowy snow. Then she shut the door and leaned hard against it, her breathing rapid.

"All the great bakers are men. . . ." she muttered aloud as she bent to pet the goat as it took an idle nibble of her skirts. "We'll show him, Miss Blinks, even though you are a little traitor, letting him pet you." Then she stood and put the wrapped plate on the table and tried to ignore the fact that the man had stroked her skin, as well. . . . *One tan finger down my cheek . . . No man has touched me since Seth. . . .*

She pushed aside the nagging thought and hurriedly swept up the remains of the blue bowl from the kitchen floor. Then she reached with determination for her recipe box and turned up a lamp.

CHAPTER 2

"*All the great bakers are men. . . .*" Daniel almost laughed out loud when he recalled his words to Clara as he mounted the steps to the family store later that evening. Although he knew he was a good baker, primarily out of necessity since childhood, neither he nor his family had ever admitted the fact to anyone else. While some Amisch men might help out around the kitchen now and then, with firewood or fetching water, Daniel knew the idea of a man baking on a regular basis wouldn't be widely accepted. *And here I've proclaimed it on the mountaintop to Clara Loftus. . . .*

But, I did get her . . . goat. He smiled grimly in the darkness. *I certainly made a better impression on her today than I did two years ago. . . . Gott . . . I'm sorry, Seth. I haven't cared for her in the way you wanted. . . . But you were right,* auld *friend. . . . She is beautiful.* And tonight there'd been a snap of life in her large gray eyes that had transmitted itself like a wash of intimacy down the center of his back and he'd shivered beneath his heavy coat, feeling unaccountably pleasured.

He tried to put aside the remembered sensation as he opened the heavy white door and the familiar jangle of an overhead bell greeted him. His *daed,* Ben Kauffman, popped his large frame out from behind some shelving, obviously thinking it was some late customer.

"*Ach,* Dan . . . turn the CLOSED sign over, will you? I've got to finish stocking these jellies and then your *mamm* has supper going though she's waiting on you to whip up some angel biscuits. Where have you been, *sohn?*"

Daniel turned the sign, though he knew his *daed* would open for anyone on the mountain, no matter the time, in the event of a sudden or urgent need. He walked across the wooden floor, knowing its creaks by heart, and automatically bent to help his *fater* finish stocking the jelly jars that bore homemade labels from several of the local women.

"I was up near the timberline, Daed. Having a bit of a walk."

His father eyed him directly. "*Ach* . . . well, then, I hope you stopped by to cut Clara Loftus a load of firewood."

Daniel felt a sudden tightness in his chest as he looked away. "*Nee,* Daed. I'll not cut timber up near that spot again."

His *fater's* big brown eyes immediately welled with emotion as he reached out to touch Daniel's shoulder. "Forgive me then, *sohn.* I forget that it's been only two years since Seth . . . and you . . ."

Daniel quickly embraced his *daed,* then pulled away. "It's all right, Daed. Look, I'd better get at those biscuits, okay?"

His *fater* nodded, pulling his white store apron up

to wipe his nose; Daniel patted his back, then walked away through the store to the back kitchen, mentally preparing the ingredients for angel biscuits to go with the fragrant venison stew his *mamm* was stirring over the woodstove.

Daniel slipped off his coat and hat and hung them on the wooden pegs near the store's entrance. He called out greetings to his numerous siblings, who were already seated around the table with a general air of expectation.

"The *kinner* be hungry tonight," his mother observed as Daniel bent to kiss her plump cheek. "Can you whip up those angel biscuits of yours?"

"Sure, Mamm."

He'd learned to bake angel biscuits and a myriad of other things, mainly by trial and taste, when he was ten years *auld*. His mother had been on necessary bed rest with one of her pregnancies, and while his *daed* was busy at the store, it had fallen on Daniel, as the eldest child, to become "the *mamm*" for a time.

Now he rolled up his blue shirtsleeves as he grabbed the homemade soap and started to wash his hands at the pump sink. He was drying off on an old tea towel when he remembered something vital to his recipe.

"I need my secret ingredient, Mamm. I'll just run back into the store for a minute."

There was a flatteringly collective groan from the hungry *kinner* at the table, and Daniel had to smile. Then he wondered with a sudden shiver of warmth whether Clara Loftus might have any secret ingredients of her own. . . .

* * *

Long after midnight, Clara sought the relative comfort of the wood-framed bed that she and Seth had once shared. Blinks was settled in her usual mound of quilts on the floor, gently snoring. "I'm glad you can sleep," Clara whispered to the animal, then sighed heavily in the dimness of the moonlit room.

Okay . . . okay, Gott . . . so having Daniel Kauffman appear on my front porch today was odd. It made me . . . unsettled.

She glanced over at Seth's feather pillow, the one she faithfully changed the case on every week, and gave it a sudden thump that oddly made her feel better for a moment. Then she laid her head down on her own pillow, closed her eyes resolutely, and drifted into fitful sleep.

She dreamed that an angel with wings like ice stood beside her bed, bending with tender, luminescent fingers to gently stroke her forehead, stirring up memories and bringing back a past she didn't want to face. . . .

"Try," the angel urged in a voice that pulsed with white light. "Try to bear remembering."

They wouldn't let her see him, no matter how much she fought. She wanted to see all of him—crushed in two or not, he was still hers. . . . But not hers . . . Gott was bigger. Gott took and gave. She clawed through the red haze of the jumbled words, and then there was only green. Steady green eyes; determined, resolute . . . Marry me . . . I'll care for you. . . . I know I can never be Seth . . . but . . . Nee . . . she screamed. Again and again until the words pounded like fists on the broad shoulders of the living man and he'd turned away—leaving her alone. Time and grief convulsed with thought and purpose like labor pains must be, and she cried out, seeing herself weeping, longing . . . needing . . . Let me see him once more . . . his green eyes. Marry me; marry him. . . . She grasped the cookie plate and tried to hold it steady, but her hand shook and she watched it fall, breaking in two. . . .

Clara awoke with a gasp, staring frantically into the shadowed darkness, feeling Blinks lick her hand. She pushed her hair out of her eyes and tried to slow the racing of her heartbeat. *A dream . . . only a dream . . .* She pulled Seth's pillow close for a moment, seeking any warmth in its pristine chill, then flung it from her to land with a soft *thud* across the room.

In the cool, moonlit confines of his narrow bed, Daniel was dreaming. He knew it on some level but he couldn't wake. . . .

Hot, chocolate-drizzled cookies overflowed from Clara's hands as she reached out to him. He wanted to lick the sticky goodness that dripped between her slender fingers and twine his hands in her loose blond hair. "Clara is as shy as a doe . . . gotta take it slow." *Slow. But Daniel was hot and his mouth ached for a taste of her full lips. Seth's wife . . . Seth's wife . . . Entrusted, treasured, given . . . Mine. The word seared itself inside his eyelids, and he reached for her, intent on taking what she offered. But then a large goat blocked his way and Clara was suddenly distant and removed, half-turned from him. Absurd that a goat should stand between them. . . . He moved to push the animal away and fell on a patch of ice. Then he was a child again, making snow angels in rising biscuit dough. . . .*

He woke, sweating, and slipped on his pants. He needed a drink of water to banish the strangeness of his thoughts and crept quietly downstairs toward the kitchen.

"Can't sleep, *buwe*?"

Daniel nearly jumped as he passed his grandfater's bed in the dark living room.

"Da, you scared me to death. Are you all right?" Daniel moved through the shadows and turned a kerosene lamp up low as he blinked at his elder.

Sol Kauffman had once been a big bear of a man, but now, at nearly ninety-two, his frame had shrunk and his mind drifted between the past and the present with a lot of odd statements in between. But tonight, he looked at Daniel with seemingly lucid eyes and sat up as if wanting a midnight chat.

Daniel suppressed a sigh and sank into a nearby chair, sliding it close to the comfortable couch.

"You've been dreaming, *sohn*?"

Daniel smiled in surprise at the accurate assumption. "*Jah.*"

"*Ach.*" Sol reached a heavily veined hand to brush at his long white beard. "About a woman, no doubt."

"Yeah, I'm afraid so."

"Well, that be your problem, *buwe*. Yer afraid . . . of her?" The faded blue eyes seemed to search the heart beneath Daniel's bare chest.

Daniel looked away. "*Nee* . . . she just . . . Well, it's not an easy situation, Da."

"Because of the promise you made to Seth Loftus that day in the wood?"

Daniel turned to stare at his grandfather and felt his heart begin to pound in his throat. *I've never told a living soul what Seth asked of me the day he died—not even Clara. She just thought I was* narrisch . . . *asking her to marry me so soon—after . . .*

He cleared his throat. "Da, how do you . . . What are you talking about?"

Sol gave him a toothless smile. "You think I'm alone all *nacht* down here, *sohn? Nee* . . . when I cannot sleep, I talk with the angels. 'Twas an angel what told me about when Seth wuz dyin' and him asking you to take his Clara in marriage . . . A heavy load to bear, I'm thinkin' . . . a heavy load."

Daniel wondered if he was still dreaming when he leaned closer to the *auld* man and touched his hand. "Da . . . did . . . did the angel tell you how I can keep my promise to Seth? Because Clara won't have me, and . . ."

His grandfather startled with a jerk and a frown, his bushy white brows nearly meeting. "What? What's that you say?"

"Clara Loftus, Da . . . the angel?" Daniel felt a surge of desperation.

"You woke me up for such foolishness as this? Turn the lamp down—it be the middle of the *nacht!*"

Daniel pulled back in confusion, then hastened to rise and turn down the lamp. He had no desire to wake his folks upstairs, but he wanted desperately to keep talking with his grandfather. Yet in moments, his da was snoring and Daniel stood with his fists clenched in the dark room, unbidden tears in his eyes. *I'm going crazy,* he decided. *Truly crazy . . . Maybe I should go back to bed and pray. . . .*

But in his heart, he wondered if Gott would hear the prayers of a man who did not keep a promise that even the angels knew. . . .

CHAPTER 3

The following morning dawned bright and cold while Clara stared, vexed, into the recesses of a cabinet. She'd woken early in the hopes of banishing the vestiges of her dream and tried to focus solely on baking.

"We need pecans," she cried in sudden dismay to Blinks.

The goat lived up to her name and blinked in solemn acknowledgment.

"We have to go down to the store!" *And I might see Daniel again. . . .* The intensity of his forest-green eyes was fresh enough in her mind to make her distinctly uncomfortable, but she squared her shoulders. She could not allow the possibility of him outbaking her.

She rushed into the bedroom with Blinks at her heels and began to layer on clothing. "Sarah is right," Clara grumbled aloud. "I should keep a horse and sleigh for emergencies." She struggled to add a third skirt atop her normal dress and almost fell over.

Then she straightened and gave her normally trim hips a ruthless pat. "Okay . . . so I look like a snowman. Who cares?" But she could not deny the little voice inside her head that mocked her words. *You care . . . because you'd like to look your best in front of . . .* him.

"Bah!" she exclaimed as she tugged on her bonnet and tied the strings with a jerk. Blinks echoed her sentiment. *Baaaa . . .* Clara rolled her eyes heavenward, grabbed her pocketbook, and opened the door with the goat following. She took one determined step off the front porch and fell flat on her face. She floundered and got to her feet, realizing that she had underestimated the depth of the snow that had fallen overnight. Even when she let Blinks out to see to the animal's needs or to her milking, the powdery white was not usually so deep. She sighed, knowing she'd end up sodden and dripping by the time she got to Kauffman's store, but the thought of the necessary pecans kept her moving at a slow but determined pace.

Daniel normally cut timber or worked in Joseph King's furniture shop doing fine crafting of wood. But today he'd promised to help his *daed* for a few hours, decorating the store for Christmas. It wasn't the tradition of his people to do much more than greenery and a tree with homemade ornaments, but Daniel knew his *daed* believed that the tang of pine and cedar was an aromatic balm to the senses and made for a better shopping atmosphere.

"Daniel Kauffman, you smell like Christmas."

He turned, suppressing a faint sigh, his arms full

of greenery, when he recognized the feminine whisper of Ruby Zook.

"Hello, Ruby." He nodded, intent on getting to work, when she stepped closer, her long skirt touching his legs. *Will the girl pursue me even in the middle of my* fater*'s store?* But he knew the answer to his own internal question. Ruby was pretty and dead focused—that was being seventeen. He didn't want to be rude, but he'd become weary of late when she approached him at every gathering.

"Do you need some help placing the greens?" she asked.

"Nee, *danki*, I—"

"Now, that's a fine offer, Dan," his *daed* boomed from behind him. "Especially coming from so pretty a customer."

Daniel wanted to run. The dual implications of the customer always being of primary significance and his *fater*'s thinking that he should have long since been a grandfather could be heard in the expectant tone, not to mention the accompanying nudge to his shoulder.

Daniel forced a smile. *How am I supposed to explain that I don't want a pretty girl with eyes as focused as a cobra's? How do I say that I'm waiting for Clara, that I need to . . .*

"So, I can help?" Ruby reached for some of the boughs, her fingernails grazing his shirtfront. He wanted to roll his eyes but handed over a good number of pine branches instead.

His *daed* had backed off, and Daniel eased through the cheerful bustle of the store to the first deep-set windowsill. He'd started to lay the boughs, trying to ignore Ruby's innuendo-filled chatter, when the shop doorbell jangled and he was struck by the odd cessation of conversation behind him. He glanced over his shoulder, then took a hasty second look as he recognized the beautiful face beneath the wilting black bonnet. *Soaked* didn't even begin to describe the misshapen and dripping Clara Loftus.

He dropped the cedar branches into Ruby's arms, ignoring her hiss of protest, and started toward Clara. She was breathing in gusty little gasps, clearly worn out.

"Widow Loftus? Are you—all right?" he asked quietly. "Clara?"

He was aware of his *daed* hovering on the periphery and the slow resumption of conversation, but all he could truly see were her gray eyes and their fringe of ridiculously long black lashes. *Why haven't I pursued her? Why did I let her go so easily? Turn me away? Gott . . . Help me. Help me, Seth. Help me know what to say to her here. . . .*

"Blinks is outside. I can't take long. I need pecans." She glared up at him, and he thought of a gray kitten he'd found once in a dim cellar as a *buwe*. The small creature had swatted at his attempts to help, but he'd gradually earned her trust with gentle hands and timely persistence.

Daniel smiled with tenderness into her pink, upturned face. "Daed, she needs pecans. I'm going to take her out to the kitchen to warm up."

"I'm fine. I told you . . . Blinks—"

"We'll bring her in. Clair Bitner always runs his goat, Benny, into the store when he drops off the milk we sell."

She swallowed and he waited, wondering if he'd

pressed too hard, suggesting he take her to the back kitchen.

"Well, I could use a bit of a rest, I guess, and—"

"Why, Daniel," Ruby Zook said in a carrying tone. "What poor wet crow do we have here?"

Daniel didn't miss the way Clara's full lips set in a grim line as she swept a glance downward over her black garb, and he wanted to rap Ruby's knuckles for her calculated comment.

Instead, he reached out and gently caught one of Clara's small hands in its thin black glove and gave her an experimental pull. To his surprise, she moved, but her chin came up with determination as she passed Ruby.

Daniel was about to make some retort to the girl's crow comment, when Clara spoke in a clear voice.

"Not a crow, Ruby Zook—a raven. With hard claws."

Ruby looked abashed, and Daniel didn't hide his grin as he led the dripping Widow Loftus down the center aisle of the store, heedless of his *fater*'s dazed expression and the sensation he knew he was creating among the customers. He understood that a young, single Amisch man didn't make a show of holding a widow's hand or suggesting that he take her somewhere private to seek warmth, but he didn't care. For the first time, Clara was yielding to him and it felt more than *gut*. . . .

Clara resolutely took in the curious stares, the feeling of being frozen on the outside, and the warmth of her hand in Daniel's as he led her like some sodden prize through the fragrant store. But she didn't care . . . *He's touching me again. Why am I letting him? I'm letting him, Seth, and it seems like Christmas.* . . .

But she lost some of her nerve when he pulled her through the doorway that led to the family kitchen, fully expecting to be swarmed by the Kauffman family. She stopped still, and he seemed to understand.

"No one's back here," he soothed in a low voice that added to the sensation of water and new warmth running like a stream down the small of her back. "The *kinner* are all at school; Mamm's gone visiting somebody, and Da is snoring in the sitting room. It's just us."

She nodded. *Just us. Just us . . . when there's been just me for so long. . . . That dream last* nacht *must have rattled me more than I thought.* . . . She shook her head, feeling her bonnet sink farther onto her brow, and then he was taking it off with careful fingers. Her *kapp* came off with the wet wool, and she parted her lips to exclaim at the impropriety of a man other than her husband seeing her head uncovered. But then she stopped. *My hair isn't down,* she reasoned. *So it's all right for a few minutes while I rest.*

"You've got to get out of these wet clothes," he murmured.

She blinked as his fingers sought the hook and eye of her cape, and she took a startled step backward. "I—I—um . . . can manage."

To her surprise, his handsome face flushed and he half smiled. "Of course you can. Look, why not go into my *mamm* and *daed*'s room and undress? You can get into her housecoat and come out here by the stove while I go get Blinks."

"Uh . . . *nee*. I need to start back soon. The trip down took me longer than I thought."

"I'll take you back," he said a bit roughly. "I cannot think how you managed to hike that distance down in deep snow with a goat in tow."

She straightened her chilled spine. "Well, I did it. Besides, I need pecans so I can bake today." Her gaze inadvertently slid to the huge wooden table behind him; it had a mixing bowl, dark brown bottle of corked vanilla, and several wooden spoons, standing at the ready. She looked back up into his eyes and saw the amusement in their emerald depths.

"*Jah*," he whispered, as if telling a secret. "I'm baking today, too . . . but I'm not doing anything until you are warm and dry. Perhaps I might get a woman from the store to help you with some of the—layers. I'm sure Ruby Zook wouldn't mind. . . ."

Clara huffed at his poor joke, then nodded. She didn't want to risk catching a chill and not being able to get on with her pralines. "All right. I'll *geh* to your *mamm*'s room and, *nee,* I don't need help. . . . If you'd just . . . point me to the right door."

He touched her shoulders lightly and turned in the direction of the door off the right of the large kitchen. "Right in there, Widow Loftus . . . *Ach,* and holler, *sei se gut,* if you need . . . anything."

She rolled her eyes and then hobbled off in the direction he'd indicated, hampered by her wet skirts and trying to ignore the unaccountable merriment she felt at his easy teasing. *I do need to* kumme *down off the mountain more if it feels this nice. . . .* Then she bit her bottom lip at the errant thought and concentrated instead on dismantling her many layers.

CHAPTER 4

"Whose goat is that, Dan?"

Daniel spun from untying Blinks to stare down into the face of his ten-year-old *bruder*, Paul.

"Why aren't you in school?"

The *buwe* rubbed the outside of his black coat. "Bellyache."

Daniel wanted to laugh. "Bellyache, hmm? How about that fractions test you were studying for last *nacht* after dinner?"

"That's why I got the bellyache. I'm goin' in ta see Mamm."

"Whoa, little *bruder*. Mamm's out and we have a guest." Daniel caught the *buwe*'s shoulder gently.

The little pug nose turned up suspiciously. "A guest? Like the goat here?"

"This is Blinks. She belongs to Frau—uh—Widow Loftus, who is our guest. I was taking the goat in just now."

Paul giggled. "Into Mamm's kitchen? She'll whoop ya fer sure. I gotta see this."

Daniel ignored the premonition that his *bruder* was right and reasoned he'd have Blinks out as soon as he could. He led Paul and the goat around to the back entrance and carefully eased open the door, not wanting to startle Clara in some state of imagined undress. *Stop the fantasies, Kauffman. . . . Isn't it enough that you think she's beautiful, that you're doing the right thing for Seth, that you more than lo—*He silenced the voice in his head. *What was I about to say to myself? That I love Clara Loftus? I'm keeping a promise, that's all . . . a promise. . . .* He was so distracted by his thoughts that he let go of Blink's lead rope, then promptly tripped over it, to fall sprawling in his own kitchen, right at a pair of delicate, feminine bare feet. . . .

Clara had struggled out of the wet layers of clothing, discovering that she was soaked to the skin. She bit her bottom lip and considered opening one of the finely carved cedar dresser drawers and borrowing a shift, but then decided on simply binding herself up in Frau Kauffman's housecoat, which happened to be a startling shade of pink. She tugged it off its peg on the wall and wound its voluminous folds around her waist, finding she could tie the long belt three times about herself. Thus girded, and feeling fairly confident that she could make it to the chair by the woodstove before Daniel got in, she tiptoed barefoot out of the bedroom.

She heard a sudden tussle at the back door, and Blinks's *baa*ing, and then Daniel came through the open wood to fall at her feet. Blinks neatly jumped over his sprawled form, and Clara froze as her bare toes nearly came in contact with his long chestnut hair.

Daniel lifted his head and looked up at her, and she wrapped her arms about herself, feeling as though his keen emerald eyes might see through the bulk of the housecoat. "Are you all right?" she asked, automatically reaching down to stroke Blinks's stiff fur with nervous fingers.

Then she watched as Paul Kauffman jumped on his *bruder*'s broad back. "Gimme a ride, Dan!"

Clara stepped back as Daniel got to his hands and knees with a chuckle, then rose to his full height, his shoulders easily supporting the weight of his younger brother. *He'd make a* gut *fater. . . .* She took another step backward, horrified at her thought, and felt her face suffuse with color.

She saw Daniel eyeing her quizzically, one dark brow raised in question, even as he jostled Paul and she sank into the chair she felt at the backs of her knees.

"What is it?" he asked, and she shook her head in mute appeal.

He slid Paul to the ground, then came forward to hunch down at her knees. "Clara, really, are you all right? You look as though you might be starting a fever."

Jah . . . this is a fever . . . in my blood . . . for you. . . . She stared helplessly at his mouth, wondering how it would be to test the contours and firmness of his perfectly shaped lips, then hastily looked away at the cream-colored wall.

She almost jumped when he laid a firm hand against her brow and then her cheek.

"Hmmm . . ." he murmured. "You are hot. Perhaps we should call for your sister to *kumme* and check you over?"

Clara swallowed and smoothed the fabric of the robe over her knees. "*Nee*. I'm fine. Um . . . maybe just . . . a glass of water?"

He frowned. "Of course. I'm being thoughtless. . . . I'll make you some tea."

He got to his feet, and she watched him out of the corner of her eye as he easily navigated the kitchen as if it was second nature to him.

"I've heard some folks say you're odd, Widow Loftus. What's that mean?"

Clara turned to look at Paul and took in his wide, innocent green eyes and gap-toothed mouth. She was about to respond when Daniel snapped at his *bruder*.

"Paul—let her be. Go on out to the store and help Daed for a bit."

"*Nee*," Clara countered with a half laugh. "He's fine. Let me answer. After all, how many women *kumme* to the store with a goat?"

"Not many," Paul concluded, reaching out to pet Blinks.

"You're right," she said softly, liking the child's forthrightness. "I'm not odd, really, Paul. I'm just . . . lonely at times."

"Then why do you stay up in that cabin all by yourself 'cept for the goat?"

She wet her lips, aware that Daniel was listening as he waited for the kettle to boil. "Because it's my home and I like it—sort of. I can talk to the trees and listen to the snow fall. . . . It's beautiful really."

Paul scrunched up his pert nose. "Mebbe you are odd, after all—talkin' ta trees."

"All right, little *bruder*," Daniel said. "Out." He handed her a cup and saucer of fragrant lavender tea and sighed as Paul scampered off. "I'm sorry about that. He means no harm."

"I know," she said, taking a quick sip of the hot tea. She choked and he patted her back. She could feel the warmth of his large hand even through the thickness of the pink fabric. Her cup rattled in its saucer and she set it on the table carefully. She was about to suggest that she had dried enough when the back door banged open once more.

Clara heard Daniel's faint groan; then he spoke. "Hello, Mamm. You know Clara Loftus. . . ."

Clara rose and tried to smile into Frau Kauffman's kind but speculative eyes. "Hello."

The older woman nodded, then frowned at Daniel. "Why is that goat in my clean kitchen?"

"All in all, I think that went rather well. Don't you?" Daniel tightened the reins a bit, and the cheerful jangle of sleigh bells rang out in the snowy afternoon. He glanced at Clara and hid a smile. Her beautiful mouth was set in a straight line, and she was studiously glaring at the landscape in front of them.

"*Nee*," she said finally. "I do not think it went well."

He laughed then, a full belly laugh that made him feel good for the first time in a long time. She turned baleful gray eyes upon him, and he hastily contained his mirth.

"You enjoyed that," she accused.

"What? You mean, you sitting in my *mamm*'s pink housecoat in the middle of—how many people was it?"

"Six," she snapped tightly. "Not counting us."

Blinks grunted from her position beneath the lap robe, and Daniel had to stifle another laugh.

Clara's frown deepened. "Blinks is correct. Six people and three—unusual—goats. I cannot begin to think what your *mamm* must feel about me."

"*Ach,* so Clair Bitner came around the back of the *haus* for once with his goat's milk to sell. . . . Of course, it makes sense that Benny, Scruffy and Teddy smelled one of their own kind and had to make an appearance. I think Blinks enjoyed the company. Besides, my *mamm* likes you."

"How do you know?"

He waved a dismissive hand. "She likes everybody."

Clara sighed aloud and he leaned over to give her a spontaneous nudge with his shoulder. "And you know your sister, Sarah, was just concerned for your well-being."

"*Ach,* sure, and Edward, her big-bodied husband, simply had to *kumme* along."

Daniel nodded. "And they couldn't leave the kids at home. Then Sarah must have mentioned it when she passed Bishop Umble's, who himself only wanted to ask again for some of your, um—second best—I mean, pralines."

She ignored his teasing. "Which, come to think of it, your *fater* wouldn't let me pay for when he came in."

"Yep, and the whole crowd was bound to have woken Da on the couch, and what's a rousing lunch party without Auld Sol Kauffman, I'd like to know?"

He saw the corner of her mouth lift a bit, and his heart kindled inside his chest. "*Ach,* don't smile, Clara Loftus. That would truly be a crime after the way you held sway in my *mamm*'s housecoat. You were . . . captivating."

He saw her smile edge back into a frown, and he could have kicked himself. "*Slow . . . Gotta take it slow with Clara. . . .*"

He cleared his throat in the cold air. "So, since you reassured the bishop you'd bake for his gathering to-morrow *nacht,* I was wondering if I might *kumme* pick you up." He paused, thinking fast. *Riled. Get her riled up. . . .* "Unless you plan on backing out? I mean, my raisin-filled cookies, when warm, are absolutely the best things you've ever—"

"Six o'clock will suit me fine." She sniffed. "But only because I want my praline cookies to be at their . . . I mean . . . *Jah, danki,* in advance, for the ride."

He hid a grin and eased the horse and sleigh around a snowdrift. "No thanks needed. It'll be my pleasure."

CHAPTER 5

"What do you mean, he asked you to warm up?"

Sarah's voice was excited, and Clara blew out a breath of exasperation as she tried to concentrate on measuring sugar. "How did you get up here so fast? I just saw you at the store, and I told you—I'm fine."

Her older sister waved away her words with an impatient hand. "I know, but I want some details. I couldn't hear a thing in all the ruckus of the Kauffman kitchen . . . so, tell me! You know Daniel Kauffman is absolutely beautiful and—"

Clara gave her a sour smile. "I thought you were happily married."

"The idea is to get *you* happily married . . . again, of course."

"Of course."

"*Ach, kumme* on, Clara, he's perfect for you, and the girls have been after him for years. Maybe he finds you . . . mysterious, up here on the mountain alone, with a goat, and—"

"All right—" Clara slammed the tin measuring cup onto the table. "That's enough. I've got to bake."

Sarah flounced into a wooden chair. "You do not. You just don't want to think about what life might look like with someone other than Seth."

"From anyone else, I'd consider that hurtful."

"I'm not trying to hurt you, my love. I only want you to have joy again . . . to have the abundant life *Derr Herr* wants for you. And if Daniel Kauffman would ask you to marry him, then—"

"He already did," Clara mumbled.

"What?"

"Nothing."

Clara saw Sarah stand up and come 'round the table and soon found herself squashed in a full embrace. "Sarah . . . I can't breathe. . . ."

Her sister pulled back to smile with delight. "We'll have a winter wedding. . . . Perhaps Bishop Umble would even allow a Christmastime wedding! *Ach*, Clara, I'm so happy for you!"

"I told him no."

"You what?"

Clara frowned. "I told him *nee*. Look, it was two years ago, all right? Two years, Sarah . . . The week after Seth died, and I didn't . . . I couldn't."

Clara saw her sister's eyes fill with tears. "I understand," Sarah whispered softly. Clara felt her lean forward and place a gentle kiss on her forehead; then she eased away.

Clara drew a deep breath; she knew her sister. Despite her tears, Sarah wasn't going to let this go, and she tried to ready herself for another round of questions by counting out pecans with unsteady hands.

But to Clara's surprise, her sister merely gathered her heavy cloak and moved to the door.

"I'll see you tomorrow at the bishop's."

Clara nodded, watching her go, then swiped angrily at a stray tear that suddenly fell from her eyes. "Two years . . ." she muttered aloud, feeling Blinks press against her skirts. "Two years is too long." The goat made a small sound of commiseration, and Clara went back to resolutely counting pecans.

The following morning, Daniel rose early to bake before he went to work that day. His plan was to get the raisin-filled cookies done before the *kinner* woke up. Then he would take the cookies with him over to Joe King's woodworking shop to save them from being devoured.

"I should have known better," he groaned to himself when he heard the patter of small feet coming downstairs.

It was Paul, still clad in his *nacht* shirt and somehow managing to look both endearing and mischievous at the same time. The *buwe* clambered onto the bench by the table and gave Daniel a wide grin. "You startin' to make Christmas cookies, Dan?"

"*Nee.*"

"You bakin' for that woman and her goat, then?"

Daniel felt himself flush unaccountably but had to smile. "*Nee.* I'm trying to outbake her."

Paul pulled a face and casually snatched a plump raisin from the bowl. "What'cha mean?"

"Stay out of the filling. . . . I mean, that I want to—well, sort of rile her up a bit by proving that I'm a better baker than she is."

"You love her," Paul stated flatly, shaking his head as if Daniel was lost at sea.

Daniel sank down on the bench beside his *bruder,* automatically beginning to roll out the dough. "I do not love her," he whispered in case anyone else decided to make a sudden appearance in the kitchen.

Paul raised a minute brow. "Uh-huh."

"Look, I like her, okay? That's all. And since when have you become such an expert on . . . love?"

The child shrugged and snagged a piece of dough. "I jest know. It's like we learn in church—ya tell the truth about what you know. And I know that you love that lady who talks to trees . . . and goats."

Daniel frowned, staring down into the resolute little face, then he shook his head. "Go back to bed before Mamm catches you up this early."

"Naw. I might as well get dressed and start my chores before school. Thanks fer talkin', Dan."

Daniel couldn't resist returning the hug Paul threw at him, and he thanked *Gott* for having a little *bruder* who wasn't afraid to tell the truth.

Clara told herself that she was being ridiculous when she checked her dress for the fourth time in the *auld* mirror above her dresser. She'd chosen to wear a cheerful dark green blouse beneath her dress and knew that the color did something for the paleness of her skin. As a widow, she did have to avoid the paler pastel colors, but the *gut* Bishop Umble was even lenient in this regard, so she knew he wouldn't mind what she was wearing. *But will Daniel notice?*

She scowled in the mirror and tried to push away the thought, but there was no denying that the man had gotten under her skin somehow. She sighed aloud, then nearly jumped when the sound of muffled, merry sleigh bells rang from outside. She hurried to swing on her cloak when there was a brisk knock at the door.

She opened it and gazed up at Daniel's ruddy handsomeness. He'd taken his hat off, and his chestnut hair caught the light from the lantern and shone with faint strands of red.

"Hello," he said with a smile, breaking into her wayward thoughts.

"Hello. I'm—uh—ready," she announced, tugging on her bonnet.

He reached a hand up to graze her cheek, and she had the ridiculously exciting notion that he might be preparing to kiss her when he tucked her *kapp* string within the confines of her bonnet. "Are you really ready?" he asked in a husky tone and she nodded, flushing . . . hoping.

"*Nee,* you're not," he declared with a whimsical smile, and she felt herself look at him blankly. "You need your cookies, right? Unless you've decided to bow out gracefully?"

She felt her flush deepen, and she spun on her heel to grab the tinfoil-wrapped platter from the kitchen table. She turned back to face him just as Blinks chose that moment to butt her unflatteringly from behind, and she watched in dismay while the platter went flying.

Daniel caught it with remarkable deftness and she gasped in relief.

"No worries. I couldn't let my competition lose out so unfairly. And"—he held up a hand when she would have made some rejoinder—"I need to let you know that we Kauffmans always let everyone assume that the cookies or whatever might be baked *kumm* from Mamm—not me."

She took her platter from his outstretched hand and gave him a saucy smile. "I have never truly seen you bake."

He bowed his head in acknowledgment, then put his hat on. "That's a situation we'll have to remedy sometime . . . if you'd like?"

His question hung in the frosty air, warm and inviting.

She lowered her lashes, then looked at him directly. "I'd like."

"*Gut,*" he said briskly. "And I imagine Blinks comes tonight, too?"

"If you don't mind?"

He looked down at her, and she thought he was going to say something teasing, but instead he merely smiled and widened the door for her goat.

"Absolutely . . . You have absolutely outdone yourself, Esther. These raisin cookies are superb!" Bishop Umble made the declaration with obvious pleasure, and Daniel shot a grin in Clara's direction.

He found her to be as beautiful and tantalizing to his senses as the coming Christmas season could be, and he was still warm inside from the closeness of their sleigh ride down from the high timber.

"So, Daniel, have you tried Clara's cookies?" Sarah King asked, coming up beside him. "My little sister is a *wunderbar* baker."

Daniel smiled, easing the cut-glass cup of punch that he held from one hand to the other as he greeted Ice

Mountain's local healer and her husband, Edward King. "She is, indeed," Daniel agreed, shaking Edward's hand.

"We have to thank you again for offering her the chance to warm up yesterday," Sarah said, giving Edward a none-too-circumspect poke in the ribs, but the big man, as usual, seemed to have difficulty dragging his attention from his wife.

"It was my pleasure," Daniel said, noting that Clara was fast approaching through the pleasant throng gathered, almost as if she was afraid that her big sister might be talking about her. "And here's Clara now," he murmured warmly. "We were just discussing your baking—er—talents."

He had to hide a grin at the frown she threw in his direction, but she recovered nicely when Bishop Umble joined them, a praline cookie in his hand.

"Mmmm . . . mmmm, Widow Loftus. I have to tell you that your pralines are a perfect match for Daniel's *mamm*'s raisin-filled cookies. Both simply delightful!"

Daniel secretly thrilled to the arch look Clara gave him, then cleared his throat. "I'm sure we—uh—Mamm might not be put out by a cookie bake off of sorts, Bishop Umble."

The *auld* man's blue eyes twinkled in sudden delight. "What an excellent thought, Daniel! Indeed, I'm sure all the ladies hereabouts would enjoy such a thing. Now, let me think of a *gut* cause. . . ."

"Why the school, of course," Daniel heard Clara declare sweetly, while her eyes shot daggers in his direction. "Perhaps we might offer the *buwes* cooking classes?"

Daniel hastily joined in the round of good-natured

laughter as he noticed Clara did, as well. *The little minx . . . She can give as* gut *as she gets!*

Bishop Umble stroked his beard as the laughing trailed off. "I do think the school is a *gut* idea, though. Although the community provides teaching supplies, there's always some new book Jude Lyons wants the *kinner* to read. In fact, I'll talk to him about having the cookie bake off on the *nacht* of the school Christmas play."

"*Wunderbar* idea," Daniel agreed, noticing that he spoke nearly in time with Clara's similar words.

The bishop shot a glance between them, then smiled a gentle smile. "There's a storm brewing, so I hear, Daniel, up in the high timber. So, if you've a mind to take Clara home tonight, you may want to leave early."

"Of course, sir. Sarah and Edward, I'll see Clara safely home, I promise."

Edward spoke up idly. "We can take her, Dan."

Daniel had to conceal another smile as Edward received his second poke of the evening from his petite wife.

"We're grateful, Daniel," Sarah said in clear tones.

"*Jah,* very grateful," Clara declared, but he knew that there'd be fireworks on the sled ride home if he gauged her temper right, and he looked forward to the cold *nacht* with abject pleasure.

CHAPTER 6

They had almost reached her cabin when the storm broke loose and Blinks jumped out of the sleigh.

"You head inside. I'll get the goat and stable the horse," Daniel hollered to her over the whipping wind.

Clara nodded, already feeling the icy sting of snow particles down the back of her neck. She paused only long enough to see him grab the lantern from the sleigh, then hurried indoors. The howl of the storm was a dim roar outside that seemed to taunt her with its power as the minutes passed. She bit her lip and found herself praying for Daniel and Blinks. Then she could stand the wait no longer and grabbed her own lantern from the tabletop and headed back outside.

The snow was near-blinding and took her breath away with its intensity. She knew how easy it was to get lost in a storm, so she carefully navigated to the clothesline that was stretched from the side of the cabin to one of the small, unused outbuildings, and grabbed hold of the rope like a lifeline. She tried to call out for Daniel, but her voice was carried away by the wind. Then she felt something warm inside her chest, almost as if she were being given a massage from the inside out. She stood still a moment, confused, then looked up and saw the ready glow of Daniel's lantern reflecting from the deserted shed in front of her. And she moved on in haste.

She eased open the door to what had once been a small barn and entered in time to see Daniel climbing a rickety ladder to a second-floor overhang that held a few bales of musty hay, some spare wood, and a very determined-looking goat.

She slid the door closed behind her, shutting out most of the wind, then listened worriedly as Daniel tested the worn floorboards of the ladder.

She caught her breath when he took a second step and the wood creaked alarmingly, releasing a fall of dust to the pile of hay beneath; Blinks *baa*ed piteously.

"It's all right," Daniel soothed the animal as Clara watched him risk another step.

He'd nearly reached the goat, when a sudden gust of wind blew a few shingles off overhead. Clara glanced up, then looked back in time to see the whole of the overhang collapse at the center. She watched Daniel move fast to scoop up Blinks, and then they were falling to the hay beneath, with Daniel taking the brunt of the fall on his back while his strong arms held her pet close.

Clara gasped and hurried through the debris, flinging away pieces of wood, while Blinks leapt with nimble feet, obviously unharmed, past her to go and stand by the door.

"*Ach*, Daniel, are you all right?" She dropped to her knees beside his big body.

He laughed from the depths of the old hay and propped himself up on his elbows, blowing a stray piece of straw from his lips. "That goat is a trickster."

"You might have been badly hurt, but you saved her. . . . Why did you do that?"

His expression softened and Clara wanted to duck her head away from the warmth in his green eyes. "Because she matters to you, and because I wouldn't let any animal risk suffering from such a fall."

"You're a *gut* man." The soft words were out of her mouth before she could even think, and she curved her mouth at his deepening smile.

"Did you just compliment me, Clara?"

She shook her head, belying her words, but he'd leaned upward to sit next to her, his legs pressed against her knees.

"*Jah*, you did," he whispered, tilting his head. "And it felt good."

Her mind raced suddenly, to some sweet, sugary place where more than words tasted good—like the lips of a man. She clenched her jaw as he reached his callused hand up to stroke her soft cheek.

"*Ach*, Clara . . ." His lashes lowered as he moved even closer, and she suddenly woke to more than sensory awareness.

"Listen," she cried, ignoring his faint groan. "The storm's stopped."

He frowned and gazed upward for a moment. "So it has." He sighed and got to his feet, reaching a hand down to help her up.

Her fingers tingled in his grasp, and she felt she

had nowhere to hide when he bent his broad back to her and brushed a piece of hay from her cloak front. "One storm's stopped, sweet Clara—but another rages on."

She swallowed hard. "I—don't—know what you mean."

He smiled a gentle smile and pulled her from the straw toward her now-impatient pet; Blinks was butting at the door.

"You know exactly what I mean, but . . . perhaps you can tell me with your sweet baking until you feel ready to tell me with your lips."

She smiled uncertainly at his teasing, but in her heart, she felt that she had been close to betraying Seth with the kiss of one who had been his best friend. . . . *I'll have to be more careful in the future,* she concluded to herself, but she knew it would be no easy task with someone like Daniel Kauffman.

"Ya say she's got a goat? Well, why not a beaver, then?"

Daniel sighed and worked the ground cloves into the gingerbread drop dough while his da sat in affable midnight companionship at the kitchen table. Daniel had returned from Clara's too keyed up to sleep and had decided to start a batch of an old-fashioned cookie favorite.

"No beavers. One goat."

"No husband. One admirer," Sol laughed, pleased with his own humor.

Daniel had to smile. His da's presence of mind was quicksilver at best, but it was still a joy to hear the grandfather he knew break through now and then.

He uncorked the bottle of molasses and added a liberal amount before starting to tell his da about the cookie bake off.

Sol scratched his grizzled head. "When I was courtin', we kissed not cooked."

I'd like to be kissing Clara. . . . His mind flashed back to the moments in the hay when he thought he'd had a chance at such pleasurable activity, but she'd shied away as usual. "*Clara's as shy as a doe . . . as shy as a doe. . . .*"

"Yer missin' Seth," his da said flatly, startling him.

Daniel swallowed and tried to concentrate on stirring in the remaining flour with a wooden spoon. "*Jah,*" he choked, telling himself it was from the flour dust and not the realization that he did miss his best friend. He wondered bleakly how far heaven was from earth and whether Seth could even see or know what happened on Ice Mountain.

His grandfather laid a big hand over his, and Daniel looked into the bleary *auld* eyes. "Ye're too hard on yerself, *buwe.* You don't have to have all the answers—only *Gott* knows," Sol smiled. "Only *Gott* knows the difference between a beaver and a goat, and that's what matters."

Daniel nodded, realizing it was time to lead the *auld* man back to bed, but he was grateful for the blessing of their talk all the same.

CHAPTER 7

The next day was Saturday and Clara found herself in a bad mood. She groaned in exasperation as she burnt her second kettle of candy. She flung open the cabin door and tossed the whole mess, kettle and all, out into the cold snow and returned to glare at an innocent-eyed Blinks.

"I am not concentrating," she declared. "And it's all because of that . . . man."

Blinks gave a gentle grunt and settled down on the floor near the woodstove while Clara went back to her third try at making Amisch Shatter Candy. When she'd spoken with Sarah last *nacht* at the bishop's, her sister had invited her to come down for a visit today to do some sled-riding with the little ones.

"More likely Sarah wants a *gut* gossip—not that there's anything to say," she grumbled aloud as she measured corn syrup into the heavy pan. She wanted to make the hard candy favorite for the *kinner* and hoped to have it set up before Edward came to get her. This time, she watched the sugary liquid boil with extra care and then poured the whole lot onto a powdered sugar cookie sheet. She spread the cinnamon-flavored redness out, and it soon engulfed the tin.

"There!" she cried, pleased, and whipped off her apron in time to hear the jangle of harness and sleigh bells outside. She took a quick peek outside through the kitchen window, half-hoping to see Daniel instead of her blond-haired *bruder*-in-law. But it was Edward, and she hurried to sling on her cloak before he knocked at the door.

"You ready, Clara?" he asked when she opened the wood.

"*Jah.*" She met his single blue eye for a moment, amazed, as always by its keen intensity. He wore a rather dashing eye patch to hide the loss of his other eye, which had been damaged in an accident several years before. "I made Shatter Candy for the *kinner,* but I'll wait to let them crack it once we're at your *haus.*"

She pulled on her bonnet while Edward held the cookie sheet for her, and then they went out to the sled with Blinks jumping in to take a front-row seat.

As they set out, Clara didn't really expect Edward to talk much, as he usually was a quiet man, but today he seemed to be inclined to chat—about Daniel Kauffman.

"Dan's a *gut* man," Edward said.

Clara longed to roll her eyeballs. Obviously Sarah had drilled her husband on what the subject of conversation on the sled ride should be. . . .

"Uh-huh," she muttered.

She felt Edward give her an appraising, sidelong glance. "But nobody'll do after Seth, huh?"

Clara blustered in surprise. "Did Sarah tell you to say that?"

"*Nee,*" Edward replied calmly, reminding Clara that as the healer's husband, he was probably more than used to women's emotions.

"Well, I never said anything about anyone 'doing' or 'not doing' after Seth. Seth's gone. . . ." *Seth's gone. He's gone, but I will not betray his memory. . . .*

"He's gone," Edward agreed.

"But I know firsthand how the past can put a damper on the present and the abundant life that Derr Herr wants us to have. Your sister taught me that."

Blinks bleated in seeming agreement, and Clara glared momentarily at her pet, clutching the cookie sheet tighter. "Well, I've never understood much about abundant life, even though the bishop talks about it a lot. Abundance is for crops or food . . . or . . . something, but not life, not people." She realized she sounded rather glum and straightened her spine.

But Edward merely nodded. "I know. It's hard to understand until you've experienced abundance, and I guess maybe you have a lot to carry, becoming a widow only shortly after being a bride. . . . If I were you, I guess I'd be pretty mad at *Gott* and His suggestion of abundance."

Clara felt her eyes well with unbidden tears. Her big, brooding *bruder*-in-law was touching things in her heart and soul that she'd never been willing to overturn, like big stones in a rushing creek, and it hurt.

He must have realized because he soon dropped the matter and pulled up on the reins as they reached the cabin where her sister and he lived with their two children. He set the brake and came around the sleigh to help her down, reaching for the cookie sheet and then offering her one of his large, gloved hands.

She took a deep breath and accepted his help, then paused to look up into his single blue eye. "*Danki,* Edward," she murmured.

He nodded. "Anytime, sweet sister. Now, let's go in and shatter some candy."

She agreed with a small smile and started up the steps to the porch when she noticed Daniel Kauffman step 'round a stand of trees and come toward the cabin on the snow path.

Daniel had awoken early that morning after a plaguing *nacht*'s sleep of tantalizing near dream kisses with Clara. Consequently, he took himself off to Joseph King's woodworking shop with only half the focus he normally had.

"Rough *nacht?*" Joe asked affably when Daniel arrived.

Daniel shrugged. "In one way."

Joseph laughed and Daniel had to smile when the dark-haired man nodded in understanding. "*Ach,* so you've been lovestruck. . . . Family rumor has it that Clara Loftus might figure into your tossing at night."

Daniel had forgotten for a moment that Joseph was Edward's big *bruder* and bound to hear the latest gossip through Sarah. "I might be tossing and turning, but I doubt that she is," he admitted to his boss and friend.

Joseph clapped him on the shoulder. "No man can figure what runs through a woman's mind—you might well be surprised."

"I'd like to be."

"Well, *kumme* and finish your work on that sweet gum dresser for the order down Williamsport way."

"*Danki*, Joe. I'll get right to it," Daniel said as he slipped off his coat and hat and hung them on the pegs near the door.

Other men were carving, as well, and Daniel exchanged cheerful greetings before going to his workbench. The dresser he was carving was of sweet gum, sometimes called "American Mahogany" due to its occasional dark streaks and red color. It was a good wood to work with and would take any variety of finishes once he'd finished the commissioned carving of sun, moon, and stars on its drawer fronts.

He'd been carving carefully for about an hour when his mind drifted a bit to Clara and the skew chisel he held slipped for an instant, slashing the top of his wrist. He sighed and put down the tool to grab a rag, quickly applying pressure to the wound, which was bleeding fast.

Joseph came over and lifted the rag, then hastily reapplied it. "Kind of deep, Dan. You'd better head over to Sarah's and have her put in a stitch or two."

"Sorry, Joe." Daniel knew that his boss ran a clean operation and wanted accidents kept to a minimum.

Joe smiled at him and spoke low. "No worries, Dan. At least I know where your mind was—just save that for some *nacht* in the future, all right?"

"Right."

Daniel got to the door when Joseph called after

him, "And take the rest of the day off, Dan. Just get some sleep."

Daniel smiled and nodded. "Will do, Joe."

He headed out into the snow, his coat slung over his arm as he walked, and kept pressure on the wound. He made the short hike to Sarah's, not bothering to stop in at home when he passed the store—he didn't want his *daed* to worry or his *mamm* to fuss. He passed the last stand of trees and turned onto the snow-bright path in time to see Clara mounting the steps to the door, and his heart began to pound in his pulse points—a delicious torment.

CHAPTER 8

"Can you peel back the rag while I check out how deep the cut is?"

Clara stared at her older sister in dismay. Sarah knew how weak-stomached she usually was when it came to blood—and here was Daniel bleeding all over the place. But then she looked at the slight pallor of his handsome face as he sat at the kitchen table with Blinks at his knee and she strengthened her resolve.

"*Ach,* all right. Let me wash my hands."

"Of course," Sarah said, stepping back from the pump at the sink.

Clara didn't know how her sister could work in the chaos of the confines of the cabin. Elijah, her nephew of five, was in and out of everything and his little sister, Anne, was right behind him. But Sarah and Edward acted as if the constant babbling and tumult was of no special concern. Born parents, Clara thought ruefully as she scrubbed her hands. *I wish I had gotten the chance to parent someone other than a goat, but Seth died before I could—we could* . . . She flushed as she turned from the sink and found Daniel's keen emerald eyes on her. *It's almost like he can tell what I'm thinking.* . . . Then she told herself that she was being ridiculous and moved resolutely to the table.

Daniel was seated sideways to the table, his bent legs sprawled, and she found that she had to move between his knees in order to reach his arm properly while Edward held up a lantern. Was it her imagination, or did Daniel move his knees ever so slightly to press against the length of her skirts so that she felt caught in a wicked flash of delight, wondering what his bare skin would feel like in such a position. She knew her cheeks flamed, but then she lifted the rag and revealed the deep gash in his arm. She swallowed hard as Sarah considered and probed, then felt herself grow weak and faint.

"I'm sorry, Sarah, I—"

"Just sit down right here," Daniel whispered low and she found herself seated on his knee like some child preparing for a bedtime tuck up. "It's a nasty cut and my own fault. I don't want you to faint over it, though."

"I—I'm fine." She struggled a bit to rise but found herself inexorably trapped with the pressure of his muscular thigh beneath the curve of her bottom as his free arm cuddled her firmly in cozy proximity.

"You are indeed fine," he purred close to the shell of her ear and she blew out a held breath, amazed that he would risk such talk even beneath the clamor of the children playing at banging wooden spoons against upturned pots.

"Daniel . . ." she gasped.

But then she saw the muscles in his fine jaw tighten

and glanced back to the table in time to see Sarah begin to stitch his skin with a whiskey-soaked piece of thread and a sharp needle. Clara thought she might faint, but then her queasiness fell away in a rush of intimate concern for Daniel's pain. The noise of the children and the presence of Sarah and Edward seemed to fade away in her consciousness as she instinctively looped an arm around Daniel's broad shoulders.

She felt him shiver at her touch and leaned closer to him in concern. "Is it very bad, Daniel?" she whispered.

"Very," he said tightly, not looking at her.

She ran a finger around the curve of his ear and watched him close his eyes in what she thought was abject misery.

"*Ach*, Daniel . . ."

He was miserable, consumed with raw, aching desire and frozen in a situation where he could do absolutely nothing to assuage his want. Was Clara Loftus really sitting on his knee, leaning close enough so that he could feel her light breath in his ear? Was she making tiny circular patterns around the back of his neck with slender fingers that seemed to touch him in perfect strokes until he felt like he wanted to scream?

He squeezed his eyes shut and tried doing multiplication tables backward in his head. "Are you all right, Daniel?" Sarah's clear voice broke through the haze in his brain. "I've finished. Five neat stitches, if I do say so myself."

He almost cried out when Clara got up from his

knee; he was utterly bereft and had forgotten completely about the pain of having his skin stitched.

"Yeah." He swallowed, drinking in Clara's every movement with his eyes. "Uh, *danki,* Sarah. What do I owe you?"

"A sled ride with my baby sister," Sarah said brightly.

Daniel smiled slowly, ignoring Clara's mingled expression of both surprise and ready denial. "You know," he said casually. "A *gut* sled ride might help me forget the pain of my arm."

Blinks bleated loudly, adding to the tumult of the room, and Daniel watched in fascination as Clara hesitated, then nodded her *kapped* head. "If it'll help your arm," she had to half yell. "I guess one ride wouldn't hurt."

Before they could bundle up and go outside, little Elijah insisted on being able to break the Shatter Candy with his sister, Anne.

"Very well," Clara agreed, smiling down at her niece and nephew. *They really are dears,* she thought as she placed the cookie sheet on the cleaned kitchen table. "Use the bottom of the wooden spoons," she instructed as the *kinner* scrambled close. "All right . . . *Geh!*"

The pounding of the spoons quickly shattered the candy into a myriad of shapes and sizes. Clara redusted the lot with powdered sugar and then allowed everyone to select a piece. She watched Daniel take a large sliver, his white bandage readily apparent on his tanned skin.

"Mmmm—mmm," he approved and she had to

look away from watching his throat work as he sucked at the sweet.

She took her own small piece, then let Sarah put the candy up for later.

"Now"—Sarah clapped her hands—"we need to bundle up for sled-riding. And, Daniel, you've got to be careful of that arm."

"*Jah,*" he agreed.

"*Ach,* and Clara, I've got a surprise for you!"

Oh boy . . . Clara thought, not liking the secretive smile playing about her sister's pretty lips.

"Edward's frozen over the back field, and we're going to have a bonfire and ice-skating tonight!"

"But—I've got to get home," Clara cried in dismay, not liking the feeling of being cornered.

"I'll take you home—if you really want to *geh.*" Daniel spoke softly, but something in his face, perhaps a lingering trace of pain, made her slowly shake her head.

"*Nee, danki,* Daniel. I—if Sarah's planned such a treat, I wouldn't want to disappoint everyone. I'll stay over *nacht* here."

She couldn't miss the look of pure pleasure on his face and was glad when Sarah grabbed her hands in excitement.

"*Ach,* Clara, Edward can sleep in front of the fireplace and we'll share the bed and talk like *auld* times. And perhaps you'll *geh* to church with us in the morning?"

"Uh . . ." Clara paused, then looked around at the happy, expectant faces surrounding her. *Gott has blessed me with family who loves me, and Daniel lo—likes me as well, I suppose. Just as a friend. Surely it wouldn't dishonor Seth's memory to spend some time in his best friend's company. . . . "Jah,* I'll go to church."

Everyone cheered boisterously, and Clara felt her cheeks redden, but she met Daniel's approving gaze and knew peace inside for the moment.

Daniel loved the feel of her as she sat between his legs, her skirts tucked protectively around her, her spine straight. They were on the large runner sled at the top of the snowy pasture hill behind Sarah and Edward's *haus.*

"Relax," he chided cheerfully, jostling her a bit with his arms as he held the lead rope.

"I can't," he heard her bite out.

"Why?"

"Because you—you're all around me and I'm rather scared of going fast."

He felt her sigh at the admission, and he eased back on the rope. "It's all right," he soothed. "I won't let us go too fast, and you can imagine that you're on the sled alone, okay? Just enjoy the ride."

"*Jah,*" she said, sounding resigned.

He smiled, determined to make it the most unforgettable sled ride of her life.

"Lemme give you a push, Aenti Clara!"

Daniel felt Elijah's small but strong hands on his back as the sturdy child threw all of his weight against the sleigh. They were off, tipping then sliding down the high hill. Daniel gained control of the sled and rode the brake so that gumdrop-like snow mounds passed leisurely by and the wind blew softly on their faces. They were about halfway down when Clara gasped, then cried out.

"*Ach,* no!"

"What?" Daniel glanced around and tried to see if she'd been hurt in some way. "What is it?"

"Blinks—dead-ahead!" she screamed.

"We'll turn," he promised, then felt the sudden, jarring impact as they plowed into a snowbank.

Clara groaned, and Daniel saw Blinks standing to their left, completely unscathed. He felt Clara shaking while Blinks bleated a rapid song.

"Clara, are you all right?" Her shoulders still shook against him, and he anxiously ran his hands up and down her arms.

"I'm—fine," she gurgled. "I'm just laughing, that's all."

"*Ach* . . ." He relaxed and reached to pet Blinks's head. "I'm glad." Then, at the unfamiliar sound of her melodic laughter, he found himself joining in, full of amazing good cheer on account of a wonderful woman and a pain-in-the-neck goat.

CHAPTER 9

Daniel walked home later that morning feeling as if anything were possible now that Clara seemed to be softening toward him. Then he walked into his *daed*'s store and mentally groaned. He'd forgotten that once a month on Saturday, his *fater* got together a crew of friends to sit around and play checkers and talk. The local customers were used to the loud, masculine laughter and the wait for their purchases to be rung up, but Daniel tried to avoid the whole thing. He always managed to get sucked in and then riled up with enough advice about life, love, and women to choke a horse. So now, he tried to back out of the door without being seen, but it was too late.

"Dan! Dan, *buwe!* Ye're just in time," his *daed* hollered. "*Kumme* on in!"

Daniel sighed. His thoughts of spending a few hours relaxing and fantasizing about Clara soon dissolved as he was practically pulled into a chair in the circle of men near the woodstove.

"How're ya doin, Danny?" Clair Bitner wanted to

know. "And what's that on your wrist?" He stared at Daniel while stroking Benny the goat's coarse neck. Teddy and Scruffy lay nearby.

"*Ach,* a cut from work, that's all."

"Are you all right, *sohn?*" his *fater* asked low, leaning toward him.

"*Jah,* Daed. Fine. I just wasn't concentrating."

"Ya got women fever! That's what," Bottleneck Joe declared, loud enough to be heard in the high timber.

Daniel suppressed a groan as Meatball Summerson clapped him hard on the shoulder with a thick hand. "Flee, *buwe.* Women ain't nuthin' but trouble."

"Now, now," Clair Bitner grinned with a gap-toothed smile as he stroked his sparse gray beard. "Mebbe they are but mebbe they aren't. It all depends on how ya look at things, Dan. Now, if I was ta tell ya a story about a certain woman, ya might have to think twice about things. Because sometimes there's more to folks than what we figure. . . ."

Daniel hung his head. He knew what was coming. Some long, tormented tale of the mountain . . .

Clair cleared his scratchy throat. "Now, you take the panther woman of Tamarack Swamp . . ." He leaned back in his chair, and the others did the same, with relaxing creaks of wood and an expectant mood to set the story. Daniel shook his head but lifted his gaze to the *auld* man as he began to spin one of the older yarns of Ice Mountain.

"Ya know that Tamarack Swamp be mostly deserted now—nobody goes in there to hunt, because that swamp runs fiercely deep in some places. A man could get sucked alive into the mud and never be heard from again . . . but I'm getting off the point. . . .

There once was a man and wife who settled on the edge of the swamp. They lived alone; no *kinner*, no folks and they liked it that way. But things got tough one winter—food was scarce. The fella went out ta hunt day after day and came back empty-handed. Well, it got so bad that they were eatin' the corn for the stock and then something . . . different . . . began to happen. The woman started to go out at *nacht*. At first, the man didn't realize, for she'd wait until he was dead asleep and then take her leave. And, in the morning when the man woke, there'd be a chicken, or a shank of lamb, or a goat. . . . No offense meant, Benny. The woman pretended she didn't know where the things *kumme* from and jest praised Derr Herr like her husband did as they ate the *gut* food.

"But then one day, there came a solitary knock at the couple's cabin door. It was another settler and he held a gun. 'You folks better be careful livin' this far back in the swamp,' he said.

"'Why?' the husband asked. 'Is there trouble hereabouts?'

"'A big black panther's been takin' stock from all around. Big animal, sleek and black as sin. I almost had a shot at it the other *nacht,* but it was too fast. Took one of my finest layin' hens. I tracked it out here to the swamp.

"The husband shook his head. 'I'll keep a careful watch. *Danki* for the warning.'

"Well, the other settler went away, and the husband, unknown to his wife, set a few metal traps about in the icy snow far out in the swamp. Then he came back to the cabin. Night fell and the husband and *frau* went to bed as usual. A few hours passed, and then the husband woke to the bone-chillin' sound of a woman screamin'—that's how a panther sounds when it's about to take its prey or is riled up about something. The man saw that the wife was not in the cabin and he grabbed his rifle and ran out, following the bloodcurdlin' screams into the swamp. He got near enough to where he thought the panther was by the yellow shine of its eyes and fired off a shot. The cries stopped and the man's shoulders sagged. He didn't know if the panther had killed his wife, and he couldn't find out the truth until first light.

"As he was walkin' home through the darkness, he had the strange feelin' that he was bein' followed somehow and he hurried along, but the dog he had with him didn't bark so he figured it was just his imagination. But when he got home, the cabin door stood wide open and light poured out onto the snow from several lanterns lit inside. The man walked in to discover his wife bleedin' from her leg and hand. He saw that she'd been shot and that her hand looked like it had taken the brunt of a piece of metal. He looked into her eyes and saw a strange glow, and he knew that his wife was really the panther of Tamarack Swamp."

Daniel had to join in with the round of clapping at Clair's dramatic intonation at the finish of the tale, but then he looked the storyteller in the eye. "So, basically women are no more than animals to be trapped and shot."

A hush descended on the store and Daniel knew he'd crossed a line, but he was thinking of Clara and his recent pursuit of her. He fully expected Clair to knock him down a few pegs and waited for the return of words.

But the *auld* man merely smiled and stroked Benny's head. "Ya don't understand the point of the tale, Dan . . . It's more about women being both wild and free, as well as wives who make a home and hearth. There's many sides to a woman—and if you truly love her, you'll spend a lifetime discoverin' who she really be . . . that's all."

Dan nodded ruefully, recognizing the gentle truth of the older man's words. "I'm sorry, Clair. You know I meant no disrespect."

There was a brief silence until Clair laughed, breaking the tension and *gut* humor was restored to all.

Clara sat in her sister's kitchen with Martha Umble—the bishop's eccentric but kind wife—and listened to the *auld* woman as she helped make jam thumbprint cookies for the evening's skating.

"Yes sir, when I was a girl, Joel Umble was the finest man on the mountain—still is, truth to tell. Though it would do no good to let him know and give him a swollen head as bishop, mind you." Martha stuck her finger into the jar of blueberry jam and had a loud taste.

Clara realized that there was a deep kinship between her sister and Martha and felt happy that they were willing to let her join in the chorus of friendship.

"Are you going to skate tonight, Martha?" Sarah asked while Clara looked at her sister in surprise. A fall on the ice for one as *auld* as Martha would surely be dangerous to say the least.

"What are you talking about, Sarah King? You

know I can skate blindfolded if I've a mind to. Of course I'll be skating. And what about you, Clara? Rumor has it hereabouts that you might circle the ice with Daniel Kauffman a time or two?"

Clara felt herself flush. There was absolutely no place to hide anything of a person's private life on Ice Mountain, but she knew that Martha meant no harm.

"I don't know. Daniel's a *gut* . . . friend," she finished rather lamely. *Is he a friend? What is he to me? And how can he be anything to me when Seth is still my hus—No, he's not, yet I cannot dishonor his memory. I cannot . . .*

"I can hear your thoughts churn like fresh butter, child," Martha said, laying a blue-veined hand on Clara's. "Don't think so much. Don't fear. Derr Herr has a plan for your life, and you can't hurry His hand none, either."

Clara wet her lips. "I—I guess I've had trouble yielding to *Gott* much since Seth—well, because of the way he died."

Martha nodded, a wise look in her faded brown eyes. "Not only the way, but the timing of his death, I'd imagine . . . with you two married for not nearly a year. *Nee*, it is hard to understand *Gott*'s ways and His timing and sometimes everything looks like a mess. But He's still around. Still has your hand, child. You'll see. You can mark my words on that."

Clara nodded, feeling some of the ice in her heart begin to melt under the other woman's tender instruction. She realized that what her sister said about her becoming reclusive was more than true. *I never let anyone in when Seth died. I didn't want to talk about it, but now . . .*

Blinks *baa*ed loudly, disrupting her thoughts. She realized that much to the *kinner*'s delight, the goat had edged a cookie sheet to the side of the table and was making merry with some of the raspberry jam thumbprint cookies.

Clara sighed and swatted her away, then helplessly joined in the infectious laughter surrounding her.

CHAPTER 10

Daniel was waved off by Edward when he would have helped carry wood to the bonfire setup.

"*Geh* make out with Clara," Edward suggested with a grin, and Dan rolled his eyes in response. He'd forgotten that Edward had spent some time in the Englisch world working on the gas rigs, so his vernacular was just a bit inappropriate.

"Yeah," Daniel replied. "Like you wouldn't kill me for that."

"I wouldn't," Edward said in a surprisingly level voice. "My sister-in-law needs a *gut* kiss, I think. And Sarah agrees. Tonight while you're skating together might be the right time."

Daniel shrugged, watching the smoke from the fire mingle with the cold of his breath in the dusky air. "Sometimes I think I'm getting close and then—well, she's off like some wild thing that I cannot ever hope to match."

"You've been listening to Clair Bitner, haven't you?" Edward asked.

"Well, it's true either way, and I—" He broke off as the women and children started coming from the cabin.

Soon, many others from the community had gathered, holding the young *kinner* back from the allure of the fire and busily tying on skates to the soles of their solid boots and high black shoes. Daniel realized that old married sweethearts and young couples as well as children were taking to the large space of clean ice, and he automatically scanned the dimly lit crowd for Clara.

He finally saw Sarah, holding little Anne up on double-bladed skates. "Sarah," he called. "Do you know where your sister is?"

"Inside. Alone. She wanted to finish the last of the cookies." She gave him what appeared to be an encouraging smile and he nodded and turned toward the cabin.

He walked up the back steps quietly and then gave a soft knock on the door. He heard her footsteps as she crossed the kitchen, and he whipped his hat off.

She looked up at him blankly, obviously surprised, and he smiled down at her. "You're missing all the fun."

"*Kumme* in. I've got to get the last lot of the sand tarts out of the oven before they burn." She turned away from him and hurried to grab a pot holder from the table. He came in and shut the door, hanging up his coat and hat as she pulled the cookie sheet from the cookstove.

He gazed with some astonishment at the array and number of cookies she'd managed to bake with Sarah—gingerbread men with raisin eyes, almond shortbread, jam thumbprints, pinwheel cookies, sea foam, and Amish snowballs. "Wow," he said in open admiration.

She smiled at him then, blowing at a tendril of loose blond hair that had worked itself loose from her *kapp*.

He walked toward her, moving slowly, and reached out to tuck the loose curl of hair behind her ear. Then he gently traced the shell-like contours of her small ear with his fingertips, lightly touching her until her gray eyes half closed and her breathing came rapid and shallow.

"You touched me like this today," he murmured. "Do you know what that did to me?"

Her eyelids flew open and she took a step backward, but he wasn't going to let that stop him.

"*Ne—ee*," she stuttered.

"It turned me upside down inside, Clara. I felt like I was coming apart and didn't even remember how to breathe. Why did you do that, hmmm?" He stepped closer to her once more, and he watched her swallow, a gentle movement down the ivory fineness of her throat.

"I—you were in pain."

"And you didn't want that?" He lifted his hand to stroke down the line of her throat, stopping at the collar of her dress but so wishing that he might go further.

"*Nee*."

"Then don't let me be in pain now, sweet Clara."

"What—I mean—does your arm hurt?"

He smiled at her tenderly. "*Nee*, but I hurt. . . ."

Her beautiful cheeks pinkened; she obviously knew what he meant and yet she stood steady.

"Clara, let me kiss you. Just one time. Please . . ."

She moistened her lips with the tip of her tongue, and he made a choked sound from the back of his throat. He didn't care that he was begging; he felt as if he'd die from want if she denied him. But she lifted her chin slightly, a faint permission—and he took it with frantic movements, slanting his head, deepening the kiss; he drank from her like summer dandelion wine, all sweetness and wet heat.

The cabin door banged open, bringing in a rush of cold air and his *bruder* Paul, bawling like a young calf. Daniel broke away from her in mute frustration, torn between the dazed expression in Clara's eyes and the obvious immediate need of his younger sibling.

Paul's tears won out based on pure insistence. "What is wrong?" Daniel asked above the din.

"My skate broke and now I can't skate and I cried in front of the other fellas. They'll never let me forget that and—"

"Wait." Daniel put up a weary hand. "I bet Sarah's got extra skates lying around, and I'll take you out to your friends and have a word with them. Okay?" He looked at Clara. "I'm sorry," he whispered.

She nodded and Daniel went out to help his little *bruder*.

Clara touched her lips with shaking fingertips. She was staggered by the intensity of Daniel's kiss and felt shaken to the core.

She understood the kiss of a man and had enjoyed kissing Seth a great deal, but she'd never known herself to so hungrily return a kiss. *I'm wan-*

ton, she thought frantically. *Wanton . . . wanton . . . wanting the touch of a man who is not my husband and—*

"Clara, *geh* on outside," Martha Umble ordered, closing the door behind her. "I'll see to passing out the cookies. You have some fun and skate. I'll be joining you later."

Clara agreed, still feeling rather dazed, and went outside, carrying her skates. Many folks were still on the ice, skating in the cheerful glow of the bonfire, while still more were heading in, seeking a cookie and some hot cocoa.

She was debating about actually going out on the ice, not wanting Daniel to think that she was pursuing him in any way, when he skated up to where she stood in the snow.

"Need some help with your skates, Clara?" he asked in a perfectly natural tone so that she wondered if the kiss in the kitchen had actually shaken him as much as it had her.

But then he bent to help her on with her skates, the firelight playing on the dark sheen of his hair, and he looked up at her. She saw the slow simmer of heat in his green eyes and bit her lip in uncertainty, but he quickly took her hand and pulled her out onto the ice. For all his size, he was a masterful and easy skater, guiding her effortlessly out beyond where the *kinner* were darting to the shadowed outskirts of the frozen field.

They skated in pleasant unison for a few moments, and as she listened to the movement of their blades on the ice, she thought back to all the times she'd skated as a younger girl, longing for someone to want her and to skate with her as a sweetheart. Seth had died before they could ever skate together as a couple, she thought, and was about to speak when Daniel brought them to a gliding standstill.

She looked up into his handsome face, illuminated by the light of the moon and stars. "Look, Clara, I'm sorry about earlier with Paul. I couldn't let him cry. . . ."

"I like you all the more for helping him," she said in a sudden burst of honesty.

He smiled at her. "*Danki* . . . and I—uh—wanted to say that I thought it was perfect that our first amazing kiss was in a kitchen surrounded by cookies." He shrugged his broad shoulders. "It seems to suit us, I think."

"Daniel, I want—"

"Another kiss, perhaps? I do, too, my sweet Clara." He bent his head but she stopped him with a hand on his chest. "What is it?" he asked.

"Daniel, I can't do this. It's not fair to you. I—our first kiss will have to be our last. I'm sorry. . . ." She turned and skated quickly from his grasp before she could change her mind, then gained the bank on the far side of the field. She stumbled into the snow, and Sarah caught her arm.

"Clara, what is it? Why are you crying?"

"Crying? I'm not." But then she reached to feel the tears that were quickly changing to ice on her cheeks. "I—Sarah, can we just *geh* inside? I'm rather tired."

"Of course," Sarah said in a bewildered tone.

All Clara wanted was to get away from the ice and the haunting emerald eyes that she knew followed her through the firelit *nacht*.

CHAPTER 11

Daniel was too deeply asleep, worn out with grief over Clara's words, to try to wake from the dream he was having.

An angel with wings like ice stood near his bed, speaking to him. I'm crazy like Da, he heard himself say and the angel laughed, a crystalline sound that penetrated his soul and reverberated like the strike of an ax against a tree.

"No, you're not crazy . . . merely in love. Deeply in love."

"What can I do?" he cried out. "She won't have me."

"She won't have herself—the truth of herself and what she really feels. You can't give up. You cannot. . . ." The icy wings pulsed with rainbow-like colors and Daniel turned in his sleep, breaking the dream.

Clara settled between the comfortable pile of quilts and crisp sheets with a faint sigh. It was long after midnight, and she and Sarah had put the last touches on restoring the kitchen to order while Edward had gotten the *kinner* ready for bed.

"Oooh, this is like *auld* times, isn't it?" Sarah yawned from her place in the big bed.

"*Jah*," Clara said quietly, unable to truly think of much more than the shine of Daniel's eyes.

"What happened with you and Daniel tonight on the ice?"

"Nothing, really. I told him that I wasn't interested in—well, pursuing a relationship."

Sarah gave a delicate groan of frustration. "But, Clara, why?"

Because of Seth and because I'm scared and because . . .

"Because what if there's another tree?"

"Another tree?" Sarah asked, puzzled.

"Like the one that killed Seth. Another tree or an illness or an accident, then what?"

"Clara." Her sister's voice was gentle. "You can't live and be afraid constantly. Loving someone is always a risk, and there's the potential for pain, yes. But love is worth it."

"I—I don't know that."

Sarah cuddled closer to give her a hug. "But you will, sweet sister. You will."

"*Gott* says, 'Behold, I make all things new.' "

Daniel tried to focus as Bishop Umble expounded upon the message the following morning. In truth, though, it was difficult to do anything more than think of Clara, who was sitting with the other widows somewhere behind him.

Bishop Umble's voice carried across the expanse of the Troyers' snug barn and Daniel felt himself caught by the wise *auld* man's words.

"How does *Gott* make something new out of something old? Or unwanted? Or unloved?"

Unbidden, Daniel found himself having to blink back tears. *How I wish I could take back that hasty proposal of two years ago and spend the time wooing her. . . . Why didn't I think? But maybe,* Gott *can even make that time new again. . . . Give me a second chance. . . .*

"*Gott* is the *Gott* of second chances," Bishop Umble said. "He takes what we think is a mess in our lives and cleans it up—makes it new. Remember that today."

Daniel closed his eyes and prayed, longing for the truth of *Gott*'s newness in both his and Clara's lives.

She'd been married in the spring on Ice Mountain—surely one of the busiest and most beautiful times of the year. But Seth had persuaded the bishop, and Sarah had helped her to make up her dress—a vivid royal blue. A welter of pink apple blossoms had fallen on the ground as she'd walked to the Kauffmans' barn. It was strange, how Daniel stood as Seth's attendant, yet she couldn't remember him at all—only Seth's dear, sweet face and the new warmth of the day. . . .

A blast of cold air broke into her thoughts as the barn doors were slid open, signaling that church was over. She rose and found Daniel staring at her across the expanse of backless benches and bustling people. She stared back, feeling mesmerized, then Sarah touched her arm.

"Clara, are you ready?" her sister asked.

"*Jah,* sure."

"Edward will take you back up the mountain after dinner."

"Excuse me, Sarah—I couldn't help overhearing. If you don't mind, I'll see Clara home," Daniel said in a brisk tone.

Clara turned 'round to stare up at him.

"*Ach,* that will be great."

Clara felt her sister's unladylike poke and frowned. "I suppose," she muttered.

Daniel smiled. "It'll be my pleasure."

That afternoon, Daniel blinked in the snow glare and pulled the brim of his hat down a bit further. He had to glance over Blinks's head to get a look at Clara, and her beautiful mouth appeared set as it usually was. *Unless she's kissing me, then her lips are soft and wet and . . .* He drew himself up sharply; he needed to focus on talking with her.

"You know, I've been thinking," he began.

"And . . . ?" she asked in a stiff little voice.

"It's simple, really. If I win the cookie bake off, then you have to agree to court with me."

She sniffed delicately. "But you won't win."

"*Ach,* but there are always miracles at Christmastime." He grinned, admiring her pluck.

"And when I win?" she asked after a moment.

"Then I agree to leave you to your baking and goat and cabin and never bother your—uh—person again."

"Done," she snapped.

"You want to shake on that?"

"*Nee.*"

"All right," he agreed. "A man, er, a woman's word is her bond."

They arrived at the little cabin, which somehow looked a bit forlorn, and his heart ached at leaving her there all alone except for a goat as company. But he knew that she'd push him away if he pressed to stay for a while. So, he merely offered his hand and helped her to the door. Then he unlatched the wood and peered around inside, satisfying himself that all was safe.

"*Gut* day then, Clara Loftus. I guess I'll see you at the bake off. Would you care for a ride that evening?"

He was sure she'd refuse, but then she nodded slowly. "*Jah*, but only so you can know you're riding with the winner."

"I'll take my chances on that. Until later, sweet Clara."

He stepped out to the sled, feeling that things were pretty much all right with the world for once.

When he'd gone, Clara lit the woodstove and set about fiercely cleaning the little cabin, even though she knew she was breaking the Sabbath by working so heartily on a Sunday. But she didn't want to have time to think. And, when all was in perfect neatness, she drew down her recipe box and began to study its contents with grim intensity, knowing she had a bake off to win—even if it would break her heart.

CHAPTER 12

The school Christmas pageant and Cookie Bake Off were set for the following Friday evening. Daniel busied himself at work and helping out in the store, trying not to think about Clara up in the high timber alone. But he wanted to give her space and time to think. . . . And, he wanted to bake his raisin-filled cookie recipe to perfection. He never would have guessed that his future love would be riding on a cookie, but it was nonetheless.

Friday morning dawned bright and clear, and Daniel went down before anyone else was awake to make the all-important batch of cookies. He'd just started the filling, using a combination of black and golden raisins, when his da shuffled out into the kitchen.

"Still courtin' by cookin', *buwe?*"

"Maybe, Da," Daniel laughed, flouring the table.

"Well, the angel says that ya can't force the widow's hand. She's got to choose. Do you understand?"

His grandfather scratched his beard and ambled

back out of the kitchen as Daniel's hand hovered over the secret ingredient that made the cookies so *gut. She's got to choose. . . .* Bowing his head for a moment, he pushed aside the container, knowing he was leaving the contest wide open for Clara to win— and for him to lose—forever.

Clara was plagued by an insistent thought, but she tried to push it aside a hundred times. *Leave out the secret ingredient in the praline cookies? Let Daniel win, and then he . . . and I . . .* He'd be so happy, she thought with sudden clarity, and pushed the glass jar away from her.

Blinks bleated.

"*Ach,* shush," Clara scolded lightly. "I know what I'm doing."

She finished the rest of the recipe, then baked the cookies and pulled them out to rest on cooling racks while she went about her normal chores. And then, somehow, the day had flown by and she had to hurry to finish getting ready to go to the school with Daniel.

He arrived on time, as usual, and she had just put on her bonnet when his firm knock sounded at the door. She gathered up her foil-covered cookie platter and opened the door. She didn't know what she'd been expecting, but after not seeing him for nearly five days, she was unprepared for his quiet words of greeting.

"Hello, Clara. You look beautiful tonight."

"*Danki,*" she said, feeling shy around him. She wet her lips and indicated her cookie tray. "I made the pralines."

"And I made my raisin-filled cookies."

She wondered why he sounded faintly sad, but then he smiled as usual and helped her into the sleigh. They were both quiet on the way down, but it was a comfortable silence—like that of two old friends, she thought, wondering why the thought depressed her. She stroked Blinks's fur with her free hand and the goat *baa*ed gently into the *nacht* air.

The schoolhouse was ablaze with lantern light when they arrived, and folks were pulling up before the garland-wrapped front step banisters and exchanging festive greetings.

"I'll stable Blinks with my horse," Daniel said as he helped Clara down. He turned for a moment to watch her mount the school steps, feeling that he was letting her go forever and it hurt him deeply inside. But, just the same, he went through the motions of housing the animals and returning the greetings that came his way.

He met his *mamm* on the way in and quickly took the cookie plates from her hands as she juggled two of his fussing siblings at her skirts. "I'll put the cookies on the table, Mamm," he said.

"*Jah, sohn.*" She leaned close. "And *gut* luck to ya tonight."

He smiled and entered the school to discover a wonderland of light and decorations. Although his people normally didn't decorate much for Christmas, Jude Lyons and the *kinner* had outdone themselves with green and red loops of cut paper, festive ribbons, and a large hand-painted banner that hung atop the long tables lining the walls where the cookies were being placed by eager participants.

Obviously, the idea of a Cookie Bake Off appealed to the bakers of Ice Mountain, as nearly everyone he knew had turned out to pay their dollar entry fee and accept a number for their tray.

He saw that Clara must have already placed her dish and was seated near Sarah and Mary, the schoolmaster's wife, in one of the many folded wooden chairs assembled in neat rows. He wanted to wish her luck and then prayed that she'd lose somehow as he made his way to the back of the room, where the young men usually stood for such doings.

The judge was Bishop Umble, and he was taking a long time savoring his job. There was a sense of expectancy and fun in the air as the bishop teased and took drinks of water between tastings. At long last, he reached the last plate of cookies and took a bite. Then he held up his aged hand for silence.

The room rumbled to an excited quiet as the bishop began to speak. "Well, this was no easy decision, I'll tell you. The bakers of Ice Mountain have truly outdone themselves tonight. But there can be only one winner."

Daniel noticed that Clara had turned in her chair and was looking at him. He smiled at her, feeling as if they were the only two in the room for the moment.

The bishop cleared his throat. "And the winner is—"

A blast of cold air and the loud bleating of what sounded like a herd of goats shook the room. Blinks ran in and headed for the first table of cookies, neatly overturning the whole setup and proceeding to munch with enthusiastic relish. Then Clair Bitner's Teddy, Benny, and Scruffy followed, each tearing up a table and feasting on the creations of the evening. It happened so fast that the audience sat stunned; then pandemonium ensued as the men made a mad scramble for the goats and the ladies for their respective cookies. *Kinner* joined in the free-for-all and sampled cookies from the floor, then started sliding them across the polished wooden boards like hockey pucks.

Daniel sidestepped as much of the mess as he could and got to Clara, who was standing by her chair, desperately trying to scold Blinks. She gave up when Daniel drew near and instead stretched out a hand to him. He took her fingers in his, heedless of the chaos around him.

"I just saw my pralines go down," she laughed. "But, *ach,* I wanted you to win, Daniel. I knew it would make you happy. So I left out my secret ingredient."

"What?" he almost had to holler. "I did the same thing so that you would win."

"But that would mean—" She broke off in sudden thought. "What is your secret ingredient?"

"What's yours?" He laughed.

They both cried out in unison: "Goat's milk!"

Then she was in his arms, hugging him, and he pulled her through the throng and outside into the relatively quiet night air.

"I see we've been working at cross purposes," he said, loving the feel of her slender form against him.

"But if I'd won, you'd never see me again. Why did you want that?" she asked, pulling back from him.

He grew serious. "Because I wanted you to choose. . . . Clara, listen. Please listen. Will you marry me? I love you. I think I've loved you for a very long time."

He felt his chest work when her eyes filled with tears and she withdrew even further.

"Daniel—I can't. I cannot help but think that Seth—well, that he wouldn't approve, what with you being his best friend. *Ach,* I love you, too, but I . . ."

Daniel smiled and felt happiness flood his veins. He framed her beautiful face with both hands and bent close to her. "Clara, listen. Do you know why I came to ask you to marry me two years ago?"

"*Nee* . . . I thought you felt sorry for me."

"*Nee,* never that. *Nee.* Seth asked me to marry you—to take care of you." His voice broke. "He wanted us to be together. With his dying breath, he wanted it."

Daniel saw the burden lift from her almost as if it were a tangible thing, and she melted against him.

"*Ach,* Daniel, then *jah.* Yes, I will marry you!" She threw back her head and laughed exultantly and he kissed her with rough tenderness.

"Let's *geh* tell the bishop," Daniel said, grabbing her hands.

"No need." Bishop Umble spoke from where he'd come out onto the school porch. He was munching a cookie and his bright blue eyes shone. "As I said, *Gott* can make all things new."

Daniel shook the wise *auld* man's hand and Clara giggled. "Who won the cookie bake off?" she asked.

Bishop Umble stroked his beard. "Hands-down—it was the goats."

EPILOGUE

December, Two Years Later

"It's a funny thing," Daniel said as he stole a too-hot cookie from his wife's baking sheet and popped it into his mouth.

"What's that?" she asked, merely shaking her *kapped* head at his theft as she maneuvered the cookie sheet next to the others to cool.

"I used to love your cookies," he confided with a grin and a flash of his bright green eyes.

She pouted on purpose. "Used to?"

"Uh-huh." He swiped a sweet kiss across her lips. "But now I love you even more than your baking."

Clara giggled with happiness at his words. "I love our Christmas seasons together."

"And I do, too, sweet Clara."

His big hands encircled her rounded belly as he bent to nuzzle her neck. "It's the perfect time for baking love. . . ." he said with undisguised heat.

And she turned to begin gathering ingredients in his arms. . . .

AMISH SNOWBALLS

INGREDIENTS

1 cup butter or margarine, softened
½ cup powdered sugar
1½ teaspoons vanilla
2¼ cups all-purpose flour
¾ cup finely chopped nuts
¼ teaspoon salt
Powdered sugar

DIRECTIONS

1. Heat oven to 400 degrees Fahrenheit.

2. Mix butter, powdered sugar, and vanilla in a large bowl. Stir in flour, nuts, and salt until dough holds together.

3. Shape dough into one-inch balls. Place about one inch apart on an ungreased cookie sheet.

4. Bake 10 to 12 minutes or until set but not brown. Remove from cookie sheet. Cool slightly on wire rack.

5. Roll warm cookies in powdered sugar; cool on wire rack. Roll in powdered sugar again.

THE CHRISTMAS BAKERY
ON HUCKLEBERRY HILL

JENNIFER BECKSTRAND

CHAPTER 1

"What does the *Ordnung* say about Vikings, Felty?" Anna Helmuth said, straightening her glasses to get a better look at her husband. Sometimes she wasn't sure what the *Ordnung*—the rules of their Old Order Amish community—did and did not allow.

Felty didn't even glance up from his paper. "What's a Viking, Annie-banannie?"

"You know. Those men with horns on their hats."

"Horns? That doesn't sound very safe. What if you bent over and poked your friend in the eye?"

"Now, Felty." Anna tied off the final strand of yarn and leaned back in her rocking chair. She had finally mastered the art of crochet, and this Viking beanie she'd made for her grandson proved it. She had always been a knitter. Felty had told her she knitted as if she were born with a pair of needles in her hand, and up until last year, her knitting had been sufficient. But then she had realized that if she wanted to find her grandson Titus the perfect wife, she would need more than knitting and cooking skills.

Last March, Anna had pulled out all the stops, bought an instruction book, and taught herself how to crochet.

All for Titus's sake.

She hoped he appreciated it.

"Look, Felty," she said, holding up her latest creation.

Her husband of nearly sixty-five years lowered his paper and peered over his reading glasses. "That is wonderful-gute, Annie. I ain't never seen no one as talented as you." He raised his eyebrows. "What is it?"

"It's a Viking beanie." The beanie was gray with little nubs and nobs and post stitches to make it look like a helmet with two crocheted white horns poking out either side at the top. It was truly formidable. Surely the bishop couldn't disapprove after she'd spent so much time making it.

"Very nice. Those horns wouldn't poke out anyone's eye."

Anna stabbed her crochet hook into the ball of yarn. "Do you think Titus will like it?"

Felty squinted as if he were trying to get a better look at the Viking horns. "Titus adores everything you make for him, Annie, but he usually wears a beanie beneath his straw hat when he does winter chores. I don't think the horns will fit under his hat."

Anna furrowed her brow. "Oh dear. Maybe I should have made him a Minion scarf."

Felty looked at Anna with an appreciative glint in his eye. "Annie, you're so smart. I don't know what a Viking *or* a Minion is."

Anna waved away his praise. "It's in the new crochet pattern book that Cassie gave me. I just follow the directions. You can do anything if you just read the directions."

"Not me. I've tried knitting, and I don't dare to try crocheting. Are you sorry you didn't marry someone smarter, Banannie?"

"Just because you can't knit doesn't mean you're not smart. *Gotte* gives each one of us our own gifts. I can cook and knit and crochet. You never saw a horse you couldn't calm or a gadget you couldn't figure out. *Gotte* has been very generous with both of us."

Felty stroked the long gray beard on his chin. "Indeed He has. The best gift He ever gave me was you, Annie. I'd be greedy to wish for more."

"Now, Felty. Don't tease."

Felty folded his paper, and it only took him three tries to get out of his recliner. He shuffled to Anna's rocker, grunted as he braced himself on the arm of her chair, and planted a kiss on her cheek. "I wouldn't tease you about a thing like that."

Anna giggled. "You were such a handsome boy. I thought you were delirious with a fever when you asked if you could drive me home from the *singeon*. I nearly keeled over dead from surprise."

"And I nearly floated off the ground when you said yes."

Anna stuffed her yarn and Titus's new beanie into the canvas bag she kept near her rocking chair. "I want Titus to be that happy, and he needs this beanie."

"Do you still think we need to find him a wife?"

"*Ach,* I've already found him a wife, dear. It's just going to be a little tricky getting them together. I don't know if I have the crocheting skills to do it."

Felty went into the kitchen and retrieved a ginger

snap from the cookie jar. Like any true Amish *mammi,* Anna always kept her cookie jar full. "If anyone has the right crocheting skills, it's you, Annie," Felty said, taking a hearty bite. His teeth scraped against the cookie. Anna smiled. He liked his cookies hard. "Who is the girl you have your sights set on?" he said.

"Adam Wengerd's fiancée."

Felty choked on his ginger snap, and Anna had to get up and pat him on the back until he could catch his breath. "Annie, I know you're worried about finding the right girl for Titus, but it doesn't seem very nice to steal another boy's fiancée."

Anna sighed. "You're right as usual, Felty. I suppose I should have mentioned that she's not Adam's fiancée yet, and quite honestly, she and Adam don't suit each other at all. Katie Rose is a shy, sweet little thing who will be able to see Titus for the wonderful-*gute* boy he is." Anna picked up an envelope from the table next to her rocking chair. "Katie Rose's *mater* has written me a letter. You remember the Gingeriches, don't you, Felty?"

Felty closed one eye in concentration. "Samuel and Martha Gingerich?"

"*Jah.* They used to be in our district."

"They moved to Augusta eight or nine years ago."

Anna nodded and slipped three pieces of handwritten pink paper out of the envelope. "Martha wants to send her daughter Katie Rose to stay with us so that Katie can secure a marriage proposal from Adam during the Christmas holidays."

"Why Christmas?"

"Everyone knows that Christmas is the most romantic time of the year," Anna said.

"And you want Titus to be the one to propose instead?"

"*Jah,* but Martha wants Adam Wengerd. Adam and Katie Rose played together as children, and their *maters* practically have them engaged already."

"What does Adam think of all this?"

Anna shrugged. "He's willing. Katie Rose was thirteen when she left Bonduel, and she was pretty, even then. Adam's had a hard time finding a wife in Bonduel, he's going to be in a hurry to propose before Katie gets to know him very well."

"Now, Annie-girl, Adam is a very nice boy."

Anna scrunched her lips together. "Well, dear, we're all entitled to our own opinion. I'll never breathe a word to anyone about how I feel about Adam Wengerd, even though everyone knows he's too big for his britches."

Felty stroked his long beard. "I don't wonder but you'll be able to bring Titus and Katie Rose together, Annie, but what will Martha Gingerich think if her daughter comes home engaged to the wrong boy?"

"We'll cross that bridge when we come to it. I've got bigger fish to fry just now. Titus will be here any minute, and I've got to think of a way to keep him coming back to Huckleberry Hill every day until Christmas."

"Why don't you just tell him you've found a girl for him?" Felty said.

Anna practically squeaked her disapproval. "I can't do that, Felty. Titus is a *gute* boy, but if he thinks we expect anything from him, he'll run for the hills. Katie is shy. They've got to get together without knowing we want them to."

Felty took another bite, scraping his teeth against

his cookie. "I would say it's impossible, but that's how most of your matches have worked out, Annie. If anyone can bring two people together who would rather not, it's you."

"*Denki,* dear. I've worked very hard to hone my skills, and not just the knitting and crocheting ones."

"Titus comes up once a week to help with chores yet," Felty said.

Anna shook her head. "We need him on Huckleberry Hill every day. Katie will only be here until Christmas. Romance takes time." Anna clutched her chest when a knock came at the door. "*Ach, du lieva.* He's here already. I'll just have to make it up as I go. You'll play along, won't you, Felty?"

Felty ambled to the door. "I'll follow wherever you lead, Banannie."

Titus stood on the porch wrapped in his heavy black coat with a straw hat on his head and a toothpick in his mouth. He was never far from a toothpick. "Hullo, Mammi. Hullo, Dawdi. It's a wonderful cold day, and it ain't even December yet." Titus's toothpick hung from his bottom lip and looked as if it would tumble at any minute, but it never did and he seemed to have no problem talking with it dangling from his mouth. Such a dear boy.

Anna bustled to the door to give Titus his weekly hug. "How is my very favorite grandson named Titus?"

Titus furrowed his brow before bursting into a smile. The toothpick stayed put. "Mammi, I'm your only grandson named Titus."

"That is *gute.* I wouldn't want to offend any of my other grandchildren. *Cum reu,*" Anna said, ushering him into the house before all the warm air escaped.

A house heated by a woodstove couldn't afford to lose even a trickle of warmth.

Before coming in, Titus stomped the snow off his boots. He was always wonderful thoughtful like that. Felty helped him off with his coat and took his hat. He did indeed have a bright red beanie on underneath his straw hat. Anna recognized it immediately. It was one she had knitted for him last year.

"Can I help you off with your boots?" Felty said. Anna pursed her lips. Felty had never taken Titus's coat and hat before, and he had certainly never offered to help him with his boots. Felty was trying too hard, and for sure and certain, Titus would notice.

Ach, du lieva, he did. His eyes darted suspiciously between Felty and Anna, and his toothpick quivered on his lip.

She'd have to think fast if she didn't want him to get scared off. "*Cum,*" she said, pulling a chair from under the table and motioning for Titus to sit.

Not taking his eyes from Anna, Titus sat as if he was afraid the chair might bite him. Anna poured him a glass of milk and grabbed three cookies from the cookie jar. Maybe she could soften Titus up with a hard cookie. She and Felty created further suspicion when they sat down at the table on either side of their grandson. Anna tried to smile as if nothing was out of the ordinary, as if Titus's entire future didn't hang in the balance. She'd never get him to agree to anything if he was suspicious.

Unable to relax in the face of so much attention, Titus shoved one of the cookies between his back molars and bit down hard. "Have you got a list of chores for me, Dawdi, or should I just do the regular ones?"

"Your *mammi* has something she wants to ask you," Felty said, pinning Anna with a significant look as if to say that if she hadn't thought of a plan, now would be a *gute* time to do it.

"*Ach, jah,* of course," Anna said, clearing her throat and hoping by sheer willpower that something brilliant would come to her. Titus's happiness depended on it. "Titus, you know we love you."

Felty nodded eagerly, encouraging Anna with his eyes. "In the past year, you have done more work around our farm than anyone else."

"It's no burden," Titus said. "You and Mammi treat me nice. Mamm says I'm scatterbrained."

Anna reached out and patted Titus's hand. "You're no such thing. You just have a lively mind, that's all, and I need your help with something."

"What is it?"

"I hesitate to ask, because it means you would have to come here every day. It's a big commitment."

"I'll do anything for you, Mammi. Just say the word. Dat says we must help the elderly any way we can."

Felty frowned. "I'm only eighty-six. Don't put me in my grave just yet."

"You see," Anna said, fidgeting while waiting for an idea to come to her. "You see, I am going to need a great deal of help with our Christmas . . . goat."

Felty kept a smile plastered on his lips as his brows inched toward the sky.

Anna stole a glance at Felty and shrugged. A Christmas goat was the only thing that had come to her. Crocheting that Vikings hat had drained her of all her creative juices.

Titus's mouth fell open. The toothpick balanced precariously on his bottom lip. "Christmas what?"

"Our Christmas goat. It's a family tradition."

"Family tradition?" Titus said, scratching his head. "I don't remember that tradition."

"We're starting a new one. There's nothing like a goat to perk up the Christmas season."

"But, Mammi, you don't have a goat."

"We will buy one. That's why it's called a Christmas goat, because we get it at Christmastime to fill our hearts with cheer."

Titus looked excessively concerned and even more confused. "I've never heard of a goat filling hearts with cheer."

"That's why it's important that we start this new tradition. You've been missing out on half the fun of Christmas for far too long."

"I had no idea," Titus said.

Anna poured more milk into Titus's nearly full glass. "I will need you to come up every day in December to feed it and milk it and take care of it. I'll be too busy, and Felty is too old to learn how to milk a goat."

"I'm only eighty-six," Felty said.

Oh dear. She hoped she hadn't offended Felty, but it couldn't be helped. They needed Titus to come to Huckleberry Hill, and Felty's age would have to be the excuse, no matter how weak it sounded.

Titus pinched his toothpick between his thumb and index finger. "I really want to help you, Mammi, but there's one problem. Once when I was little, a goat tried to eat me."

"A goat tried to eat you?" Felty said.

Titus's head bobbed up and down like a buoy on

the lake. "I was five years old. He jumped and rested his hooves on my shoulders and knocked me to the ground. Then he snatched the lollipop out of my mouth with his teeth and ate it, stick and all. I've been afraid of goats ever since. Maybe we should ask Ben to help you with your goat. I don't know if I'm brave enough."

Anna swiped at the air as if pushing that suggestion as far from her mind as possible. "Ben has a wife, a little one, and another on the way. He couldn't possibly come every day." She squeezed his hand, probably a little too hard, because her knuckles turned white. "Titus, I need all the courage you can muster. Our goat needs you. You're the only one who can save Christmas."

"You need me to save Christmas?" Titus stared at her for a few moments as the toothpick between his lips bobbed up and down like the second hand on a watch. "You're not planning on eating this goat, are you, Mammi? I don't like to eat a pet once I've named it."

"Eating it? Titus, I could never eat our Christmas goat. Christmas is a time for peace on earth and goodwill toward men . . . and goats."

Titus nodded as the uncertainty in his eyes gave way to calm determination. "I'll do it, but only because I love you so much, Mammi."

"*Wunderbarr,*" Anna said. "You won't regret it."

Concern passed across Titus's features. "I'll be okay. I just have to remember to leave my lollipops at home. No sense in looking for trouble."

"*Gute* idea," Anna said. "Now. I want to talk to you about a special Christmas beanie."

CHAPTER 2

Trina Benson rolled her car to a stop in front of the gravel road that led up to Huckleberry Hill. She bent her head to peer up the snow-covered lane. "Katie Rose, I hate to say this, but I don't think my little hatchback is going to make it up that hill, even with snow tires. I'm sorry, but can you manage?"

Katie peered up the hill. It had been eight years since she'd been to Bonduel, but she still remembered the steep and long walk up Huckleberry Hill. She had a large, heavy suitcase to drag up with her, but she would be in trouble if Trina got stuck in the snow or lost control and slid down the hill and into a tree.

"The older I am, the more nervous I get driving in the snow," Trina said. "I should probably quit driving altogether and move to Florida."

Katie fished into her pocket and handed Trina some money. "I could use a little fresh air after that stuffy bus."

Her heart only started galloping when she got out

of the car and pulled her small traveling bag and her giant brown suitcase out of Trina's trunk. For once, she regretted being such an obedient child. If she'd had her way, she'd be at home baking cookies for the school Christmas program or delivering Christmas fudge to her neighbors and friends. Instead, she was standing at the bottom of a daunting hill contemplating the miserable task before her.

Get a proposal from Adam Wengerd by Christmastime or die an old maedle, Mamm had warned.

The thought of dying an old maid had been enough to get Katie out of Augusta and back to Bonduel. She wasn't brave enough by half to try to get a husband, but she didn't want to end up an old *maedle,* either. In her Amish community, old maids lived off of the kindness of their brothers and sisters, never having a home of their own or respect from their neighbors. Old maids ended up keeping house and taking care of other people's children. Katie would do just about anything to keep from becoming an old maid.

Even marry Adam Wengerd.

It wasn't that Katie was against Adam Wengerd as a husband, but she didn't know him that well. They had been friends in sixth and seventh grade, before Katie had moved away. All Katie could remember was that Adam had been handsome and tall and that he liked to talk about softball and hunting. Now she had to make him fall in love with her.

What if he didn't? What if he found her boring and awkward? He might decide she was too quiet. Her brothers scolded her constantly for being mousy and shy. "What boy will try for a date if you won't talk to him, Katie?" her brother Mahlon had said.

But what of her feelings? She didn't want to be an old maid, but that didn't mean she should settle for just anyone, did it? What if Adam turned out to be mean or lazy? How could she even know such a thing before she married him?

Maybe there was still time to find someone in Augusta.

She shook her head. She was twenty-four years old, timid, and quiet. Adam Wengerd was the boy who could save her from dreaded spinsterhood, but the thought of trying to convince him to marry her made her sick.

Being the seventh of ten children, Katie had been all but ignored by her parents. Mamm had always been too busy running the house to give Katie or her siblings much attention, but Katie didn't mind being insignificant. As long as Mamm would let her cook for the family and try out new recipes, she was perfectly content. The thought of trying to win a husband terrified her. She'd cried all night the night before she'd left home. How could she bear the embarrassment of it all? Cooking all her best dishes to wheedle a proposal out of Adam, trying to come up with interesting things to say, and Adam all the while knowing she was so desperate that she had to come all the way to Bonduel to find a husband.

Maybe being an old maid wouldn't be so bad.

Katie exhaled slowly and picked up her bag and her suitcase. She'd better get going. Mamm said Adam would arrive at Huckleberry Hill in time for dinner, and Katie was expected to cook for him. That's how Mamm said Katie would win Adam's heart—with her cooking. What boy could resist Katie's sour cream apple pie?

Her suitcase clattered as she hefted it in her hand and began her journey up the hill. She certainly hoped Anna Helmuth was expecting her. What would she do if she showed up and Anna had no place to put her? Katie imagined trudging back down the hill and going from house to house in search of a job as a cook or a maid. What would Mamm think if she walked all the way back to Augusta?

The suitcase got heavier and heavier as she hiked up Huckleberry Hill. Katie almost regretted bringing it, but she had to impress Adam with her cooking skills. For sure and certain, she wouldn't win Adam's heart with clever conversation. Her *mater* had made that perfectly clear.

With her arms shaking and her legs feeling like jelly, Katie finally made it to the top of the hill. A friendly white clapboard house with a big front window stood to her left, and a red barn with white trim sat farther down the lane directly in front of her. In such a pretty place, perhaps she could convince Adam to fall in love with her.

A caramel-and-white blur of hair and legs ran toward her, bleating as if it was very happy to see her. She caught her breath as the floppy-eared goat jumped up and propped its hooves on her legs just above her knees. In surprise, she dropped her travel bag and suitcase, and they clattered into the snow. "*Ach!*"

"Beth, stop!"

Katie tensed as a young man, probably about her age, with long legs and a gray beanie with horns came running toward her. The goat was either playing a game of tag or wanted to escape. It pushed off and ran down the hill as fast as its little legs would go, *baa*ing all the way.

The young man, who seemed very intent on catching the goat, took a *gute* look at Katie and stopped as if he'd run into an invisible brick wall. His eyes grew wide, and the toothpick between his lips tumbled to the ground. His beanie was the most unusual thing Katie had ever seen—gray and lumpy, with what looked like two horns sticking out of either side. She thought it was sort of cute, as if she could tell he was good-natured just from his choice of beanies. Surely no one who wore a beanie like that would take himself very seriously. He stood frozen to the ground and stared at her, as if he wouldn't mind being there all day. As if he hadn't just been chasing a goat.

Katie wasn't sure if it would be more awkward to say something or remain silent, but if they did remain silent, he would definitely lose his goat. She gave him a tentative smile. "Do you . . . do you want me to help you catch your goat?"

He seemed to snap out of his stunned daze. "*Ach* . . . uh . . . *jah*. That would be wonderful-*gute*. My *mammi* would be heartbroken if I lost her special Christmas goat. It's a new family tradition." He reached down and picked up her suitcase and her travel bag. "Can I help you into the house with these first?"

It was a very thoughtful gesture, considering he might lose his goat with further delay. "Maybe we should find your goat first."

He nodded as if he thought that was a very *gute* idea, set her bags on the ground, and started jogging down the hill. "Her name is Beth. Sometimes she'll come when I call. Mostly she likes to run away. Don't be afraid of her, though. She doesn't steal lollipops or beanies."

He seemed like a very nice young man, not the type to expect her to say something clever or entertaining every time she opened her mouth. She followed him down the hill, calling the goat's name and listening for a sign that she was near. They followed her tracks halfway down the hill, where they veered off into the bushes that grew along the steep incline on the right side of the lane.

The young man stopped and stared at her for a second too long. Had he forgotten about the goat again? She nearly forgot about the goat herself. His eyes were the color of a deep blue lake.

"I don't want you to slip," he said. "What if I hike down and herd Beth up here to the lane?"

Katie nodded. "I'll try to grab her before she runs away."

"There's a red Christmas ribbon around her neck. Hook your hand onto that."

The young man crunched through the snow and into the bushes. Katie stood with her arms wrapped around herself to keep warm, trying to breathe quietly so she would be able to hear the goat coming back through the snow. She didn't want to risk losing someone's special Christmas goat.

"Beth," the young man called again.

Soon Katie heard the muted clatter of hooves in the snow, and the goat appeared from between the bushes. Katie gasped and reached for the red ribbon around the goat's neck.

Red ribbon with a bright red Christmas bow.

Despite the goat's quick reflexes, Katie caught her on the first try. Beth didn't resist so much as drag

Katie along with her, farther down the hill and on to a new adventure. Katie planted her feet and held on with all her might, but her winter boots met a patch of hard ice. A squeak escaped her lips as her feet slipped from under her and she plummeted to the ground, grunting as her backside met with the hard-packed snow. She'd have a very impressive bruise that she wouldn't be able to show anyone, but at least she still had hold of the goat. Beth stopped trying to go anywhere, gazed at Katie as if Katie had just done something terribly embarrassing, and started nibbling on Katie's coat sleeve.

"*Ach.* Don't do that, little goat," Katie said, making her voice as sweet as possible. "Mamm would never approve if I came home with one sleeve missing."

The young man trudged out from the bushes and immediately ran to her when he saw her predicament. "Are you all right?" He offered a hand and pulled Katie to her feet. With a look of deep concern, he cupped his fingers around her elbow until he was sure she was securely on her feet. "Did Beth knock you over? I'm wonderful sorry."

Once the young man had a firm hold of Beth's ribbon, Katie let go and brushed the snow from her dress and coat. "Beth behaved as well as she could for being a goat. I slipped on the ice, and then she tried to eat my coat."

"Goats will eat lollipops, but they don't usually eat coats, even if they smell good, like yours does." He turned bright red and stared faithfully at his boots. "I mean, even if your coat smelled good—which I can't say that it does, because who ever notices how a coat smells?—but even if your coat smelled like chocolate and lilacs, Beth wouldn't eat it." He lifted his eyes and grinned at her. "Goats are like babies. Babies put everything in their mouths. Goats nibble on stuff to find out what it is. At least that's what the man at the dairy told me."

"Beth seems like a nice goat, except it was naughty of her to run away."

"She can jump over any fence and wriggle through small holes. I think it's what she does for fun. And I think she likes to see me run." He motioned up the hill. "Are you here to see my *mammi?*"

Katie nodded.

He tugged on Beth's ribbon, and the three of them started walking.

"What is a Christmas goat?" Katie said. "I've never heard of such a thing."

The young man stuffed his hand into his pocket, pulled out a toothpick, and stuck it between his teeth. "Mammi says it's a family tradition to have a Christmas goat. The man from the dairy brought it last week. I'm taking care of her because I don't want to be the reason that everyone's Christmas is ruined."

Katie furrowed her brow. "It would be terrible if Christmas got ruined."

He reached down and patted the goat on the head. "Mammi let me name it even though it's her goat."

"Beth is a very nice name."

"It's short for 'Bethlehem.' I figured that since it's a Christmas goat, it should have a Christmas kind of name."

"That's very clever of you," Katie said. Bethlehem was the perfect name for a Christmas goat. She'd never been half that clever. "Is Anna Helmuth your *mammi?*"

"Oh, *sis yuscht.* I never even told you my name." He snatched off his horned beanie as if he wanted her to get a complete and *gute* look at him. His white-blond hair stuck out all over his head, brought to life by static electricity. A boyish cowlick made the hair in front tumble in unruly tufts over his forehead. "I'm Titus Helmuth. Anna and Felty's grandson. Mammi didn't tell me anyone was coming today, or I would have come down the hill to help you with your bags."

"Trina's car couldn't make it up the hill, and how could you have known what time I'd be coming?"

"I suppose that's so. Still, I'm wonderful sorry you had to carry them up the hill by yourself."

They made it to the crest of the hill, where Katie had dropped her bags. With one hand clasped firmly around Beth's ribbon, Titus picked up the bulky suitcase.

"You don't need to do that," Katie said. She hated to be a burden on someone who already had the important responsibility of a Christmas goat.

His toothpick pointed upward when he smiled. "You shouldn't have to carry something this heavy when I'm happy to carry it for you. My *dawdi* taught me better than that." He drew his brows together in concentration. "Or maybe it was my *mammi.* Anyways, one of them taught me better than that. Or both of them. I can't remember."

Katie picked up her travel bag. "It's so kind of you, especially with a Christmas goat to mind."

"You look familiar," Titus said. "Do I know you?"

"I used to live in Bonduel, but my family moved away nine years ago."

The front door of the house opened, and Anna Helmuth, looking older but as radiant and delighted as ever, bounded down the porch steps like a sixty-year-old. She wore a bright red sweater and a hunter green dress. With her white *kapp* and equally-as-white hair, she looked as festive as a Christmas ornament. Everything about Anna felt as warm and inviting as Christmastime. Her blue eyes twinkled merrily, and the lines on her face looked as if she hadn't frowned a day in her life.

Anna threw out her hands and squealed as if Katie were one of her own grandchildren. "Katie Rose Gingerich, all grown up. I was thrilled when your *mamm* wrote and asked if you could stay over Christmas."

Christmas. Katie would be away from home for Christmas, trying to snag a boy who probably wouldn't even like her. She couldn't think of anything more depressing. Unwanted tears pooled in her eyes.

Anna wrapped her short arms tightly around Katie's waist. "Is everything all right, dear?"

Titus frowned. "Was it the goat? I'm sorry if it was the goat. I can take her back to the barn."

Katie blinked away the tears. Titus and Anna didn't need to hear how worried she was about getting a husband—or not getting one. "*Nae. Nae.* I am just missing home, I suppose." She sniffed and wiped her eyes. "It's silly. I've only been gone a few hours."

"It's not silly," Titus said. "Everybody misses home. I cried like a baby the last time we went camping."

Anna's eyes danced. "I thought you liked to camp, Titus."

"I do." He raised his index finger. "But I nearly chopped my finger off with my hatchet."

"That would make anybody cry," Katie said, grateful Titus had taken the attention off of her. It was childish of her to cry, anyway. Who cried over a humiliation that hadn't even happened yet?

A fluffy white dog wearing a red doggy sweater bounced down the porch steps. Beth bleated loudly, and the dog jumped out of its skin and yelped as if it had been stuck with a pin. Whining as if it had lost a fight, it ran back up the porch steps and into the safety of the house.

"Now, Beth," Anna scolded with a twinkle in her eye, "I'm afraid being the special Christmas goat has gone to your head. You know how upset Sparky gets when you talk like that. Please try to have some consideration for her feelings."

"*Maa*," Bethlehem said, with a blank stare as if Anna's lecture had no effect on her whatsoever.

Anna wrapped a grandmotherly arm around Katie and looked at Titus. "Katie will be staying with us for four weeks. I know you'll make her feel welcome."

Titus's toothpick traveled up and down as he nodded eagerly. "I hope you like goats."

Katie felt her face get warm, though she couldn't figure out exactly why. Maybe it was the way Titus looked at her, or the embarrassment she'd feel if Titus knew why she was staying with the Helmuths. "Your goat seems very nice."

Anna nodded as if she was extremely satisfied with that answer. "We've already got four gallons of goat's milk. *Cum*, let's get you into the house. My feet are freezing."

Katie looked down and realized that Anna wore only stockings, and they were now soaking wet. "Oh dear, Anna. Your stockings."

Anna tiptoed along the sidewalk. "I didn't have time to put on my boots. I can't even bend over to put on my boots. It's a *gute* thing stockings dry so fast. Felty will be so glad to see you."

Titus followed them up the steps. Anna opened the front door. "Your clothes are wonderful heavy," Titus said, setting the suitcase just inside the door. He still had one hand attached to the goat, which stood on the porch. "I guess I haven't carried a girl's suitcase before. But I'm not complaining." He blushed and smiled sheepishly. "It's been an honor to carry your suitcase. I'll gladly do it anytime. I didn't mean to offend you about the heaviness of your suitcase. It wasn't heavy at all."

Katie giggled. She'd never met someone so eager to please. "No need to worry." She lifted her travel bag. "I have all my clothes in here. This suitcase is full of gadgets."

"Gadgets?" Felty Helmuth, with eyes as twinkly as Anna's, sat in a recliner in the great room. He pulled the lever on his chair, and it catapulted him to his feet. "I love gadgets. What did you bring?"

Katie grabbed the suitcase handle to lift it onto the table. Titus, still holding on to the goat, nudged her hand aside, leaned over, and lifted the suitcase for her. This meant that Beth had to come into the kitchen with him. Her hooves clomped on the wood floor as she stepped into the house.

Whining and carrying on, Sparky jumped from her perch on the rug in the great room and tore down the hall, out of sight.

"Now, Titus," Anna said, "you're going to give Sparky a conniption. The special Christmas goat cannot come into the house."

"Sorry, Mammi." Titus looked at Katie like a little kid who wanted some candy. "Can I see the gadgets sometime?"

"Tie Beth to one of the porch railings," Felty said, "then come and have a look."

With a spring in his step, Titus was out and back in two shakes of a goat's tail.

Katie opened her suitcase, and the four of them gathered around it as if it were a treasure chest. Katie pointed to the box containing one of her favorite gadgets. "This is an apple peeler, corer, and slicer." She pulled it out of the box. "You stick the apple here and turn this crank, and it peels, slices, and cores the apple for you. It saves hours if you make a lot of apple pie."

"That's a handy invention," Felty said, taking it from her and turning it over in his hand.

"This is a garlic press for fresh garlic," Katie said, pointing to her treasures, "and this is a pomegranate de-seeder. Here is a digital thermometer for candy and cheese-making and a meat grinder to make sausage." She rummaged through the suitcase. "I also brought a pasta maker, a lemon zester, and my maple rolling pin. I hope it's all right I brought all this. I . . . I thought I'd need it. . . ." To impress Adam.

Anna slid an arm around her. "Of course, dear. Never underestimate the power of a good kitchen gadget."

"Do you know how to use all of these?" Titus said.
Katie nodded.

"You must be a genius," he said, admiration evident in his eyes. She didn't deserve it, but it made her feel strangely warm and tingly. No one at home ever said such things to her.

But would Adam agree with Titus and save her from becoming an old maid?

She glanced at the bird clock on the wall. She wouldn't have much time to wonder. "I'd better get to work. He'll be here in less than two hours."

Titus suddenly looked concerned. His toothpick drooped on his lip. "Who'll be here?"

"Adam Wengerd," Anna said, when Katie didn't answer. "Katie is making him dinner."

Katie couldn't have answered. She'd been rendered speechless by the thought of the boy she hoped would fall madly in love with her chocolate chip cookies.

She really didn't want to be an old maid.

CHAPTER 3

Titus chewed on his toothpick. Why was Adam Wengerd coming to Huckleberry Hill? Adam and Katie must be cousins. That was the only explanation for it. Titus thought about some of the cousins he hadn't seen for a while. Max and Mary. Gideon and Aaron. If they came to town, for sure and certain he'd be up to see them in a heartbeat. With other relatives, like Norman Coblenz and Aunt Esther, he might take his time. Adam and Katie must be very close.

Titus vaguely remembered Katie from when she lived in Bonduel. They hadn't gone to the same school or been in the same district, and he hadn't known that Katie and Adam were cousins, and that had to be his excuse, because Titus couldn't fathom why he hadn't fallen in love with Katie Rose Gingerich nine years ago. Not that he was in love with her now or anything, but he surely would have fallen nine years ago. Katie had the silkiest chocolate-brown eyes he'd ever seen and the silkiest chocolate-brown hair. Not to mention she smelled like chocolate.

He probably shouldn't mention to her that chocolate was his favorite thing ever. She might get suspicious.

But that wasn't the reason he would have fallen in love with her nine years ago. In the fifteen short minutes he'd known her, she'd been kind and sweet and didn't think she was better than other people. She'd helped him catch Bethlehem, and she hadn't even gotten annoyed when she fell. Titus was sort of growing attached to Bethlehem, and he appreciated that Katie was nice to his goat.

Of course, that would have been nine years ago. Now he didn't know whether he would fall in love with her or not. "What are you going to make for dinner?" Titus asked.

Katie's eyes nearly popped out of her head, and that would have been very bad. "What am I going to make for dinner?"

Titus clamped his mouth shut. He hadn't meant to upset her. He always seemed to say the wrong thing.

Katie glanced at the clock again. "I'm so sorry, Anna, but do we have time to go to the store?"

"I can go to the store, if you need me to," Titus said, feeling sorry for how pale Katie looked all of a sudden.

Katie sighed as if she'd been holding her breath for a long time. "Oh, Titus. Would you?"

Mammi didn't seem the least bit ruffled by Katie's sudden panic. "Why don't we see what we've got in the fridge? And I've got a whole cellar full of maple syrup, huckleberry jelly, and green beans. We should be able to come up with something."

Katie nodded. "Okay. That is a *gute* idea. I'm sorry to be so difficult, but I want to make a *gute* impression."

"Of course you do, dear," Mammi said, patting Katie on the arm.

She must be wonderful excited to see her cousin.

Mammi's fridge was crammed full of bottles. Titus moved in for a better look. Three bottles of ketchup, at least that many of mustard, salad dressing, mayonnaise, Tabasco sauce, horseradish. Titus couldn't see anything but condiments and a bag of carrots. If Katie couldn't come up with an idea, maybe he could help. He was very *gute* with ketchup.

Did she know that ketchup and carrots made a *gute* appetizer?

Mammi opened the freezer for good measure. Peas, corn, a bag of something icy, another bag of something icier, and an actual bag of ice.

A deep line appeared between Mammi's eyebrows as she and Katie stared at the contents of the freezer. "You could make green bean and corn casserole with ketchup sauce."

"I love that one," Felty said.

Katie slid her arm around Mammi's shoulder and planted a kiss on her cheek. "You are so kind, Anna." She poked at one of the icy packages in the freezer. "Is this chicken?"

"*Jah,*" Mammi said. "But it's been sitting in the freezer for almost a year."

Katie smiled a tentative, hopeful smile. Titus thought it was the prettiest thing he'd ever seen next to her chocolate-brown eyes. "I won't tell if you won't."

"Tell what?" Mammi said.

Katie's smile grew in strength. "Do you have shortening?"

"I eat it on my toast every morning," Dawdi said.

"Instead of butter?" Katie said.

Dawdi shrugged. "They taste the same to me."

Katie glanced once again at the clock. "I might have time. . . ."

"I'll help you any way I can," Mammi said.

"What do you want me to do?" Titus chimed in. He'd do anything to keep that smile on Katie's face.

Katie's gaze was as soft and mushy as chocolate pudding. "You want to help?"

"Of course. I'm *gute* at celery. I once chopped ten pounds for my cousin's wedding."

Katie's eyes pooled with moisture before she looked away and swiped her hand across her face.

A lump grew in his throat, and he couldn't swallow. He was always saying the wrong thing. "I don't have to chop celery if you don't want me to."

She reached out and touched his arm. "I don't mind. I'm just missing home, I guess." She picked up her small travel bag, pulled out a light pink apron, and put it on. On the bib of the apron were three embroidered hearts, one red, one pink, and one purple. "I think I'll make chicken potpies. Do you . . . do you think that's good enough?"

"I love chicken potpies," was all Titus could think to say. His arm was still tingling from where she had touched him, and he felt a little dizzy in the head, as if his brother Ben had smacked him in the head with a two-by-four—which had actually happened once.

Titus slipped outside and quickly put Bethlehem in the barn, then he sprinted back to the house to help Katie with dinner. She needed him. He didn't want to spend an extra minute lollygagging in the snow.

He carried a bag of flour from the cellar for Katie's piecrust, and she smiled at him as if he'd done something really important. She wasn't mad at him for the celery remark, because she asked him to chop the celery and the carrots and didn't boss him around or tell him he was doing it the wrong way.

Katie worked with sure purpose, rolling out the dough while Mammi sprinkled flour and measured the peas. Katie obviously wanted to impress Adam Wengerd. They must be very close cousins.

Katie kept glancing at the clock, but it seemed like she dreaded the passage of time rather than anticipated it. Once the pies were in the oven, Titus washed dishes while Kate dried and Dawdi swept the floor.

Titus had just drained the sink and wiped his hands as a knock came at the door. Katie stiffened beside him and turned as pale as that apron she had on. She really must have been anxious to see her cousin. Titus felt sort of sorry for her. Maybe Adam was a cousin like Norman. Norman had once told Titus that Titus's brains must have fallen out of his ear as a baby. It sort of put a damper on their relationship.

Mammi and Dawdi smiled as if they were very excited about Adam's visit, but they made no move to answer the door, and Katie looked to be in no condition to answer it, either. Titus glanced down at his hands, wrinkly from being submerged in the water so long. Norman would make fun of him for wrinkly hands. What would Adam say?

It didn't matter, because Katie needed help, and Titus was the one to give it, wrinkles or no wrinkles.

He glanced at Katie and flashed a reassuring smile.
Adam was a nice person. He wouldn't be anything
like Norman.

Adam stood on the porch, a smile stretched across
those brilliant white teeth. "Titus Helmuth," Adam
said, "*Wie gehts?*" Without waiting for an answer, he
strolled into the room as if the house were his. "So,
where is the girl I've been waiting for?"

Katie didn't even smile. She stood behind the
counter as if she was afraid to come out from its pro-
tection.

Titus was pretty sure she was going to faint.

And he was pretty sure Adam's eyes were going to
fall out of his head. "My *mamm* said you had turned
out well, Katie, but I told her I wouldn't commit to
anything until I saw for myself."

Katie still didn't move a muscle, though Titus
might have seen her lip twitch slightly. Mammi and
Dawdi stood silently as if they were watching one of
their grandchildren perform in a school program.

Couldn't Mammi and Dawdi see how upset Katie
was? Somebody had to do something to help her feel
more at ease with her cousin. "Would you like to see
my Christmas goat, Adam?" Titus said. "It's in the
barn."

"What's a Christmas goat?"

Katie forced a smile, which came out more like a
grimace. At least she was able to find her voice. "It's . . .
it's a special Helmuth Christmas tradition."

Adam patted Titus on the shoulder. "Maybe later,
kid. It's cold, and I'm hungry."

Kid? Had Adam forgotten that he and Titus were
the same age? Titus chewed on his toothpick. Didn't
Adam remember all those games of softball at recess?

Didn't he notice that Titus was a good four inches taller than him?

Adam sniffed the air. "Mamm says you're a fine cook, Katie. It smells *gute* enough to eat."

Katie's fingers were clenched so tightly together, Titus feared her circulation would be cut off. "*Denki.* I made chicken potpie."

"And snickerdoodles," Titus volunteered. He loved snickerdoodles.

Adam puckered his whole face until he looked like a shriveled apple. "*Ach.* I hate chicken potpie."

Katie seemed to wither like a flower in the heat. "I'm sorry."

Oh, *sis yuscht.* If Adam turned out to be like Titus's cousin Norman, poor Katie didn't stand a chance. "I love chicken potpies," Titus said. "Can I eat yours?"

For the first time since Adam had come in, he seemed to sense Katie's discomfort. He smiled at her. "I'm just teasing. I can tolerate chicken potpies as long as they don't have carrots. I hate cooked carrots."

It was Titus's turn to wither. If only he hadn't been such a *gute* chopper. . . .

Katie glanced at Titus with a look of sympathy in her eyes. He stood up straighter and winked at her. He didn't want her to think he was upset. Something told him it would only make her more nervous.

"Katie has made chicken potpies for dinner," Dawdi said. "I have a box of Bran Flakes in the cupboard if you'd rather eat those. They'll keep you regular."

Adam glanced around the room and gave Dawdi

an awkward laugh. "I suppose I could pick out the carrots. I do that all the time at home."

Adam stuck out his hand toward Titus. Titus figured Adam wanted him to take it. He did. Adam's handshake was firm and determined. "Nice to see you again, Titus. Tell that Christmas goat hello for me." He chuckled, and Titus got the very unchristian impression that Adam was trying to get rid of him.

Titus felt his face get warm. He had overstayed his welcome. Adam and Katie wanted to catch up with each other without Titus's interference. He slowly backed up toward the hook that held his coat and the Viking beanie Mammi had made for him. "I suppose I'll be going, then."

"But, Titus," Katie said, fingering the ties of her apron, "you can't go. I made one for you."

Warmth twisted up Titus's spine like a strand of chocolate-flavored licorice. Katie had been in a hurry with dinner, but she had still found the time to make him a potpie—probably his favorite food in the world.

Adam squinted and pressed his lips together. "*Ach, vell.* I had hoped it could just be Katie and me. I mean, so we can get to know each other better."

Didn't they know each other well enough already? Titus was pretty close to all his cousins. Even the ones who lived far away. Pretty close to all of them but Norman, and Norman had once told him he was dumber than a post.

Adam smiled like a tomcat. "Do you think you could all find somewhere else to go, and let me and Katie be alone? We've only got a month."

Dawdi's beard twitched slightly. "I always enjoy eating my dinner in the bedroom."

"Do you, Felty?" Anna said. "I never knew."

Titus didn't want to be in the way, but Katie looked positively terrified, as if being alone with her cousin was worse than being alone with a roomful of goats. He swallowed hard. Adam wasn't going to like it. "I'd better stay. Who else will eat your leftover carrots?"

Katie's gaze flew to his face, and she smiled. "*Jah*. Titus should eat all the leftover carrots. We don't want them to go to waste."

Adam did most of the talking during dinner, speaking as if he were applying for a job while the rest of them ate. He sat between Titus and Katie and across from Mammi and Dawdi. Titus's grandparents stared at Adam as if they weren't quite sure what to do with him. It was the way Titus's *mamm* looked at him when he tried to fold laundry.

"I like hunting," Adam said, "but I don't like fishing. I shot a four-point buck in October. My *dat* wanted to mount its head in our kitchen, but my *mamm* said she didn't want a dead animal looking down on her while she ate. I said if she didn't like it looking down on her, then she shouldn't look up."

"I suppose that would solve the problem," Mammi said.

Titus glanced at Katie. She had relaxed enough that her knuckles were no longer white around her fork, but she was still staring faithfully at her plate. Titus might have thought she was studying the pattern if not for the fact that the plates were plain white. She certainly wasn't very comfortable with her cousin. Titus again wished he could think of something that would help her not be so homesick.

Mammi skewered a carrot with her fork. "This chicken potpie is delicious, Katie. Don't you think it's delicious, Titus?"

"It's my favorite food ever," he said, taking a hearty bite just to prove his point. If that didn't cheer Katie up, he didn't know what would.

"My favorite food is chocolate cake," Adam announced, methodically separating the cooked carrots from his potpie and sliding them onto Titus's plate. "One of the children in my class brought me a whole cake as a gift last year at the end of school."

Katie perked up a bit, as if she finally had something to say. Even though her lips were quivering slightly, she smiled at Adam. "My *mamm* told me you are a teacher. My sister is a teacher."

"I have twenty-nine students," Adam said.

Katie seemed to be trying real hard to find something to say. "Do you enjoy being a teacher?"

"It's not a bad job, but I'm quitting after this school year. I can make more money shingling roofs. I like being outside." He wiped his face with one of Mammi's cheery yellow napkins. "Do you like being outside, Katie?"

"*Jah.* I like—"

"Though I guess it doesn't matter. I don't suppose you'll ever want to go hunting with me. Girls kind of slow you down on a hunting trip." Adam leaned over and elbowed Titus's arm. "Right, Titus?"

"I don't hunt," Titus said. Dawdi didn't like killing animals. Titus had taken after him.

One side of Adam's lip curled. "Not a hunter? It's because you haven't done it before. I'll have to take you out sometime."

It was wonderful nice of Adam to offer, but Titus

wasn't interested. Could he tell Adam no without hurting his feelings?

Once Adam had cleaned his plate and stacked his carrots onto Titus's, he laid his fork and knife on the table, laced his fingers together, and stared at Katie as if she were a horse he was thinking of buying. Did Adam always inspect his cousins this way? "Tell me about you, Katie. I've hardly been able to get you to say a word this whole time. What do you like to do?"

Katie looked as if she'd rather chase Beth around Huckleberry Hill than have to answer any more questions. Titus gave her a slight nod of encouragement. Mammi and Dawdi were about as fearsome as two fuzzy white kittens, Titus already thought she was *wunderbarr,* and surely there was nothing to fear from her cousin Adam.

"I like to cook," she said softly.

"You're very *gute* at it." Titus said, nodding again just in case she hadn't seen his first nod. What the world needed was a lot more nodding.

"Except for the carrots," Adam said, folding his arms across his chest. "Next time remember about the carrots."

Katie lowered her eyes. "I won't forget."

"You're a wonderful-*gute* cook," Adam said. "I couldn't be happier about it. Except for the carrots."

If Titus had a toothpick in his mouth, he would have broken it in half with his teeth. Couldn't Adam stop with the carrots? Katie looked as if she were about to cry.

Cousins could be so thick in the head.

Titus retrieved a toothpick from his pocket and stuck it in his mouth. "You can't make a chicken pot-pie without carrots. It would be like eating apple pie without cheese or a peanut butter sandwich without potato chips on top."

Adam gave Titus the look that Norman often gave him. "Whatever you say, kid." He grinned at Katie and winked as if she were in on some secret.

But Katie wasn't even looking at Adam. Her eyes were squarely focused on Titus, and behind the distress in her eyes, he could see a little sparkle, too.

It might be a *gute* idea to change the subject, just in case Adam decided to cast aspersions on the celery next. "So, how are you two related?" Titus asked. "On your *mater*'s side or your *fater*'s side?" He furrowed his brow. Maybe he should have said "*Adam's* mater *and Katie's* mater," or "*Adam's* mater *and Katie's* fater" or the other way around. There were actually several ways Katie and Adam could be cousins.

He gazed around the table. Even Adam had fallen silent, and all eyes were on Titus, including Mammi's and Dawdi's.

"Who do you mean, Titus?" Mammi prodded.

Titus hesitated. He was always saying the wrong thing, but he couldn't think of a reason why his question should offend anyone. "Adam and Katie. Are they cousins on their *mamm*'s side or their *dat*'s side?"

Adam exploded into loud, uncontrollable laughter, throwing his head back so far, Titus feared his chair might tip over backward. Dawdi looked mildly surprised, and Mammi smiled that grandmotherly smile that meant that no matter what he did, she still loved him. Katie's eyes were full of worry, as if he'd just told her he had some dreaded disease.

Titus had obviously said something very funny. Adam was laughing so hard, he couldn't speak for several seconds. After sitting up straight in his chair, he wiped the tears from his eyes and stifled the chuckles. "We're not cousins. It wonders me what gave you that idea."

Titus's heart suddenly felt as heavy as Katie's suitcase full of gadgets. Whatever it was, he'd made a horrible mistake. "I thought you said . . . maybe I heard you wrong."

Adam smirked and laid a hand over the one Katie was resting on the table. "Katie and I aren't cousins. We're sweethearts."

CHAPTER 4

Katie stuffed a hearty bite of scrambled eggs into her mouth and gagged it down with a swig of goat's milk. By drowning the mouthful with milk, she barely noticed how the slimy, undercooked eggs slid down her throat and came to rest in her stomach. Right after breakfast, she would volunteer to take over all the cooking for Anna.

"How are your eggs, dear?" Anna said, spreading a dollop of jelly on her toast.

"Best I've ever tasted," Felty said. He was on his second helping, shoveling eggs into his mouth like a starving man. "You are the best cook in the world, Annie."

Katie could barely keep the surprise from showing on her face. Did Felty really like the eggs, or was he just pretending? He must be pretending. Katie loved him instantly for that alone. Nothing made a cook feel so happy as knowing someone liked her food, and nothing made her so miserable as thinking her food tasted terrible.

"And what about you, Katie?" Anna said, turning her bright eyes to Katie. "Are your eggs the way you like them?"

"Delicious," Katie said, sure that *Gotte* would forgive her for fibbing to spare Anna's feelings. "Nothing like farm-fresh eggs." Katie gave up on trying to eat something so runny with a fork. She picked up her spoon, determined to finish every bite, no matter how unpleasant.

How had Anna raised thirteen children without ever learning how to cook? Perhaps it was her children who had needed to learn something—like how to eat barely edible food and still be grateful and kind to the cook. Kindness and gratitude were never wasted lessons.

She polished off her eggs, every bite, then stood and collected the plates from the table. Anna got up to help her, and Katie waved her back down. "You made a wonderful-*gute* breakfast," she said. "The least I can do is clean the kitchen."

Anna tapped her finger to her chin. "It will give me more time for crocheting. I'm making a surprise for someone special."

"For Christmas?" Felty said.

Anna grinned. "You'll see."

A stiff and cold wind blew into the house as Titus opened the door. Wearing the beanie with horns, he stomped the snow off his boots and came into the kitchen. Before he could shut the door, Beth galloped in with him and clomped around the great room as if she were frolicking in the pasture.

"Titus!" Anna squealed. "The special Christmas goat is not allowed in the house."

Sparky, the dog, yelped, shot onto Felty's recliner, and barked at Beth as if her life depended on it.

"I'm sorry, Mammi," Titus said over the din of goat hooves and barking dogs. "She keeps sneaking out and following me." Titus slammed the door, waved hello to Katie, and chased the goat around the room. His winter boots slowed him down, and Beth would not be caught. She dodged his every attempt to catch hold of her and ran this way and that, up-ending the magazine rack next to Felty's recliner, bumping into the walls, and nearly toppling over the propane floor lantern.

Katie gasped as Titus caught the toe of his boot on the rug and fell hard. He rolled over onto his back and groaned. "Ow." Beth hopped right over him. Titus had been right. Bethlehem seemed to enjoy watching him run.

"Oh dear, Felty. Help!" Anna said, scurrying to her rocker and gathering up her crochet hook and three balls of yarn.

Felty leaped from his chair, surprisingly spry for an eighty-six-year-old, and joined Titus in the chase. Bethlehem jumped up and ran across the sofa, her hard hooves sinking into the stuffing with each step. The special Christmas goat was a very *gute* runner. Sparky was nearly hysterical, climbing onto the recliner's headrest and barking with all her might.

Katie snatched a snickerdoodle from the cookie jar and broke it in half. She stepped into the great room and held the cookie in front of her. "Here, Beth. Yum, yum. Come get a cookie."

Beth immediately slowed down, changed direction, and strutted over to Katie. She snatched the cookie out of Katie's hand with her rubbery lips.

Katie grabbed the red ribbon around Beth's neck and held on tight.

Titus grinned at Katie as if she had just worked a miracle. A toothpick had somehow managed to stay intact between his nice white teeth. "Look, Mammi," he said. "She's done it."

Anna propped her hands on her hips and scolded Beth with her eyes. "Bethlehem C. Helmuth, you are a very naughty goat. And you scared poor Sparky to death."

Titus got to his feet and took the goat from Katie. "I'm sorry, Mammi. She keeps escaping the barn. I should probably keep her tied up, but it makes me sad that she can't roam free, at least around the barn."

Anna sighed with her whole body. "Thank the *gute* Lord that Katie knows how to catch a goat. Beth might have broken something."

Titus turned his full attention and his heart-stopping blue eyes to Katie. "*Denki* for catching the Christmas goat. I hope she didn't scare you."

"I've tussled with a few stubborn cows in my day," Katie said. "Beth is cute."

Titus nodded. "She is pretty cute, even though a goat tried to eat me once."

He strolled out of the house with Beth in tow, and Katie helped Anna and Felty put the room to rights. Titus came back shortly thereafter without a goat and with a bucket of milk.

"I got almost half a gallon of milk from Beth this morning," he said, placing the milk on the floor next to the table.

"What are we going to do with all this goat's milk?"

Anna said. "We've already got more than we need from the cow."

Katie smiled. "I could make cheese. Mozzarella, ricotta. Goat cheese is delicious."

"What a *gute* idea, Katie," Anna said. "We have enough milk. You could probably sell some."

Titus nodded and slid his beanie off his head. "People pay lots of money at fancy stores for goat cheese. That's what they told me at the dairy."

Katie fingered her *kapp* string. "I do need to make some money for my wedding."

Titus cleared his throat and stared down at the beanie strangled between his fingers. "So, you and Adam are engaged?"

"We . . . uh . . . plan to get engaged at Christmastime."

No one mentioned that it was already Christmastime. Katie decided not to point that out. She felt her face get warm. Why should she be embarrassed about getting engaged to Adam?

Anna waved her hands in the air and spoke a little too loudly. "There's still plenty of time to make that decision. There are so many other people you have to get to know and so many crochet projects I need to finish."

"If you need money for your wedding," Felty said, "why don't you make more than cheese to sell? You're a fine cook, Katie. I know one or two neighbors who would buy your snickerdoodles."

Katie drew her brows together. "I don't know. I should probably be spending my time making cakes and goodies for Adam." The way to a man's heart was through his stomach, Mamm always said. *"No girl who can cook will ever be without a husband if she just tries hard enough, Katie. Boys will take a full belly over a beautiful* fraa *any day.*"

"You can only cook so many cakes for Adam Wengerd," Anna said. "What about all those other people who need a Christmas cake?"

Titus gave her a half smile. "You should start a bakery. It might help you feel closer to home."

"Oh, Titus," Anna said, clapping her hands in delight. "You are smarter than a raccoon in the rain. Katie could start a bakery to pass the time while she's waiting for Adam to pop the question." She looked at Katie with such eagerness in her eyes that Katie couldn't have contradicted her if she'd wanted to.

Anything would be better than sitting around waiting for Adam to propose, and starting a bakery would feel like a little slice of heaven right here on Huckleberry Hill. She couldn't keep her lips from curling. "Do you think I could? I mean, how would people know about my bakery? What if nobody wanted to buy anything?"

Titus's eyes widened with excitement. "If you make me a list of things you want to sell, I'll go around the community and ask people what they want to buy. Lots of the mothers would be happy for some help with their Christmas baking."

"But . . . but that's so kind of you," she said, as if that would dissuade him from helping her. She didn't want to take advantage of him.

"Kind?" His lips vibrated as he blew air from between them. His toothpick stayed put. "I'm not kind. It would be a sin to keep all your talent a secret. Your food could bring so much happiness to people."

Katie had known Titus for twenty-four hours, and he had already shown himself to be one of the kindest boys ever. How many boys would take care of a Christmas goat for their *mammi?* Titus was thoughtful and kind to his grandparents, and he didn't look at her as if he judged everything she did with a critical eye.

That was her *mamm*'s job. And Adam's, it seemed. The dread she had been trying to tamp down all morning surfaced before she could gather her thoughts. Titus was wonderful nice. She felt comfortable with him, and she didn't feel the least bit comfortable with Adam. But surely that was because Adam was her intended fiancé. There were no expectations with Titus, so they could just be friends.

She would learn to love Adam. He had all sorts of interesting stories, and he didn't expect her to talk much, which was *gute* because she didn't like the pressure of trying to carry on a witty conversation. Adam was very handsome, with his chestnut hair and caramel-colored eyes. She couldn't imagine why some girl in Bonduel hadn't already snatched him up. Surely Katie was the most blessed girl in the world. She couldn't have been happier.

"Is everything okay?" Titus said, studying her face as if he didn't like what he saw in her expression. "Are you missing home again?"

"I think maybe I am."

He winced. "It was me, wasn't it? I'm sorry about what I said about sin. I didn't mean you are a sinner. It's just an expression, but you have probably only committed like one sin in your whole life . . . not that I'm saying you have ever committed a sin."

Katie frowned. Titus took too much on himself. "*Nae*, Titus. You haven't done anything wrong. I was just thinking about home." The home she would be making with Adam. Would it be happy? Did it even matter?

Titus gazed at her with genuine concern and stuffed his hand in his pocket. "I'm sorry you're so sad about leaving home. I hope you don't mind, but I wrote you a poem."

"For me?"

His blush traveled to the tips of his ears. "It's not very *gute*, but I hope it might make you feel better."

Warm electricity traveled clear to her toes. Titus had written a poem for her? She already felt better. "Oh. That is so nice of you."

He pulled a sheet of lined paper from his pocket, unfolded it, and gave her a sheepish glance. "*Katie came to Bonduel with a suitcase full of gadgets. Being in Wisconsin is the greatest adventure she's had yet.*"

"What a clever rhyme," Felty said.

Anna immediately shushed her husband.

"*She's lonely for her family, and her heart feels sort of melty. But now she's made some new friends; Titus, Anna, Beth, and Felty.*"

Titus glanced at Katie doubtfully before continuing. "*And so when she is very sad and thinking of Augusta, I hope that she will think of us, and not cry on her custard.*"

CHAPTER 5

Felty Helmuth loved to sing. He sang while milking the cow. He sang while setting the table. He sang to Anna while she sat in her rocker and crocheted. And he loved the Christmas songs, even if he made up his own words to almost every one.

Katie put the finishing touches on Adam's cake while Anna slid cookies onto a plate with her spatula and covered them with plastic wrap. Felty readied all the bakery deliveries in three large cardboard boxes on the table, all the while singing at the top of his lungs.

"O little inn of Bethlehem, how much we are like you. Our lives are crowded very full with all we have to do. To our King we're not unfriendly, we love without a doubt. We have no unkind feelings, we simply crowd Him out."

Maybe Titus had gotten his knack for poetry from his *dawdi*. They were both very clever with a rhyme. Her heart swelled. Nobody had ever written a poem for her before Titus. The thought was thrilling and exhilarating, like jumping into a cold river on a hot summer day.

Had she ever met such a smart boy? She bet there wasn't a boy in Augusta who would have been able to rhyme *gadget* with *had yet*. It was brilliant.

After all, the bakery had been his idea, and it couldn't have been going any better. She already had as many orders as she could manage, even with the Helmuths' help.

Katie spread the last bit of chocolate frosting on Adam's triple chocolate cake. No coconut, no chocolate sprinkles, and no fruit on top. At least three times a week, she made Adam a small cake that he could eat himself, no bigger than two cans of tuna fish stacked on top of each other.

She frowned. Things couldn't have been going better with Adam. He had come to dinner six times in the last two weeks, and he'd spent last Saturday on Huckleberry Hill visiting with Katie while she kneaded bread and made cookies for her bakery orders. It didn't seem to bother him that she said so little. He filled up any awkward silences with his own stories. He had a very interesting life, and he loved to talk about hunting and his students at school. Little Mahlon Zook had gotten a splinter just last Friday. Dinah Neuenschwander had lost her coat. Marvin Glick couldn't understand fractions.

Katie found it fascinating.

At least she tried to.

She ignored the fact that her heart felt as heavy as a plow in the mud. She was simply worried about being an old maid. That was all. But why was she worried? Adam was thrilled that she could cook, even when she forgot and put raisins in his oatmeal raisin cookies. If he didn't like how she made something, he always let her know. He was helping her improve her recipes.

He also seemed very excited about the money the bakery was making, because she'd have more money for the wedding. He was already anticipating marriage. Tears stung her eyes. She was overjoyed.

She finished frosting Adam's cake and slid it over to Anna, who placed it in a little cardboard box. Titus had found the boxes at Walmart, and they had turned out to be the perfect size for mini-cakes and blocks of fudge. Titus could deliver baked goods without smashing them.

While Anna boxed up the cake, Katie leaned against the counter and pulled a crumpled piece of lined paper from her pocket.

Katie makes delicious cakes and fudge and cheese and pies. She misses home but if she left, we'd all cry out our eyes. Each day the people look to see just what she has in store. Because of her delicious food, we'll weigh a whole lot more.

She smiled to herself and stuffed the poem back into her pocket. Titus had written her seven poems since she'd been here, each one better than the last. She marveled that he still had any ideas or rhymes left.

Her heart fluttered like a moth to the light when Titus stomped into the kitchen wearing the Vikings beanie that Anna had made him. His coat collar was pulled up around his ears. A flurry of snow blew in with him. "It's wonderful cold out there," he said. "Like an icicle."

"Titus, you're such a dear to take care of our special Christmas goat," Anna said, handing Felty the box with Adam's cake in it. "It's going to be the best Christmas ever." Anna winked at Felty. "Isn't it, Felty dear?"

"For sure and certain, Annie-banannie."

Titus had been, in a word, *wunderbarr* these last two weeks. In addition to his poems, he had gone to several neighbors in the community, both Amish and non-Amish, and had taken orders for baked goods. Then he had made deliveries every day but Sunday, even in the bitter cold, and brought back the money for Katie. When she had expressed concern that he was spending too much time on a bakery that wasn't even his, he'd simply shrugged and said that the world should not be deprived of Katie Gingerich's baked goods. Even though she knew he would never do it on purpose, he always seemed to know how to make her blush.

Katie's eyes widened. Titus carried a full bucket of milk in one hand. "Bethlehem has never produced that much in one milking before."

Titus unzipped his coat and grinned—with a toothpick between his teeth, of course. "That fancy restaurant in Shawano wants as much mozzarella as you can make and as fast as you can make it. So I bought another goat."

Anna's jaw dropped to the floor. "Another goat?"

Titus nodded. "Katie needs the milk."

"But you're spending so much time already," Katie said. "How can I ask you to milk another goat every day?"

"It only takes me seven minutes to milk Bethlehem. It's not that much more time. And that restaurant in Shawano pays *gute* money."

Katie could barely move her lips around her smile. "*Jah*. They do." If the restaurant kept buying, she'd make almost three hundred dollars from her cheese alone by Christmas. There weren't enough words to thank Titus.

"Such a *gute* boy," Anna said.

Titus placed his bucket on the floor near the door. "Do you want to see the new goat, Katie, just so's you know where you're getting the milk from? She's real pretty and doesn't say a word. I think she's a little unsure of Beth."

"Of course. I'm finished with my baking for the day."

Titus motioned toward the boxes on the table. "Are these my deliveries?"

"*Jah*," Katie said. She snatched a piece of paper from the counter. "And here is the list of houses each item goes to."

Titus twirled the toothpick in his lips as he studied the list. Shuffling his feet, he cleared his throat and turned a darker shade of pink. "Would you . . . would you like to come with me?"

"To deliver?"

He nodded. "I can hitch the horse to the sleigh."

All of a sudden, Katie felt breathless. A sleigh ride with Titus Helmuth sounded like the funnest thing in the world. "I would like that very much."

His eyes shone as if there were a propane lamp inside his head. "Really? It's wonderful cold. Are you sure?"

Anna beamed. "What a *gute* idea. I bet the people who are buying all your delicious baked goods would like to meet you."

Katie pressed her lips into a hard line. What if she

couldn't think of anything to say to her customers? She didn't have a way with words like Titus did.

Titus's forehead piled up with creases. "I don't mind going by myself. They're always happy to see me when I'm bringing them a loaf of bread or one of your cakes."

Katie swallowed the lump in her throat. She really wanted to go, even if she had to speak to total strangers. She'd be okay if Titus was with her. "I'll get my coat."

She put on her coat and bonnet and wrapped the scarf Anna had given her around her neck. It was caramel brown, made with yarn as soft as baby hair. Anna had also made her matching mittens and three dishrags. Titus zipped his coat up and smiled reassuringly as he stacked two of the delivery boxes on top of each other and lifted them off the table. Katie grabbed the third box. Felty opened the door for them, and more snow blew in from outside.

"Have fun," Anna said. "There's no need to hurry back. I'll start dinner."

Katie tried to hide her distress behind her scarf. Under no circumstances should Anna make dinner.

Titus's toothpick bobbed up and down. "Don't worry, Mammi. We won't be long. I don't want Katie to freeze."

They trudged to the barn and loaded their boxes into the sleigh, then Titus slapped his gloved hands together. "Do you want to see the new goat?"

"*Jah.* Very much."

He led Katie to the corner of the barn where the two goats sat on a bed of hay. Bethlehem's red ribbon was tied to a wooden post, but Katie could see that Titus had lengthened it so that Beth had room to

roam around the barn without escaping. The new
goat had the same floppy ears as Beth, and her coat
was the same caramel brown with eyes to match.
They could have been sisters. Beth had a white patch
of hair that ran in a V right between her eyes. The
new goat had white hair on the tip of her nose. Titus
had tied a green velvety bow around her neck. Katie
reached down and took the goat's soft ears in her
hands. The goat *baa*ed a greeting.

"I like the ears," Katie said. "They look like a funny
haircut."

"She's a real nice goat," Titus said. "More sensible
than Beth and not inclined to wander. I named her
Judy. It's short for Judea, as in *Bethlehem of Judea.* I
hope Mammi doesn't mind if we have a second
Christmas goat. I'm hoping it will make Christmas
twice as special."

Titus was so clever.

He hooked up the horse to the sleigh, and Katie
held on tight as they practically flew down the hill.
The bells around the horse's neck jingled merrily,
and Katie didn't think she drew a breath until they
got to the bottom.

Titus glanced at her with a frown. "Am I going too
fast? I didn't mean to scare you."

"I forgot how the *swoosh* and the wind takes my
breath away. I like it."

Titus gave her a wide grin, snapped the reins, and
prodded Felty's horse into a gallop. It was the most
terrifying, most exhilarating feeling in the whole
world. "*Whee!*" she squeaked and threw her arms into
the air. Titus's smile couldn't have gotten any bigger
as they made their way up the road.

Katie needn't have worried about meeting people.

At the first house they went to, it was obvious that everybody loved Titus. Erda Beiler greeted them warmly at the door, and when Titus introduced Katie as the baker, the old woman threw her arms around both of them and declared she wanted to adopt them.

Titus seemed to be best friends with everyone. He was natural and likable and could keep conversations going without Katie, even while she felt included in all of them. Titus wasn't like Adam, who never stopped talking. Titus seemed eager to introduce Katie to the neighbors, but didn't act irritated if she didn't say more than hello. She found herself talking to everyone because she was genuinely interested in getting to know the people who thought so highly of Titus. Titus's endearing manner helped her forget herself and turn her heart outward.

After their fourth delivery where Mrs. Overton, an Englischer, had paid Katie ten dollars extra for a loaf of wheat bread, Titus cupped his hand around Katie's elbow and helped her back into the sleigh. Once settled in, she picked up the list and her heart sank like a stone in the pond.

Next stop, Adam Wengerd's house.

Titus was uncannily sensitive to subtle expressions on her face. "Is everything okay? Are you getting cold? We can go home, if you want, and you can stick your feet in the woodstove. I mean . . . I didn't mean *in* the woodstove. *By* the woodstove. But not too close, because you don't want to burn your toes."

"I'm fine," Katie said, because how could she explain the struggle raging inside her? Was Adam her last, best choice?

She chastised herself. How could she wonder

about such a thing after only two weeks? She needed to give the relationship more time. It was silly to entertain doubts this soon.

"Are you missing home again?" Titus said, looking at her with so much sympathy, she felt like bursting into tears.

She swallowed the lump in her throat. "Christmas will be very different this year."

"What is Christmas like at your house?"

"We have greenery and candles at every window, just like Anna does." Last week, Anna had directed Titus to hang pine boughs and adorable little Christmas bows that Anna had crocheted herself. "On Christmas Day, Mamm makes chicken and corn and butter rolls. After dinner, we set twelve candles on our table and light them one by one. The person who lights the candle gets to choose a Christmas song, and we sing it before lighting another candle. My *dat* always lights the last candle, and we sing '*Stille Nacht*' before going to bed."

"And you'll miss that."

Katie nodded and blinked away the tears in her eyes. "I suppose when I marry, I'll make new family traditions."

Titus's toothpick drooped precariously on his bottom lip. "Maybe Adam will want to carry on with your family's traditions."

She could barely force out the words in a whisper. "Maybe he will." She couldn't imagine Adam ever finding out about her family traditions. He never stayed silent long enough for her to tell him anything.

Katie bit her tongue. How could she think such a

thing about the boy who was going to save her from becoming an old maid?

Titus drew a piece of paper from his coat pocket. Snowflakes made small tapping noises as they fell onto the paper. "I was saving this for later," he said, "but maybe it will cheer you up."

The mere thought of another poem tugged a smile from Katie's lips. Did Titus ever have a selfish thought?

His cheeks glowed red from the cold. "*Katie is pretty. Katie is sweet. Eating her potpies is such a treat. I hope she'll be happy, I don't like her sad. I hope she'll discover Bonduel ain't so bad.*" He folded the paper and seemed to grow even redder. "I know *ain't* isn't a real word, but it fit with the rhythm better."

Katie didn't need her coat anymore. Her face felt as hot as if she had a fever. Did Titus really think she was pretty? Her heart knocked on her chest like a woodpecker on a telephone pole. Maybe *pretty* had been the only word that fit in the poem, but for sure and certain, she wasn't going to ask.

"It's very nice," she said.

"Not half as nice as you are." He gazed at her as if he believed every word of that poem, then seemed to remember he was supposed to be driving them somewhere. He picked up the reins, jiggled them slightly, and clicked his tongue to get the horse moving. "Where to next?"

She didn't want to say it. Titus withered like a failed soufflé every time she mentioned Adam. He practically shriveled up when Adam came over. Had Adam been mean to him in school or something? Titus was so nice, Katie couldn't imagine anyone ever being mean to him. "We . . . uh . . . next is the Wengerds."

Just as she expected, Titus seemed to shrink about five inches. He attempted a smile. "*Ach*. Okay. Adam's house next."

"I haven't been there for nine years," Katie said, as her heart did a little flip. Would she be living there someday?

Titus guided the horse onto a short driveway right off the main road. "Here it is," he said, giving her a wide smile that seemed a little sad.

Two bare oak trees stood in front of Adam's mint green–colored house with a hunter-green metal roof. A smaller house sat right beside the big one. Adam had told her that his brother and his family lived on the farm. This must be his brother's house. Directly behind the smaller house was a country red barn that looked as if it had recently been painted.

Katie pulled the small cake box from the bigger box.

"I'll wait here," Titus said, "so you and Adam can have a few minutes alone."

Katie grimaced. She wasn't particularly comfortable being alone with Adam. She never knew what to say. But what a silly thought that was. She never had to say anything when she was with Adam.

She set the cake box on the seat of the sleigh, then found the box of fudge, the nut-brown bread, and the loaf of honey wheat bread in one of the bigger boxes. Adam had hinted that his *mamm* liked whole wheat bread, and Katie was eager to please her.

She glanced at Titus. He had his toothpick clamped between his teeth. How mean *had* Adam been to him in school? She set the rest of her baked goods on the seat and jumped from the sleigh. Surely she could manage everything in one trip so Titus wouldn't have to help. If she tucked the box of fudge under her elbow, she might be able to carry it all.

Titus saw her difficulty at once. He shot to his feet so fast, he probably pulled a muscle. "Here. I can help."

She smiled sheepishly. "I'd be very sad if I dropped Adam's cake."

He returned her smile with one just as sheepish. "Last week I dropped the apple pie you made for the Johnsons."

Katie caught her breath. "*Ach, du lieva.* I hope they weren't mad about it."

Titus shook his head and grinned. "They paid full price and said they'd scrape it out of the box."

"If that ever happens again, I'd be happy to make them another one. I'm sorry, Titus. I've asked too much of you. I should be the one doing the deliveries."

"I like delivering. Folks are always wonderful happy to see me when I have a plate of your cookies in my hand. I've become very popular."

Katie studied the snow caking her boots. "I don't wonder but you were already the most popular boy in Bonduel."

He tied the reins and jumped from the sleigh. "Nah. Cousin Norman thinks I'm thickheaded, Aunt Esther scolds me, and Mammi Anna has given up on teaching me how to knit."

"That's not true. Anna can't talk about you without smiling. She thinks you're more *wunderbarr* than triple chocolate cake."

Titus's lips curled into that modest smile he often wore. "I think you're more *wunderbarr* than triple chocolate cake." He immediately swiped his hand across his mouth—without dislodging his toothpick—

and lowered his eyes. His boots must have been as interesting as hers were.

Katie felt as if she was standing right next to a glowing fire. It was turning out wonderful warm for such a cold December day. Just how much did Titus like triple chocolate cake?

Titus carried the loaves of bread, and Katie got the box of fudge and the cake. In silence they trudged across the Wengerds' lawn and up to Adam's front door. Katie felt a little flustered. Would his *mater* even remember her? Would Katie have to try to make conversation with the whole family? What if she couldn't think of anything to say?

Titus studied her face, and he seemed more worried than she was. "If you get stuck, ask them about hunting. They like to hunt. Or you could talk about food. Most everybody eats. Sometimes." He frowned. "I didn't mean that some people don't eat. I mean, I know everybody eats. They all eat, all the Wengerds. They might like to talk about it, if you can't think of anything else." He reached into his pocket. "Do you want a toothpick? Sometimes I chew on my toothpick when I don't know what to say."

Katie crinkled her brows together. "I . . . I think I'll be okay." She was only stopping by to deliver a few baked goods. They'd be here two minutes at the most. Or maybe she should try the toothpick.

"They're going to love you, all of them."

"I hope so." If they didn't, Adam would never propose.

Titus, always so kind, knocked on the door when he saw that she couldn't quite muster the courage to do it herself.

Adam immediately answered, as if he'd been waiting for her just inside. He burst into a smile. It was a very good sign. "Katie." His smile faded slightly when he glanced at Titus. "Titus brought you for a visit?"

Katie infused her voice with extra enthusiasm. "We're doing bakery deliveries."

Adam's eyebrows rose on his forehead. "Bakery deliveries? Wonderful-*gute*. Are you making lots of money?"

Katie didn't quite know how to answer that. She'd never been very *gute* at math. "I brought you some presents," she finally said, hoping Adam would forget about the money. She handed him one of her boxes. "Here is some chocolate swirl fudge."

Adam peeked inside the box. "Without nuts?"

Katie could almost feel the embarrassment travel up her neck. "*Jah*. I'm sorry about last time."

"It's okay," Adam said. "It wasn't your fault. You didn't know I don't like fudge with nuts."

Katie relaxed slightly. It was *wunderbarr* of him to be so forgiving. She handed him the other box. "And this is a triple chocolate cake with no sprinkles, no coconut, and no chocolate chips. I hope you like it."

Adam smiled, showing all his straight white teeth. "Like it? I'll love it. You know chocolate cake is my favorite."

"And these," Katie said, taking the loaves of bread from Titus's arms, "are for your *mamm*. Honey whole wheat and nut-brown bread."

Adam set the two boxes on the small table next to the front door and took the loaves from Katie. "This is perfect, Katie. My *mamm* will be pleased. I don't think she'll like the nut bread, but you made the effort and that's what's important."

Titus took a small step closer to Katie. "The nut-brown bread is so *gute*, I can eat a whole loaf by my-self."

Adam acted as if Titus hadn't said anything. He placed the loaves of bread on the table, opened the cake box, and took a whiff. "Smells *gute* and looks *gute*, too. A little small, but that gives me a good excuse not to have to share with my *bruders*."

Katie glanced at Titus with an apology in her eyes.

He smiled and winked at her.

She melted like butter on the griddle.

And almost forgot Adam was standing there.

Katie pried her gaze from Titus and back to Adam. "Well then, I hope you enjoy the food." Adam didn't offer to pay her. He never paid, and she didn't expect him to. The baked goods were in exchange for a possible proposal.

Adam's expression brightened. "Why don't you stay? My *mamm* hasn't seen you since you got back, and my brothers have been asking about you."

Panic tightened a hand around Katie's throat. She had only planned on being here for two minutes. "Well . . . we . . . have to finish our deliveries."

Adam cocked an eyebrow and laid a hand on Titus's shoulder. "You don't mind making the deliveries by yourself, do you, kid? Katie and I want to spend some time together."

Katie tried to hide her reluctance. "I should help Titus finish."

Titus's toothpick trembled. "I can do the deliveries. Nothing should stand in the way of true love."

True love? Was that what this was?

Adam smiled. Or smirked. Sometimes Katie couldn't tell the difference. "Okay then, kid. Make your deliveries, and be back in an hour."

Titus didn't seem the least bit embarrassed at being bossed around. He gave Katie a boyish grin that made her feel better about her staying. If a boy as kind and thoughtful as Titus thought she was as *wunderbarr* as triple chocolate cake, then maybe Adam would come to see her that way, too. The thought gave her confidence.

"I will come in an hour," Titus said, giving her one last nod before trudging back across the snow-covered lawn.

Adam invited her into the house. He picked up the two loaves of bread and led her down a dark hall to the kitchen. Adam's *mamm* stood at the sink, three of his brothers sat at the table, and his sister swept the floor. Katie held her breath. They looked up when she and Adam entered the room.

"You remember Katie," Adam said, nudging her forward.

An awkward silence fell as they stared at her, no doubt expecting her to say something clever. She felt like she had a mouthful of sawdust. Could she turn around and march out the door?

Not without ruining her chances with Adam.

She'd have to be extra brave.

"So," she said, her heart beating in her throat, "I hear you like to hunt."

CHAPTER 6

Adam Wengerd was a real nice guy. Titus had always thought so. He was one of the best softball players in school, he had nice teeth, and word was that he was a *gute* shot with his rifle.

Would Adam mind very much if Titus courted his fiancée?

Of course, Titus didn't want to hurt Adam's feelings or anything like that, but something niggling at the back of Titus's brain told him that Adam and Katie wouldn't suit each other. It didn't seem right that Katie should marry someone who didn't like fudge with nuts.

Titus adored fudge with nuts. It was probably his favorite food ever.

He rubbed the stubble along his jaw. He should feel guilty for wanting to court Adam's girlfriend. If Adam and Katie were meant for each other, *Gotte* would not like it if Titus got in the way. But Titus couldn't stop thinking about Katie or stop writing poems about her. Poems just came to him when he milked the goats. They reminded him of Katie.

Not that she looked like a goat. Katie was prettier than any grand-prize goat at any county fair. Katie wasn't mischievous like Beth or always hungry like Judy. She baked delicious cakes and cookies and breads. The goats could only make milk. Katie's eyes were brown, and neither of his goats had such chocolaty-brown eyes. And she was so kind, she could have been an angel. Titus liked her kindness most of all.

Come to think of it, he wasn't sure why his goats reminded him of Katie. She was nothing like them. But he liked her all the same.

He liked her more than a million goats and a million blocks of fudge with nuts.

A lot more.

Would that make Adam mad?

Of course, a girl like Katie probably wasn't interested in Titus. Cousin Norman often reminded Titus how thick he was, and Katie was so smart, she could add fractions in her head. He'd seen her do it just the other day when she needed to double a recipe. A girl like Katie deserved a bishop's son and a thousand goats.

Norman was right. How could Titus be so dim-witted as to think that Katie would even give him a second glance?

Titus tromped toward the barn through the waist-deep snow with his shovel in one hand. Last night had made down hard with over three feet of snow. Titus had risen extra early this morning to come up to Huckleberry Hill and shovel the sidewalk so

Dawdi wouldn't have to. Of course, the lane was still buried in snow, but the sidewalk was clear if Katie needed to use it.

He had left the horse and buggy at home and hiked up the hill in his snowshoes. The snow was too deep for the horse, but Titus managed well enough with his snowshoes. He'd retrieved the shovel from Dawdi's toolshed and shoveled the walk in almost complete darkness and heavy snowfall. *Gute* thing he had his Viking beanie. The strap to his headlamp rested right on top of his beanie and the Viking horns held it in place. Mammi probably didn't even realize how smart she was.

Titus paused to shovel the snow away from the barn door so he could open it. Then he pulled it open and stepped inside. With the light of his headlamp, he located the matches and lit the propane lantern. Judy and Beth both greeted him with a *baa*, and Iris, the cow, swished her tail.

Dawdi would be in to milk Iris soon. Titus would have gladly done it for him, but Dawdi said milking the cow every morning kept him young and that Titus had the Christmas goats to look after and they were quite enough for one boy to take care of.

Titus didn't think it was too much at all. Taking care of the Christmas goats meant he got to see Katie every day. He got to deliver her goodies. Even though she had only gone with him on deliveries three separate days, he liked to pretend she sat beside him every time. He imagined that smile and those brown eyes and the way the wind teased little wisps of her hair out from under her bonnet.

He could feel another poem coming on.

Titus glanced around, as if more than Judy, Beth,

and Iris might see him, and pulled a cardboard box from under Dawdi's workbench. He set it on the bench and pulled out two pieces of fudge with nuts, half a round of mozzarella cheese, and a loaf of Katie's famous cinnamon bread.

He hardly dared hope for a day when Katie would make something special just for him, the way she made Adam a triple chocolate cake almost every day. But for now, he was content to secretly buy her baked goods and keep them stashed in the barn.

He sat down on the old chair next to the workbench, and Judy immediately came close, wanting some of his breakfast. Not wanting to be left out, Beth nudged his leg with her nose. Titus took a piece of cinnamon bread, tore it in half, and fed a half of that to each of his goats. It was Christmastime. They deserved special treats too.

An old, rusty toolbox sat on Dawdi's workbench. Titus lifted the top shelf and set it aside. In the bottom of the toolbox was where he kept all the poems he'd written about Katie. He unfolded one and read it while he ate.

Katie's eyes are brown, her hair is brown too.
I like her a lot, and Adam does too.

It was one of his shorter poems and the rhyme wasn't very *gute*, but he'd put a lot of thought into it. Maybe he should show it to Adam.

Adam, I'm thinking of courting Katie at the same time you are courting her. Is that okay with you?

Something told him Adam wouldn't like that very much. He still called Titus "kid."

After eating, Titus milked the goats. He found the *plip-plop* of goat's milk in the bucket very peaceful. It reminded him of Katie. He wasn't sure why, unless it

was because Titus found Katie's voice just as sooth-
ing. Maybe it wasn't the sound particularly. Maybe
everything reminded him of Katie.

Beth was the mischievous goat who didn't like to
stay still, even during milking. Judy was cuddly and
would eat almost anything. Beth was so picky, she
picked out the spent barley from the feed corn in
her trough. Once he'd milked them both, he tied
Beth back up to her post, picked up paper and pencil, and jotted down a poem he'd thought of while
milking.

Titus donned his heavy gloves and wrapped his
scarf tighter around his neck. From the sound of the
wind against the slats of the barn, the snow was still
blowing. He hoped he wouldn't have to put on his
snowshoes to make it to the house.

He pushed the barn door open. Another foot of
snow had piled up against the outside since he'd
been inside. He'd have to shovel again. Katie deserved a clear sidewalk. Pressing his scarf over his
face to keep the blowing ice from his eyes and grasp-
ing the bucket of goats' milk in his other hand, he
waded through the snow toward the house. Through
the blizzard, he saw a dark figure struggling up the
hill. Was it Katie? Had she needed to go down the
hill for some reason earlier this morning? The figure
stumbled and fell into a bank of snow, but quickly
stood and kept walking.

Titus set down his pail of milk and ran toward her
as fast as he could through the deep snow. He
reached out and wrapped his gloved hand around
Katie's arm, just in case she needed someone to
steady her. But it wasn't Katie. Even though she

kneaded a lot of bread, she didn't have arms quite that thick.

"Kid," Adam Wengerd said. "I'm fine. You can let go. You're going to give me a bruise."

"Sorry, Adam. I thought you were Katie."

Titus couldn't see the expression under Adam's scarf, but he sounded irritated. "Do I look like Katie?"

Not in the least, except they both had nice teeth.

Titus followed as Adam slogged through the snow toward the house. "What are you doing here?" Adam said. "You shouldn't be out in this weather."

"I milk the goats twice a day."

"*Ach,* I forgot." Adam kept walking. "It picked an inconvenient day to snow. Katie promised to make me breakfast, and I didn't want to miss out on her French toast, but I shouldn't have come. I can see her any day."

If Titus were engaged to Katie, he'd make an excuse to see her every day, even if he had to walk across the North Pole to get to her.

"Jason Pyne drove me to the bottom of the hill on his four-wheeler, but I had to walk the rest of the way. I shouldn't have come."

Titus retrieved his bucket of milk and followed Adam up the sidewalk. Another four or five inches of snow had accumulated, but at least it wasn't a struggle to make it to the porch.

Adam knocked, and Mammi opened the door and ushered them in before her kitchen floor was covered with a drift of snow. "Adam and Titus, how nice to see both of you on such a fearsome day. The snow will be up to the tops of the windows before it's over."

Titus set the milk bucket in its usual place by the door and peeled off his gloves and hat and scarf, being careful to stay on the rug so he wouldn't drip on Mammi's floor. His boots and coat came off next.

Dawdi sat on the sofa lacing up his boots. For sure and certain, he was getting ready to go out and milk the cow.

Katie stood at the kitchen counter looking very pretty in a drab gray dress with her hair tied up in a just-as-drab scarf. Gray suddenly became Titus's favorite color. She smiled doubtfully at Titus and then at Adam. "I hope you didn't have too rough a time coming up the hill."

"I'm looking forward to that French toast," Adam said. "A tornado couldn't have kept me away."

"What I want to know," Mammi said, "is who was the Good Samaritan who shoveled our sidewalk this morning. It must have taken at least an hour."

Adam spread his hands wide and gave Mammi a modest bow. "I didn't want my sweetheart and her grandparents to be buried in the snow."

If Titus had been chewing on a toothpick, he would have swallowed it.

Dawdi looked up from his boots and raised his eyebrows until they were nearly on top of his head.

Katie glanced at Titus before turning a smile on Adam. "How very nice."

Adam made a show of bending over to loosen the laces on his boots. The motion brought him closer to Titus. "You don't mind, do you, kid? I'm trying to impress Katie."

Titus frowned. A nice boy like Adam shouldn't lie to impress a girl, even one as *wunderbarr* as Katie Rose Gingerich. Hadn't he ever listened in church?

Adam took off his coat and shook it hard. Droplets of water flew in every direction. He didn't even seem to notice. He left his boots by the door and sat in one of the kitchen chairs.

Titus hurried into the kitchen and grabbed a towel from the drawer. Getting on his hands and knees, he wiped up the water from Mammi's wood floor. How could Adam know that Mammi was a little unstable on her feet since her surgery in February? She was sure to slip on a wet floor.

Dawdi tromped across the room and lifted his coat from the hook. "Have you ever had Katie's French toast, Titus? She puts bananas in it."

"Titus was just leaving," Adam said. "Nice to see you again, kid. Tell the goats hello for me."

Titus didn't remember telling Adam he had to be somewhere. *Did* he have to be somewhere? Had he forgotten an important appointment?

Katie's face fell like a rotten apple from a tree. "*Ach,* really? I was hoping you would tell me what you think of this recipe. It's bananas Foster French toast with goat's milk."

Adam leaned back in his chair. "Goat's milk? Why does it always have to be goat's milk? Doesn't anybody milk cows anymore?"

Dawdi slid his hat over his head. "I'm going out right now."

"It sounds wonderful-*gute,*" Titus said. "But I should be going." Adam wanted time alone with Katie. Titus couldn't see that he blamed him. After that lie, Adam must have been desperate.

Mammi's eyes twinkled as she marched to the door, pressed her back against it, and spread her arms out wide. "I forbid you to leave," she said, looking as if a team of horses couldn't budge her. "You'll get lost in the blizzard."

Titus's mouth fell open. He was grateful for a second time that he didn't have a toothpick between his teeth. Did Mammi really want him to wrestle her? The things his grandparents expected from him!

"Won't you stay?" Katie said.

The tenderness in her eyes convinced him better than his *mammi* could. He grinned, pulled a toothpick from his pocket, and stuck it between his lips. "*Jah,* I will stay."

Adam was the only person in the room who didn't seem happy about it. Titus felt bad for hurting Adam's feelings but not bad enough to leave. After breakfast, he'd write a poem for Adam to make him feel better.

He just needed a *gute* rhyme for *shovel.*

CHAPTER 7

Katie lifted the lid of the Dutch oven and dipped her spoon into the sauce. A chasm grew in the pit of her stomach. *Ach, du lieva,* the sauce was too runny. Fifteen minutes to go, and the sauce was too runny.

She couldn't ruin the venison. She just couldn't. Adam had proudly brought her almost five pounds of it, and asked her to cook it for his siblings tonight. What would he say if the venison didn't turn out? Would he be mad or just disappointed? Would he decide he didn't want to marry her?

Titus leaned his head closer to the stove so he could get a good look at her face. "Are you okay?"

"The sauce is runny," she said.

He sniffed the air. "It smells wonderful-*gute.* Venison is just about my favorite food ever."

Katie grinned. Everything she cooked seemed to be Titus's favorite food ever. She marveled that he was so easy to please and that he always seemed to make her feel better, no matter how bad things got. When a cake fell or her cookies burned, he would smile at her and tell her things were going to be okay. Sometimes he'd read her a poem or offer to wash the dishes or show her a new trick his goats had learned. Titus never failed to make her smile.

"Do you need help?" Anna said, as she sat at the table and folded napkins. "Tomato paste is a *gute* thickener."

Dear, sweet Anna. She would have done anything for Katie, and Katie wouldn't have hurt her feelings for the world, but she couldn't let Anna near Adam's venison. Anna had a gift for making everything she touched taste worse.

With shaking breath, she slid the lid back on the Dutch oven and tried not to panic. She knew how to thicken a sauce. It wasn't that hard, and she had plenty of time. "*Denki,* Anna," Katie said, "but I think I can fix it with a little cornstarch. It should taste just fine." Though Katie would barely be able to eat, she certainly hoped everyone else would enjoy it.

Anna creased a napkin between her fingers. "I've never been able to get the lumps out when I use cornstarch."

Jah. Only last week, Anna had made gravy with lumps of cornstarch as big as quarters. At least Adam hadn't eaten with them that night, and Katie didn't mind the lumps. Anna had made them with lots of love.

Katie spooned a tablespoon of cornstarch into a mason jar. Titus, who seemed to know exactly what she needed more often than she understood, lifted the lid of the Dutch oven for her. She ladled a cup or two of the runny sauce into the mason jar, tightened the lid, and shook it vigorously.

Titus grinned at her again. "You're the smartest girl I've ever seen."

She felt her cheeks get warm. "Only if this works."

"It will work. You know everything there is to know about cooking."

"Almost as much as my Annie-banannie knows," Felty said. "Annie is the best cook in the whole world."

"But don't you think Katie takes a close second?" asked Titus.

Felty set the napkins around the table as Anna folded them. "*Jah.* I've gained five pounds since Katie's been living with us."

Katie was too busy concentrating on her sauce to respond, but her lips curled involuntarily. Titus and Felty were two of the kindest men she'd ever met. The girl Titus married would be blessed indeed.

Titus finished stirring the lemon-lime soda into the lemonade mix. "What else can I do to help?"

"Will you light the candles?"

He nodded eagerly, always so happy to do whatever he could.

The guilt that Katie had been smothering all afternoon flared to life. Titus had been there all day helping her get ready for a party he hadn't been invited to. He'd brought up the extra folding chairs and two table leaves from the cellar and helped Felty set them up. He'd swept and spot-mopped the floor, given Sparky a bath, and stirred fudge for over twenty minutes without a complaint. All the while reciting poetry and singing Christmas songs.

Katie loved Titus's poems. She could tell he had deep thoughts, like what the moon was made of and why snow was cold. He should have been a professor or something.

Or a schoolteacher.

Katie frowned. Adam was a schoolteacher. He was probably just as smart as Titus. He certainly talked as if he knew everything.

The lines between her eyebrows were no doubt piling on top of themselves. She shouldn't think such things about her boyfriend. It wasn't his fault he talked so much. Katie hardly said a word when they were together. He obviously felt the need to fill in the awkward silences. She resolved to say more when Adam came over. He shouldn't have to be responsible for every conversation, especially when they actually got married. He'd certainly expect her to give her opinion now and then.

Adam hadn't proposed yet, though everything seemed to be going according to plan. Was he falling in love with her? He seemed to like her cakes and cookies. He'd told her she was pretty.

She stole a glance at Titus out of the corner of her eye. But Adam had never written her a poem.

Anna definitely knew how to set a table. She'd made a centerpiece of three red pillar candles tied together with a ribbon, crocheted of course. A wreath of holly surrounded the candles. Titus pulled the matches out of the drawer and lit the candles. Katie's heart did a little flip. Adam's family would love it. At least she hoped they would.

Titus blew out the match just as they heard quick steps outside on the porch. Adam opened the door just wide enough to stick his head into the room. "We're here," he said, smiling as if he sat on top of the world. His gaze landed on Titus. "Titus, kid, I don't mean to be rude, but my brothers and sister are right behind me, and they want to see Katie, not you."

Katie's heart sank. Titus hadn't been invited, but he was the reason Adam's siblings were getting punch instead of water.

Titus frowned as if he'd done something wrong. "Sorry." His toothpick drooped between his lips. "I'd never stand in the way of true love."

"I know you wouldn't," Adam said, glancing behind him as if he were under attack and needed to get to safety.

Titus looked at the spent match in his hand as if he didn't know what to do with it. If he took the time to throw it in the garbage, Adam might get even more annoyed. He squeezed it into his fist.

Hopefully he hadn't burned himself.

"Titus," Adam said, with more urgency.

Titus threw one last reassuring smile in Katie's direction. He was always nice like that. "I'll go out the back door."

He was gone before Katie even had a chance to thank him—not that she would have had a chance. Seconds later, Adam's family swooped into the house. Adam had been very sensitive when Katie acted nervous about inviting his family to dinner. He'd asked his parents to stay home this time.

Adam's sister, Rebekah, who was twenty years old, came in unenthusiastically. She sort of nodded at Katie before making her way to the sofa, where she plopped down and started petting Sparky. Adam's three brothers who still lived at home, Zeb, Melvin, and Josiah, shook Felty's hand with varying degrees of enthusiasm, Zeb being the least enthusiastic, probably because he hadn't been baptized yet, and he hated it when he had to put his cell phone away to have a conversation.

Katie knew all of them from when she'd lived in Bonduel nine years ago, and she had also spent that hour last week at Adam's house getting to know his family. They were all wonderful nice, even Adam's sister. She just hadn't warmed up to Katie yet. Katie tried to be sympathetic, even though she felt smaller in Rebekah's presence. Rebekah probably just didn't like the thought of someone marrying her big brother. It would take some time for her to get used to the idea. Katie would have to make some cookies for her.

Josiah clapped his hands together. "It smells good enough to eat."

"I hope so," Adam said, raising his eyebrows in Katie's direction. He was eager for this meal to go well. He wanted his family to think he'd chosen well. Katie did, too. Her chest tightened. She would hate to embarrass Adam in front of his family.

"Let's eat, then," Adam said, not waiting for Anna to invite them to sit.

Katie, Felty, and Anna brought corn, beets, Jell-O salad, and fresh baked rolls to the table. Katie peeked into the Dutch oven before bringing it over. The sauce had thickened perfectly. That last prayer she'd uttered had worked.

"What is it?" Zeb asked.

"Braised venison with rosemary and shitake mushrooms," Katie said, trying to keep the anticipation out of her voice. *Oy*, anyhow. She wanted them to be impressed, even if the desire smacked of pride.

Adam glanced at his brothers with an apology shining in his eyes. "I told her not to get fancy."

Melvin frowned. "I like pan-fried venison with just a little salt."

Rebekah cringed. "I hate venison."

Once they said a silent blessing over the food, Katie dished up venison for everyone but Rebekah and spooned potatoes and sauce over the meat.

Zeb skewered his fork into one of the potatoes. "Did you make any cooked carrots? They're my favorite."

The kitchen suddenly felt ten degrees hotter. Adam didn't like cooked carrots, but she should have thought to throw a few in the Dutch oven for the rest of his family.

It was her first mistake. Lord willing, there wouldn't be any others.

Once Katie finished serving venison, she sat and poured herself a glass of lemonade punch. She needed something to cool her nerves. What if they didn't like it?

"This is so tender," Josiah said. "And what a wonder-ful-*gute* flavor."

Adam's smile stretched all the way across his face. "Didn't I tell you?"

"The corn is decent," Rebekah mumbled. She looked at her plate as if she hoped no one had heard her say it.

Josiah, the brother just younger than Adam, had been the nicest to Katie. When she had gone over last week, Josiah had asked about her family and whether she liked living in Augusta. "It's really *gute,* Katie," he said. "We eat a lot of venison and I've never tasted it like this. I don't think I've ever tasted a shitake mushroom."

Zeb spread a generous amount of huckleberry jelly on his roll. "I'll have to admit, Adam, when you suggested to Mamm that she write to the Gingeriches about sending Katie to Bonduel, I thought Katie would be a homely, desperate girl who no one in Augusta wanted to marry."

Adam half-growled, half-chuckled. "To be honest, I wasn't too sure myself until I laid eyes on her and tasted her cooking. I knew then it was a match made in heaven."

Katie fingered the hair at the nape of her neck. She should probably say something, but they were talking about her, not to her, and she felt as if she was eavesdropping. Had Adam really thought she was desperate?

Her face grew hot with shame.

She *was* desperate. She was a twenty-four-year-old girl whom nobody but Adam wanted to marry. She knew exactly what they thought of her—it was exactly what she thought of herself.

"You've got *gute* taste, Adam," Melvin said, almost as if Adam had baked the rolls and braised the venison himself.

Katie shouldn't have been so troubled by that. It was pride, pure and simple, to crave praise for her cooking.

"Of course," Adam said. "I always have." He took another bite, smiled at Katie, and winked.

Adam obviously couldn't have been more pleased. She was overjoyed.

Why did being overjoyed feel like a patch of mold growing in her chest and a rock around her neck?

After dinner, they moved to the great room, where they pulled their chairs around the card table, and Zeb laid out Life on the Farm.

If things hadn't been going so well, Katie might have groaned out loud. She hated Life on the Farm. She didn't like it when players went bankrupt or she couldn't afford to buy more cows, not to mention the fact that the game could go on forever. She didn't know if she could bear it.

She squared her shoulders and pasted a happy smile on her face to show Adam how happy she was to be with him. She'd made fudge without nuts and a lovely triple chocolate cake for dessert. Adam was sure to be thrilled. After tonight, she'd get her proposal.

Oh, what a happy day.

She eyed Adam as he sat down to play the game. What if she told him she didn't want to play? Would it be so bad to be an old *maedle*?

The Wengerds were not a quiet group. Adam and his *bruders* were good-naturedly yelling at each other before everyone had even taken a turn. Mammi and Dawdi played as a team, and they watched, eyes wide, as Adam accused one brother and then another of cheating. The brothers in turn teased Rebekah for being such a bad player, until she collected enough money to buy several cows and nearly win the game.

"Felty, dear," Anna said, after Zeb slapped his money onto the card table and growled while his family laughed at him. "Do you think we should buy a cow?"

After half an hour of discomfort, Katie was barely paying attention to the game when a hunter shot her last cow and she was out. It was the only good part about Life on the Farm. If she played poorly, she didn't have to suffer through it for very long.

Adam and his siblings laughed at her for getting out, but she couldn't help but rejoice inside. She tried to keep a weary smile from her lips as she stood up and went straight to the hook for her coat and scarf. She needed some air away from her boyfriend and his loud family. She needed to remind herself how much she didn't want to be an old maid.

Adam glanced up. "Where are you going?"

"I thought I might get some fresh air," she said, feeling guilty for not wanting to spend every moment she could with her boyfriend.

Though she seemed to be concentrating intently, Anna looked up from her cards. "The goats might like a visit," she said, smiling as if she had fifty-nine cows in her hand.

"Off to lick your wounds?" Adam said, flashing her a teasing grin. He liked to tease her. It was a sign of affection. He probably sensed her low mood. How sweet of him to try to cheer her up.

She gave him a weak excuse for a smile. "You are too good of a player for me."

Adam laughed. "I'm too good of a player for anybody."

His brothers protested loudly, but Katie didn't hear most of it because she quickly walked out the door and shut it behind her. She zipped up her coat and stuffed her hands into her pockets. She should have brought some gloves. She'd forgotten how cold it was today. Her breath hung in the air as she strolled down the porch steps and over the sidewalk.

Adam was going to be a wonderful-*gute* husband.

Hadn't he come all the way in the snowstorm to shovel their sidewalk? Didn't he always say nice things about her cooking? Wasn't he pleasant to look at?

The snow crunched beneath her feet. Adam *was* nice to look at, but she preferred blue eyes and white-yellow hair and dimples. Like Titus's. Titus had a *gute* face, and he always had such an eager look about him, as if he was jumping at the chance to help his fellow man.

But Adam was nice, too.

A gust of wind blew around her ankles and rustled her dress. She squeaked as the cold air seeped through her stockings. Not ready to face the noisy Wengerds, she tromped to the barn. Anna suggested she say hello to the goats. They might enjoy the company.

She opened and shut the barn door quickly so that Beth wouldn't have a chance to escape, just in case she had a mind to. Two propane lanterns burned brightly inside the barn. Katie had always found their hiss comforting, like rain on the roof or jam bubbling in a saucepan.

She jumped just a bit when she saw Titus sitting on a hay bale with two toothpicks in his mouth, jotting down something in a spiral-bound notebook. Her cold cheeks immediately warmed up. What a nice surprise. Titus could give her some *gute* advice about Adam and being an old maid. He wrote poetry all day long. Surely he knew something about love and how you knew if you were in it.

Titus sprang to his feet when he saw her, and the notebook slipped from his fingers. He attempted to catch it, whacked it with his hand, and sent it flying

into the air. Beth and Judy *baa*ed their approval
when he managed to snatch it before it fell on the
ground.

He quickly set the notebook on the hay bale behind him, rushed into the shadows, and pulled a
chair out into the light. He dragged the chair close
to a small propane space heater that sat on the floor
near the Christmas goats.

"Come warm up," he said. "You don't want to get
frostbite. A baker needs all her fingers and toes. Not
that you bake with your toes, but just because you
bake with your fingers doesn't mean that toes aren't
important."

Katie grinned. "I once checked out a book from
the library about a woman who was born without
arms. She did everything with her feet, including
change diapers."

"I hope she washed her toes when she was done."

Katie giggled. "I never thought of that."

Titus sort of helped her into the chair and then
scooted the propane heater closer to her feet. "Is
that warm enough? It's wonderful cold outside."

Katie nodded, trying not to think about why she'd
gone out in the cold in the first place.

Titus smiled at her and sat back down on his hay
bale. Judy hopped up and sat next to Titus with that
absent look in her eyes. Titus played with Judy's
floppy ears and watched Katie as if wondering why
she was out in the barn instead of at her own party.

"For sure and certain, that was a short party," he
said. "Did you have a *gute* time?"

She shrugged, trying valiantly to keep the tears
from forming in her eyes. She added a happy lilt to
her voice. Titus wouldn't suspect a thing. "They were

playing Life on the Farm, and I got out early so I decided to come and check on the goats."

"That was wonderful nice, but you don't need to worry about the goats. Goats like the cold weather. They like it better than the heat. That's what they told me at the dairy."

Beth *baa*ed and *clip-clopp*ed over to Katie's chair. Katie stroked Beth's floppy ears. "I'm glad. It doesn't seem fitting that the Christmas goats should be shivering in the cold."

Titus seemed to snap to attention. "Hey," he said, "how did the venison turn out? Did Adam and his family like it? It smelled wonderful-*gute*."

For some reason, Titus's question took the wind out of her—well, it took the rest of the wind out of her. She slumped and couldn't even muster a half smile. "*Ach, vell,* they liked it." At least this time. She'd better find several good venison recipes, because she'd be cooking venison often when she married Adam.

If she married Adam.

She crossed her arms. Of course she would marry Adam. What girl wanted to be an old maid?

"I knew they'd like it. There's nothing you cook that people don't like." He furrowed his brow in confusion. "Is that right how I said it? I meant that everything you cook, no people wouldn't like." He narrowed his eyes and drew both toothpicks from his mouth. "I mean that everybody likes what you make, except Adam, who doesn't like cooked carrots. Or nuts. Or those little coconut sprinkles."

Oh, *sis yuscht.* Before she had a chance to do that little trick where she opened her eyes extra-wide to keep herself from crying, tears were running down

Katie's face. She sniffled quietly and buried her face in Beth's neck so Titus wouldn't see them. He'd feel obligated to write another poem, and she couldn't impose upon his kindness any more than she already had.

Unfortunately, Beth did not cooperate. She *baa*ed her displeasure at being cried on and strutted away from Katie as if she saw something very interesting at the other end of the barn. Katie leaned her elbows on her knees and patted her eyes with her fingers. Maybe Titus wouldn't notice that something was wrong.

"Is something wrong?"

Ach. Titus was as smart as a tack. He always noticed.

"It's been a hard day," she said, as if that explained everything.

But how could she make Titus understand, when she knew she was being irrational? Adam was all but ready to propose, and all of a sudden she wasn't sure if she even wanted him to? Her *mamm* and his *mamm* had been making plans for months. Adam had trekked all the way to Huckleberry Hill many times, thinking she wanted him to propose. She'd made him a dozen cakes and more than a few cookies—for sure and certain a sign that she liked him and wanted to be his wife. It was deceitful, plain and simple, to have made him all those goodies without intending to marry him.

Well . . . she *had* intended to marry him. Maybe she still did. Just because she felt so low tonight didn't mean she wouldn't feel differently on Christmas Day.

A small sob escaped her lips, and she clapped her hand over her mouth. She couldn't even go about getting a husband without messing everything up. "*Ach*, Titus! I'm so selfish."

One side of his mouth drooped downward, and his sky-blue eyes glowed with concern. "You're the nicest girl I know. And I know a lot of girls. I have about two hundred cousins. I mean, not all of them are girls, but at least half of them are." He pulled a strand of hay from the bale he sat on. "I was never very *gute* with fractions, but you are. You're not only nice, but you're about the smartest girl in Wisconsin. I'm guessing you're about the smartest girl in the USA, too, but I don't know many girls outside of Bonduel, so I'll just have to limit it to Wisconsin. I don't want to be accused of exaggerating."

Katie giggled through her tears. Nobody could make her forget her troubles like Titus could.

He leaned forward, looking about as troubled as she felt. "Would a poem cheer you up?"

She took a hankie from her coat pocket and wiped her nose. "Your poems always cheer me up, but I can't ask you to sacrifice your time to write me one."

"It's no sacrifice," he said. "The words just flow when I think of you." Lowering his eyes, he pressed his lips together and fiddled with another piece of hay.

She lowered her eyes, too, as her heart seemed to *clip-clop* around in her chest like two Christmas goats on a wood floor. "Your poems are wonderful-*gute*. You should send them in to the *Budget* newspaper to be published."

"I can't take credit for them. You're my inspiration." She peeked out of the corner of her eye in time to see him turn bright red before he hopped off his hay bale and pulled his Viking beanie farther over his ears. "I know you're in Bonduel for a very important reason, but nobody should be away from home at Christmastime." He strode to the workbench, opened one of the drawers, and pulled out a small pair of pruning shears and some twine. "I'll be back. Can you wait for me?" He shuffled his feet. "If you don't want to, I'll understand. It's wonderful cold."

"I'll wait," she said, smiling so he knew he had nothing to worry about. She certainly wouldn't be going back to the house until Life on the Farm had fizzled out. She could almost talk herself into marrying Adam if she wasn't in the same room with him.

Titus was back like lightning through one of the side doors with a fistful of pine boughs. He brushed fat snowflakes off his beanie and coat and shook the pine boughs to clear the snow off them, as well. He grinned at Katie as if he hadn't expected her to be there on his return. "We need our own Christmas celebration."

Warmth skated up Katie's spine. "A celebration?"

His smile faded momentarily. "Unless you think we should invite Adam and Mammi and Dawdi, too."

"Adam would rather play games with his family, and it's too cold for Anna and Felty. They'll understand why we left them out."

His grin spread across his face, his toothpicks bobbing up and down with approval. "I brought a few decorations."

After Katie helped Titus hang the pine boughs on the wall above the propane heater, he took the green bow from Judy's neck and the red bow from Beth and tied them to the branches. It wasn't a lot, but it made their little corner of the barn look very festive.

Titus scooted a sturdy bench in between Katie's folding chair and his hay bale. "This will be our table, okay?"

She nodded, unsure what he had planned but knowing it would be fun all the same.

Titus squinted and fingered the toothpicks in his mouth. "This is going to be the tricky part yet." He took a flashlight from the workbench, turned it on, and walked all the way around the perimeter of the barn, stopping to pull things from the shelves along the wall or look into the stalls and cupboards. He even searched Anna and Felty's sleigh and Adam's buggy.

He circled back around to Katie with a small bucket in his fist. Grinning, he started pulling things from his pockets and from inside his coat. "I can't go into the house without interrupting the game, so we'll have to make do." Katie's mouth curled upward as he set three white taper candles on the bench. "These were sitting on Dawdi's workbench." He stuffed his hand into one of his coat pockets and pulled out five crayons. "These were in the drawer. I think one of the grandchildren has been coloring in here. I'm glad, because crayons make wonderful-*gute* candles."

She couldn't keep a slow smile from forming on her lips. Titus was even more clever and thoughtful than she first realized.

He tilted the bucket to show her the contents. "Three stumpy candles from Mammi's gardening shelf."

"Are these for singing?" Katie said, her heart swelling at the thought.

Titus nodded.

She very nearly forgot that she was very nearly engaged to Adam and almost gave Titus a hug. "You remembered." Her insides glowed like a warm fire on a frosty morning, and this time, she didn't try to hide the tears that pooled in her eyes.

He frowned. "I want you not to miss home so much." Titus lined the candles and crayons along the bench. The tapers were put into red clay pots that Titus retrieved from Anna's gardening shelves. He stepped outside and came back with half a bucket of snow. After forming the snow into five hard balls, he set the balls on the bench and stuck a crayon into each one. They would stand up nice and straight until the snow melted.

Titus examined the row of makeshift candles and rubbed his hand down the side of his face. "*Ach du lieva*, there's only eleven. I didn't count right. You're the one who's *gute* at arithmetic."

"Could we light one of your toothpicks?"

He shook his head in dejection. "I tried that once when I was a kid because I wanted to pretend I was smoking. Toothpicks don't burn very well."

Katie tried to smile even though she felt some of her enthusiasm wilt. "Eleven candles is *gute* enough."

"*Nae*," Titus said, a determined set to his jaw. "There has to be twelve." He gazed around the barn as if hoping an overlooked candle would catch his eye. His face suddenly brightened.

Katie's heart bounced off her ribs. She loved it when Titus got so excited. He went near the trough where the goats fed, bent over, and picked up a dried goat manure pellet. Coming back to the bench, he rolled it around in his palm and held it out for Katie to see. "I've heard these will burn, though I've never tried it myself."

Katie giggled at his clever idea. "How did you get to know so much?"

Titus shrugged. "I don't know all that much, but sometimes I remember stuff I've heard." He set the pellet of manure on the bench next to the crayon-stuffed snowballs.

"It might not burn very long," Katie said. "We should light it last."

Titus cocked an eyebrow. "Now who's the smart one?" He pulled a box of matches from Felty's work-bench. "Do you want to light the first one or me?"

"You light it," Katie said. "We wouldn't be doing this if you hadn't searched so hard for all those candles. And cut down the pine boughs. And had the idea in the first place."

With his eyes practically glowing, Titus pulled his hay bale closer to the bench and sat down. He grabbed his beanie by the horn and slid it off his head, revealing that white-blond hair and the boyish cowlick Katie liked so much.

"I like your beanie," Katie said.

Titus pulled a match from the box and grinned. "*Denki*. Mammi made it for me. She doesn't want my ears to get cold." He struck a match and lit one of the taper candles. It would burn the longest.

"Now pick a song," Katie said, "and we can sing. Unless . . . unless you don't want to sing."

Titus shook his head. "We have to sing. It's a Christmas tradition." He scratched his head. "I choose 'O Come, All Ye Faithful.'"

Katie gave him a pitch, and they began to sing. Katie could carry a tune, but she had a mousy voice that she'd never been tempted to be proud of. Titus, on the other hand, had the voice of an angel or a movie star—even with two toothpicks in his mouth. Katie melted like a snowball in a wood-burning stove. Surely the angels singing to the shepherds sounded much like this. She almost stopped singing just to listen to Titus, but she didn't want to break with tradition, so she kept up, as inadequate as her voice was.

After the first verse, Beth and Judy sidled next to Titus as if they wanted to be included in the party. Holding perfectly still, they stared at the candle, almost as if they, too, felt the Christmas spirit.

Katie lit another taper candle. She gazed into Titus's eyes as they reflected the flickering light. His look was sort of mushy, like a bowl of sweet, warm tapioca pudding. If Titus were Adam, she'd like Adam a whole lot better. "'Away in a Manger,'" she said, after a long pause. Who knew a pair of blue eyes could make her forget every Christmas song she'd ever known? They almost made her forget her own name.

Which was . . . Katie, by the way.

The goats were nearly as enthralled as Katie as she and Titus lit candles and crayons and sang Christmas song after Christmas song about the Christ child and the little stable where He was born. The propane heater became completely unnecessary by the fifth song. Memories of Christmas in Augusta as well as the new memories of carols and Titus and goats on Huckleberry Hill kept her plenty warm. It was the first time it had truly felt like Christmas since Katie had come to Huckleberry Hill.

"'Hark the herald angels sing, Glory to the newborn King!'" Titus smiled at her, concern and puzzlement mixed together on his face. "You stopped singing at the end there. Did I sing the wrong words?" He scrunched his lips together. "I'm always messing up something. Norman tells me so all the time."

Katie's face got warmer. "I'm sorry. I . . . I just wanted to listen for a minute. Your voice is like bacon sizzling in the pan."

He raised his eyebrows. "Crackly and scratchy?"

She giggled. "Not like that. Doesn't the smell of bacon make you think of every *gute* thing? Like nothing can go wrong as long as your kitchen smells like bacon?"

He ran his fingers through his hair while a grin played at his lips. "Bacon is about my favorite thing in the whole world." He handed her the matchbox. "It's your turn for the very last candle."

In unison, they looked down and eyed the goat manure pellet. "Do you think it will burn?" Katie said.

Titus lifted his upper lip. His toothpicks rose with it. "In any case, it won't smell like bacon."

It couldn't be helped. They had to sing "*Stille Nacht*" if they wanted to keep the tradition. She struck a match and held it to the edge of the pellet. There was a lot of smoke before the match sputtered and died. She lit another and then a third. Smoke, but no fire. Katie didn't know why she was so disappointed. It was only one more candle. "We could sing without lighting anything."

Titus hopped to his feet. "I just had another idea." He went to the workbench hidden in shadow, and she saw him pull something from underneath it. He came back with a stick of store-bought butter.

"Where did you get that?"

He pressed his lips together and shrugged. "I have a box."

He pulled out a pocketknife and cut the butter in half, then poked a hole down the center of one half with one of his toothpicks. He tossed the used toothpick on the floor, tore a small piece of paper from his notebook, rolled it up, and stuck it down the hole he'd made with his toothpick. The butter looked like a square candle with a real wick.

They studied Titus's candle before meeting eyes. "Titus, you are the smartest person in the world," Katie said.

Titus's grin couldn't have been pulled any wider with a pair of pliers. "I'm not even the smartest person in this barn."

Katie lit a match and held it to their makeshift wick. After two tries, the fire caught and the butter burned like a candle. She started to sing. "*Stille Nacht, Heilige Nacht. Alles schlaft, einsam wacht.*"

They sat in silence, staring at each other as the last strains of music wafted up to the ceiling. Titus propped his elbows on the bench and leaned toward her. Hopefully he wouldn't singe his eyebrows. She liked his eyebrows. They were thick and just a shade darker than his hair. She'd hate to see them catch fire.

Her name was . . . Katie . . . Gingerich. She would not forget, no matter how good a singer Titus was. With tingling fingers and toes, she rested her chin in her hand and gazed into the candlelight, stealing glances at Titus when she thought he might not be looking. Her heart skipped-to-my-Lou with every glance. He was always looking.

"Your eyes are like chocolate frosting," Titus said.

"Dark or milk?" she whispered.

She flinched as icy water soaked through her coat.

The snowballs holding the crayons had all but melted, and the crayons were about to topple onto the bench.

Titus quickly blew out the crayons and the butter candle. "I guess we shouldn't set Dawdi's bench on fire," he said, smiling at her with a sort of dazed look on his face. Beth started lapping up the water pooling on the bench while Judy eyed the smoking crayons. "Don't eat those, Judy," Titus said. "You'll burn your lips." He stood and maneuvered his way around Beth and Judy. "Would you like a Christmas treat?"

"A Christmas treat? I didn't know this would be such a fancy party."

Katie could hear shuffling and sliding as he went to the workbench in the shadows and returned with two slices of what looked like Katie's own cinnamon bread.

She widened her eyes as Titus came into the light. "Did I . . . did I make that?"

"I have something to confess." Titus set the bread on the non-soggy side of the bench as his toothpick trembled in his mouth. "I always make my own order when I give you the list." He pulled a sheet of paper from his back pocket. It was the last list of bakery orders he'd given her. He pointed to the last name on the list. "I put myself down as Frank. It's short for Frankincense."

"Oh, I see," Katie said, half-confused, half-intrigued at why Titus would be so secretive.

He gave her a half smile. "I thought it was a *gute* Christmas code name."

"But why didn't you tell me that Frank was you? Titus is just as good a name as Frank."

Titus kicked at an imaginary pebble at his feet. "Norman and Aunt Esther would say I was foolish for spending all my money on Christmas goodies—even though I'd spend my last dime for a block of your fudge. I'd feel lower than a fly on a manure pile if you thought I was a fool."

Her heart swelled like warm yeast. "Your last dime?"

Titus pulled the toothpick from his mouth. "I really, really like fudge."

Katie suddenly couldn't breathe. It was like that time she had pneumonia, but a thousand times more pleasant, until she thought of Titus believing he had to sneak around to get a loaf of bread from her. She sudden felt thoroughly ashamed of herself. She had been so anxious about making cakes and pies for Adam, she hadn't appreciated that Titus had taken dozens of orders and delivered dozens of goodies for her. Her bakery was successful, and she would have plenty of money for her wedding to Adam because of Titus. He was the one who deserved a triple chocolate cake every day.

Titus ran his fingers through his hair. "I'm sorry for pretending to be Frank. I didn't mean to hurt your feelings."

She stood up, reached across the bench, and grabbed his hand. He froze as if he were a snowman. "I'm really excited about my Christmas treat," she said. "Do you think Frank will mind if we eat his food?"

Titus's lips twitched, as if he didn't know whether he was allowed to smile or not. "Frank won't mind. It's an emergency. We have to keep up the tradition."

"Then let's eat. We can toast our bread on the propane heater."

A deep line etched itself between his brows. "Just to be clear, you know that Frank is really me in disguise, right?"

She giggled. "Merry Christmas, Frankincense."

He brightened like a flaming Christmas crayon. "Merry Christmas to you, too."

CHAPTER 8

"I am a tiny candle, not large or bright at all, but if I pass my flame around, there's light enough for all."

Mammi nudged Titus with her elbow, and Titus nearly jumped out of his skin, which would not have been appropriate at the school Christmas program. "That's my great-granddaughter," Mammi said, smiling like a goat with a mouthful of spent barley.

Titus nodded his agreement. His niece Sadie had to be the smartest eight-year-old in Bonduel. She wasn't shy about reciting her lines clear and loud, and she didn't falter on one word. When Titus was a little boy, he'd often been assigned to be the poster holder in the school Christmas programs. He wasn't real *gute* with memorization.

The other children recited their lines, and then the seventh graders sang, "This Little Light of Mine" while the next group of children filed to the front. Titus craned his neck to see Adam Wengerd kneeling in front of the scholars with a script in hand, ready to help anyone who forgot their lines.

Titus clamped down on his toothpick.

He tried not to harbor ill will for Adam, but his patience was sorely tried sometimes. Two days ago, Adam had shown up on Huckleberry Hill and offered to help Titus make bakery deliveries. Katie's face had lit up like a homemade butter candle. Once they got down the hill and onto the main road, Adam had grinned smugly, taken his own baked goods, and walked home, leaving Titus to finish the deliveries. Titus hadn't minded doing the deliveries by himself. He usually did. But he had felt a little cross about Adam taking credit for it.

Then he'd been forced to go to the bishop's house and confess to having bad thoughts about one of his fellow men. The bishop had told him not to worry, but Titus still did. He should not be having such feelings about Katie's boyfriend. Adam was a boy in love. He was trying to impress Katie the best way he knew how.

Adam was a wonderful nice boy who knew how to put on a wonderful-*gute* school Christmas program. The difficulty was that Titus was in love with Adam's girlfriend, and there didn't seem a *gute* way around that, not if he didn't want to hurt anybody's feelings.

What Titus thought really didn't matter. Adam's wishes didn't even matter all that much. What Katie wanted was most important, and she seemed to like Adam just fine. There was no way a dull-witted boy like Titus had a chance of attracting her attention or her approval. He shouldn't covet, but it didn't seem fair that Adam should get all the triple chocolate cake *and* Katie Gingerich. *Oy*, anyhow, the ache in his chest nearly made him swallow his toothpick.

Titus squinted at the children singing a happy Christmas song in the front of the classroom.

It was time to step back.

But how could he step back if he'd never really stepped forward? Maybe he should hole up in Mammi and Dawdi's barn writing poetry until Katie went back to Augusta with her fiancé and her garlic press.

The only *gute* thing about the school program, besides his niece Sadie, was that Katie sat right next to Titus and had smiled in his direction more than once. She had a wonderful pretty smile, and he liked the way her eyelashes nearly touched her cheeks every time she blinked. But he should really stop looking, because he'd made up his mind to step back.

Katie leaned over and whispered to him. "I like the part about the Christmas recipe."

The scholars sang "We Wish You a Merry Christmas" as their final number, and the parents and guests clapped with great enthusiasm.

Once the program was over, Adam announced that refreshments would be served. Three or four *maters* brought out plates of cookies and dried fruit, and another *mater* poured soda and sherbet into the punch bowl.

Katie smiled up at Titus. "That was a *wunderbarr* program. I know where Sadie got her singing voice."

Titus couldn't do anything but stare at her and smile back. Her pretty face always struck him momentarily dumb.

"She got it from Felty," Mammi said, winking at Dawdi. "He sings like he learned from the birds."

Dawdi shook his head. "Annie-banannie, you're making that up."

"I brought cookies," Katie said. "Peanut blossoms."

Titus's ears perked up. "Do you think anyone would notice if I stole the whole plate?" He could take them to the barn and eat them while he drowned his sorrows in poetry.

"Now, Titus," Mammi said. "Everyone should have a chance to enjoy Katie's cookies."

Parents and scholars crowded the eats table, visiting and filling their plates with the many varieties of cookies Amish *fraas* had made for the program.

Many of the families were Katie's customers. Titus introduced her to the ones she hadn't met yet, and she was instantly everyone's best friend.

"Katie, we love your cookies."

"Levi Junior eats his green beans when we promise him a piece of your chocolate cake."

"Adam is a lucky boy, for sure and certain."

"My *mamm* used to make bread like yours."

Katie was a little shy, but Mammi and Dawdi stayed close by, and she seemed pleased that so many people loved her bakery. She deserved to hear it firsthand. Titus heard it all the time.

Families started to leave, and the crowd in the small schoolhouse thinned.

"Shall we go, Katie?" Mammi said. "It looks like it's going to make down hard with snow."

"I'm sorry I didn't drive you here," Titus said. He was sorry for more than one reason—the biggest being that he would have been able to spend more time with Adam's almost-fiancée—even though he was resolved to take a step back.

Katie took a long drink of Christmas punch. "I suppose I should go tell Adam good-bye before we leave."

Mammi's eyes sparkled like headlights on Highway 29. "I suppose you should, dear."

Katie caught her breath. "I almost forgot, Titus. I have something for you in the buggy."

"For me?"

"*Jah.* Wait here, and I'll go get it."

"I'll come with you," Titus said. Even though he was stepping back, he couldn't let Katie march out into the cold winter's night by herself. "So you won't be lonely."

Katie grinned at him, which made him reconsider stepping back. "You're about the nicest boy I ever met."

He helped her on with her coat, and she pulled something bright yellow from her pocket and wrapped it around her neck. It was a scarf with big, googly eyes on either end. "It's a Minion scarf," she said. "Your *mammi* made it for me. Isn't it cute?"

"What's a Minion?"

"I don't know. She said it's to go with your Viking beanie."

Katie led the way to Mammi and Dawdi's buggy, slid open the door, and pulled out a square pan covered with plastic wrap. Whatever was in that pan was creamy white with chocolate sprinkles. Chocolate sprinkles were about his favorite thing in the whole world.

Katie handed Titus the pan. It was heavy. "This is for you," she said, pressing her lips together. "I am wonderful sorry about all the cakes I should have baked you but didn't. You take bakery orders and make all the deliveries, and then you had to pretend to be Frank to get anything for yourself."

Titus's heart beat as if a giant cow were tromping

around his chest in work boots. She'd made it for him, not Adam or Mammi or even Frank.

"It's called Chocolate Wonder," Katie said. "You have to eat it with a fork or a spoon because it's very messy."

"Are those real or fake chocolate sprinkles on top?"

She shrugged her shoulders coyly. "Real."

He gasped in amazement. Real chocolate sprinkles. He'd sure picked an inconvenient time to step back.

"Katie!" Adam clomped down the schoolhouse steps.

Titus stifled a groan. Couldn't Adam see that they were having an important conversation about real and fake chocolate?

"Hey, kid," Adam said, giving Titus a light punch on the arm. Adam was a real nice guy, but Titus nearly lost his toothpick every time Adam called him "kid." Then he practically turned his back on Titus to smile at Katie. "What did you think of the program, Katie? I put that recipe part in just for you."

Titus didn't want to think ill of anyone, but that was the exact same program they had done last year. He spit the toothpick out of his mouth. Better to be toothpick-less than to choke on it.

Katie gave one of her best smiles to Adam. *Jah.* It was *gute* Titus had thrown away that toothpick. "It was a *wunderbarr* program, Adam. You had them so well organized. Nobody missed any lines or anything."

Adam nodded as if he expected no less. "Not to brag, but Reuben Weaver says I'm the finest teacher this school has ever had." He glanced at the pan in Titus's hand. "What is this? A present for me?"

"It's Chocolate Wonder," Katie said.

Adam scrunched his lips together. "Milk or dark chocolate?"

Titus tilted the pan slightly so Adam could see the sprinkles better. "They're real chocolate."

"It's milk chocolate." Katie studied Adam's expression as if waiting for his approval.

Adam nearly shouted. "Yes! I love milk chocolate."

"I made it for Titus as a thank-you for making my deliveries all month."

Adam's elation died like a mosquito under a swatter. "It's not for me?"

Uncertainty filled Katie's eyes as she shook her head. "I . . . I made that plate of cookies for you for the program tonight."

Adam's lips drooped lower. "But they're all gone. Besides, those weren't really for me. They were for the parents. Didn't you think to bring anything for me?"

"I . . . I guess just the cookies," Katie said weakly, as if it was her fault they'd all been eaten.

Titus couldn't let Katie take the blame for that. "I ate your share, Adam. And Katie's share, too. They were wonderful-*gute.*"

"I've never tasted Chocolate Wonder," Adam said. "Why didn't you make me any Chocolate Wonder?"

"I suppose I was thinking of what Titus might like yet."

Adam stuck out his lower lip. "How could you think of Titus and not your boyfriend? I really want that Chocolate Wonder." He turned to Titus as if he were on the attack, even though he smiled as if they were buddies. Titus straightened his shoulders. They were buddies. They'd played softball together in school. "Don't you agree that Katie's boyfriend should get the special dessert, especially since you ate all my cookies?"

Titus glanced at Katie, but he couldn't tell what she was thinking because she was looking down at her shoes. "I don't want to cause any trouble."

Adam tugged the pan from Titus's fingers and gave him a friendly pat on the shoulder. "Then you won't mind if I take the Chocolate Wonder, will you, kid? After all, I'm Katie's boyfriend. You're just the boy who takes care of Anna's goat and writes poems."

Titus nodded dumbly, because he couldn't think of a *gute* reason that Adam shouldn't get the Chocolate Wonder. He almost couldn't bear seeing his special dessert in the wrong hands, but Adam was the boyfriend. The boyfriend should get the Chocolate Wonder and all of Katie's smiles. Titus was just a glorified goatherd.

But wait a minute. How did Adam know Titus wrote poetry? Had Katie told him?—because Titus didn't share that talent with just anybody. He hadn't shared that talent with anybody but Katie.

"But . . . Adam," Katie protested weakly. "I can make you another Chocolate Wonder. Titus deserves this."

"And you deserve this," Adam said, kneeling down on one knee and setting Titus's Chocolate Wonder on the ground next to him. He fished in his pocket and pulled out a folded piece of notebook paper and one of the gold stars that had been hanging on the bulletin board in the school.

Katie took a small step backward. Titus couldn't move a muscle.

Adam unfolded the paper and started reading. "*Katie's eyes are chocolate brown. They shine just like a star.*

I think about her all the time, whether she be near or far. I hope that she will smile at me and bake me one more cake. If I am left here all alone, I know my heart will break."

Titus's lungs were so tight, he couldn't have taken a breath if his life depended on it.

Well, his life *did* depend on it, so he drew in a breath as if he was sucking from a straw.

Adam Wengerd had stolen his poem!

Adam had probably been sneaking around the barn and found where Titus hid his poetry. Titus was truly grateful he'd discarded his toothpick. He was so shocked, he would have swallowed it, and he would have come down with a very bad stomachache. Titus couldn't utter a word, not even when Katie pursed her lips and eyed him with concern as if she wanted him to say something.

A toothpick stomachache would have been nothing compared to the ache in his heart. Adam had stolen his poem, and it wouldn't surprise Titus if that one poem won Katie's heart in the end. It had been his very best one.

Adam pressed the gold star to his heart, then handed it to Katie. She took it as if she wasn't sure what to do with it but felt guilty for not knowing. Adam grinned at Titus as if they shared a secret. *Jah,* they shared a secret. The secret that Adam was a thief and a plagiarizercist . . . or whatever that word was.

Adam picked up his pan of Chocolate Wonder and stood. He tapped Katie lightly on the nose with his finger. "We'll see you tomorrow night."

Titus surprised himself that he was able to speak. "Tomorrow night?"

Katie glanced down at her hands, then up at Titus, then down again. The smile on her face looked like she'd taped it there. "My parents are coming from Augusta, and Adam's parents will be there. For dinner."

"I'm going to propose to Katie," Adam said. "I wanted our parents to be there to see it."

Titus eyed Katie. How long had she known about this? She didn't look all that happy about it, but maybe she was just nervous. Who wouldn't be nervous anticipating a proposal?

They stood in silence for a few seconds, Titus staring at Katie, Adam staring at Titus, and Katie staring at her hands.

"Well," Adam said, "I'll see you tomorrow, Katie. And remember, no Jell-O of any kind. My *dat* hates it."

"I'll remember," Katie said as if he'd asked her to remember to muck out the barn.

Adam turned to go back into the school, stopped short, and turned around. He practically smacked Titus on the shoulder and leaned in close to whisper in his ear. "You don't mind, do you, kid? I was trying to impress my fiancée."

He jogged away, not waiting for an answer. Titus couldn't have given him one.

"I . . . uh . . . I should fetch Anna and Felty," Katie said, not looking at him. "Good night, Titus." She raised on her tiptoes and planted a kiss on his cheek. Titus stood perfectly still even though it felt like a tornado had gone through the school yard. "*Denki.* For everything."

She walked quickly back to the school as if there really was a tornado and she had to get to shelter.

Titus reached into his pocket and pulled out three toothpicks, just to calm his nerves. Adam had stolen his dessert and his poem, and Katie had kissed him. A thousand rhymes came into his head.

Adam is in love, it's true, but he stole my poem. I feel like poo.

I really should step back from this, but Katie Rose gave me a kiss.

Titus wasn't sure about it, but it didn't seem right that Adam stole people's poems. If Adam was that much in love, he should write his own. Titus pressed his lips around his three toothpicks. Not everyone had Titus's gift for poetry. Maybe Adam couldn't think of his own poem and was so desperate, he had to steal one of Titus's.

The door to the schoolhouse opened, and Dawdi appeared. He tromped down the stairs, squinting into the darkness as if he was looking for something. "Titus, there you are. I was hoping you hadn't left yet."

Titus hung his head. He shouldn't be having unkind thoughts about Adam. Dawdi wouldn't like it. "I was just headed out."

"Katie and Anna decided they should help Adam clean up. I decided we should have a talk, man to man," Dawdi said.

Titus squared his shoulders. He liked it when Dawdi wanted to talk man to man. Dawdi's respect always made Titus forget Cousin Norman's dislike.

"As soon as Katie came inside, Adam got down on one knee and recited a poem for her." Dawdi frowned and smoothed his gray beard as amusement twinkled in his eyes. "It sounded a lot like one of your poems."

Titus let out a breath it felt he'd been holding for a long time. "I don't want to talk bad about anyone, Dawdi, but it *was* one of my poems." Titus drew his brows together. "Either that or we both wrote the same poem by mistake."

Dawdi nodded as if he had answers to every question ever asked. "*Nae*, I caught him sneaking around the barn a few days ago. He must have found your stash of poems."

Titus tried to keep a straight face. "My stash of poems? What are you talking about?"

"I've been sneaking around the barn, too. I read your poems while I milk Iris. They're very creative and keep me from getting bored. It's a shame to keep all that talent to yourself. Even Adam knows it should be shared."

Titus pulled all three toothpicks out of his mouth. "But Katie thinks he wrote it. She thinks a lot of things about Adam that might not be true."

"Like the fact that he took credit for shoveling our sidewalk? Or that he let you do the deliveries even though he made Katie think he helped you?"

Titus thought his eyes would pop out of his head. "How did you know?"

Dawdi lifted his eyebrows. He always looked so smart when he did that. "Everyone thinks all I do is read the newspaper. You learn a lot when no one knows you're paying attention."

"I was happy to shovel the sidewalk and I didn't need the credit for it, but it doesn't seem fair that Adam was admired for something he didn't do." Titus quickly remembered himself and cleared his throat. "Adam Wengerd is a wonderful nice boy. For sure and certain, he knows how to put on a *wunderbarr* Christmas program."

Dawdi's lips twitched upward. "Adam is a nice boy, but Katie will never guess how you feel about her if you keep scooting out of the way for Adam. If you love her, you need to fight for her."

"Fight for her?"

"Symbolically, of course. We still believe in nonviolence."

Titus's head ached from thinking so hard. "How do I fight symbolically?"

Dawdi wrapped an arm around Titus's neck. "Maybe it means not giving up on someone you care about, even if you're afraid you'll hurt Adam's feelings. You have feelings, too."

"*Jah.* I suppose I do." And he felt like maybe, possibly, likely he was in love with Katie.

Nae. There was no maybe. His insides felt like chocolate tapioca pudding with raisins every time she smiled at him. He loved Katie Rose Gingerich, as sure as Adam Wengerd had nice teeth.

He'd almost convinced himself that he should step back so that Adam and Katie would be free to fall in love. Except now he thought maybe he should step forward. Adam was a real nice boy, but he stole other people's Chocolate Wonder and other people's hard-written poems. He didn't deserve to marry Katie.

And Titus loved her.

This time, he would not step back.

CHAPTER 9

"Annie," Felty said, scooping himself another helping of Katie's corn chowder. "You made Titus a Viking beanie and Katie a Minion scarf. Are they related somehow?"

Anna seemed to perk up her ears. "Well, Felty, they're not related yet."

"Vikings and Minions?" Adam's *mamm* said, trying hard to follow the dinner conversation.

Anna smiled sweetly. "I meant Titus and Katie. They're not related yet."

Katie was too nervous to make sense of Anna's remark. Of course she and Titus weren't related. Maybe she was hearing things.

Steam rose from the hot roll when Adam's *dat* split it in two and spread butter on it. "The minister mentioned the devil and his minions in a sermon not long ago. I think minions are evil helpers."

"*Jah,*" Mamm said, "and I don't think we need to say any more about that."

Mamm was practically glowing with anticipation and looking at Adam's parents as if they were direct descendants of Jakob Ammann, the founder of the Amish faith. Katie didn't even have the energy to sit up straight. She felt as if she were fighting against a powerful current that threatened to pull her under and drown her. How had things gone so far awry?

She picked at her vegetable medley, barely listening to the conversation that no one cared whether or not she participated in. Mamm and Dat were gushing over every word that came out of Adam's mouth. It was a lot of gushing, because Adam always had so many words.

Adam hadn't even complained about the vegetables, even though the dish was a combination of broccoli, cauliflower, carrots, and onions swimming in a pool of melted homemade mozzarella cheese. His *dat* raved about it, so Adam kept his dislike for carrots to himself.

"The chowder isn't as thick as I like it," Adam said, "but it's wonderful-*gute*, Katie."

Mamm nodded so enthusiastically, a strand of hair came loose from her *kapp*. "Katie knows her chowders. She even makes clams tasty."

Katie made a mental note. Next time, she'd have to work on making the chowder thicker, more to Adam's liking.

Ach, she would have liked to wander out to the barn and sit with Titus while he lit crayons on fire, but she hadn't seen him all day. His cousin Aden had come twice to milk the goats, and when Anna had asked about Titus, Aden had only told them that Titus was working on something big and had asked Aden to milk for him. Tomorrow was Christmas Eve.

Titus was probably getting a few presents for his family, but Katie had been disappointed all the same.

No one understood Katie like Titus did. It was easy to talk to him, and she sensed his *gute* heart every time he smiled at her. Besides that, he looked so adorable with that toothpick he always had pressed between his teeth. What more could she want?

It didn't matter, because she'd be back in Augusta in another week and wouldn't see Titus again until she and Adam moved in with his parents after the wedding.

Oy, anyhow. She would suffocate if she let herself think about the wedding. Better not to turn blue in front of her future in-laws.

Katie gave up on her dinner when everyone else finished eating. She pulled herself from her chair and retrieved the triple chocolate cake from the fridge. Adam's parents *ooh*ed and *aah*ed over the cake, while Adam smiled as if he took credit for making it. She served everyone a generous slice except herself. She had no stomach for chocolate tonight. How could she, when Adam had taken Titus's Chocolate Wonder and left Titus with nothing? She should have said something. Why had she been too chicken to say something?

"This is wonderful-*gute* cake, Katie," Adam's *mamm* said, licking her fork clean. "Next time you should make it with coconut-pecan frosting."

Katie pressed her lips together. Adam hated coconut-pecan frosting. It would be impossible to please both her mother-in-law and her husband. She'd have to avoid the whole dilemma by never making triple chocolate cake again—that or make two different cakes for every get-together.

Adam ate two pieces of cake before he crinkled his napkin into a ball, tossed it onto his plate, and scooted his chair out from under the table. He held out his hand to her. "Katie, come here," he said, with such confidence in his tone that Katie hopped to her feet and took his hand.

Her heart thumped inside her chest like a tense bunny rabbit. She wished she were anywhere but here. If she prayed hard enough, would *Gotte* have mercy on her and transport her to the barn with the goats? Adam gazed at her with something akin to love in his eyes.

She had thought she wanted Adam to propose to her. She had thought she didn't want to be an old maid, but now, at the moment of truth, she didn't know exactly what she wanted. Well . . . not exactly. She knew exactly what she *didn't* want. And that was Adam. Adam made her long to be an old maid. She couldn't marry him. She just couldn't.

But how was she going to tell him that, with his parents and her parents leaning in with such eagerness?

Katie glanced at Anna. Titus's *mammi* eyed Katie with a glint of exasperation dancing in her eyes. Katie couldn't decipher what that look meant. All she knew was that the panic rose like bile in her throat. What was she going to do? What was she going to say?

Adam took both of Katie's hands in his. She was going to throw up.

The front door crashed against the wall behind it as if a stiff wind had blown it open, and Titus Helmuth stood in the doorway wearing his Viking beanie and looking as fierce as if he were preparing for battle.

Katie thought her heart might stop. He looked so determined, so formidable. So handsome.

He took two adamant steps into the room. "Katie," he said, the toothpick quivering on his lip, "You cannot marry Adam Wengerd."

Her heart fluttered like a whole garden of butterflies and moths and spiders—*nae,* not spiders. Spiders were scary, and this was a much more pleasant feeling. "I . . . I can't?"

Adam tightened his grip on Katie's hands and stared daggers at Titus. "We're in the middle of something important here, kid."

Titus ignored Adam altogether. Always thoughtful of making sure the heat stayed inside, he closed the door behind him and swiped his battle beanie off his head. "Katie, I am . . . you are the girl . . . I need to tell you . . ." He frowned in frustration, pulled the toothpick from his mouth, and broke it into little pieces.

"Titus," Adam said, more loudly this time. "You need to leave."

Titus flung his broken toothpick to the floor and planted his feet. "Adam, you're a real nice guy, but you're a poem stealer, and I've lost all respect for you, symbolically, of course."

Adam glanced at Katie and chuckled uncomfortably. "What are you talking about?"

Titus took a piece of paper out of his pocket. "I have written another poem to tell you how I feel. I mean Katie, not Adam."

Adam's face turned as red as a Christmas bow.

"Titus, you're interrupting something very important."

Katie pulled her hands from Adam's grasp and took a step toward Titus. "I'd like to hear it." She sounded mousy and small, but at least she'd gotten the words out. Her feelings were just as important as Adam's.

Titus nodded as if preparing to deliver a sermon in church. "*Oh, Katie dear, my heart beats fast whenever I can see you. We've gone on a few fun sleigh rides and even burned some goat poo. I know you came to Bonduel to marry Adam Wengerd, but from the very first day here, my faithful heart you have stirred. And so, although I know I am not worthy of your love, my heart will break in two unless you say you'll be my wife.*" Titus folded his paper, and for the first time since he'd stormed into the room, he looked unsure of himself. "I couldn't think of a *gute* rhyme for love."

"It wasn't a very *gute* rhyme for *Wengerd,* either," Adam muttered.

The room fell silent except for the sound of Katie's heart thumping in her ears. Adam's parents looked as if they were trying to catch flies in their open mouths. Her *mamm's* eyes were as wide as peanut blossom cookies, and her *dat's* eyes were as narrow as one of Titus's toothpicks.

Only Anna and Felty seemed unruffled. Felty dished himself another piece of chocolate cake, and Anna smiled like she always did when Titus shared one of his poems. "That was lovely, Titus," Anna said, lacing her fingers together.

Katie met eyes with Titus. His expression was so full of love and determination, she thought she might faint. Titus wanted to marry her, but until this moment, she hadn't realized that she wanted to marry him, too. More than anything.

Adam looked from Katie to Titus. "Is this some kind of a joke? Because it's not funny." He was yelling by the time he said *funny*. He definitely didn't sound amused.

"*Jah*," his *dat* said. "What is going on here?" He slammed his hand against the table so hard, Katie jumped.

This was no time for smiles, but Katie couldn't help it. Titus loved her and she loved him. "There's . . . there's been a change of plans." She pursed her lips and gave Adam the look she used to scold her nephews. "Adam, it's not nice to steal other people's poems. You should be ashamed of yourself."

Adam's face only got redder, as if he had a bad case of heat rash. "I didn't steal. I borrowed. Titus didn't mind."

Titus puffed out his chest. "I'm sorry to have to say this, but he didn't shovel the sidewalk, either."

Katie's mouth fell open. Thoroughly appalled, she turned on Adam. "I wouldn't even consider marrying you now. Sorry, Mamm. Sorry, Dat, but Adam doesn't like cooked carrots, chocolate sprinkles, or fudge with nuts."

Mamm gasped as if she'd caught Adam smoking in the barn.

Dat's face was as dark as a storm cloud. "That does change things yet."

"Titus," Adam yelled, "this is the most disgraceful—"

Titus must not have closed the door tightly. With a *bang* and a *woosh* of frigid air, Judea and Bethlehem crashed into the room as if they'd come to rescue

Titus from a coyote. Judy had a new gold bow around her neck, and Beth wore a single jingle bell like a necklace—though why Katie noticed at a time like this was a mystery.

Titus's eyebrows nearly flew off his face as he tried to grab Beth, then Judy, before they escaped his grasp. He wasn't fast enough.

Katie's *mamm* squealed and jumped onto her chair. Adam's *mamm* snatched a towel from the fridge and snapped it in the goats' direction.

Beth galloped around the kitchen and the great room as if she was looking for the nearest exit. Sparky, who had been asleep on the rug, sprang to her feet and vaulted onto the sofa, barking like the world was coming to an end.

Judy *baa*ed her greeting and proceeded to lick Adam's plate and eat his napkin.

"Shoo, shoo," Katie's *mamm* yelled as she snapped her towel in an effort to herd Judy out the door.

Dat grabbed on to Judy's gold ribbon and held on tight, but Judy simply pulled him to his feet and led him around the great room with her.

"Get them out," Adam shouted. "Mamm, throw me your towel."

Beth put her head down and ran right at Adam. He held out his hands to catch her as if she were a ball, and she flattened him like a pancake.

"Help him up," someone yelled, but there was so much confusion, Katie couldn't tell who'd said it.

Titus stared at Katie as if he hadn't noticed the chaos in the room. As if Judy wasn't trying to jump up on the table for the cake and Beth wasn't drinking water from Sparky's bowl. Without taking her eyes from Titus, Katie glided breathlessly toward him. It was as if they were the only two people in the room.

"I liked your poem," she said, just as Judy ran past and snatched it out of Titus's fist with her teeth.

Titus didn't even flinch. "I meant every word."

Her heart kept rhythm with Sparky's barking and Beth's stomping. Would she ever breathe normally again? Not that she wanted to. She liked this giddy, oh-so-happy feeling she got being near Titus.

"Get a broom! Anna, do you have a broom?"

Titus took Katie's hand. The tingle went all the way up her arm. He looked down and shuffled his feet. "My *dat* is selling me a piece of property not three miles from here. Mammi says I can keep the Christmas goats. Would you be ashamed to be married to a goat farmer who can't do his fractions?"

"Think of the cheese we could make."

"Samuel," Mamm yelled, "be careful or you'll knock over that shelf, and watch the knitting needles."

Titus wrapped his arms all the way around Katie. Her knees got as wobbly as Jell-O. *Gute* thing he was holding on so tight. "Will you marry me, pretty Katie Gingerich?"

"I love cheese," she whispered, her heart so full she thought it might burst.

"And I love potpies," he whispered back.

He lowered his head and kissed her softly, making the bees and the butterflies and all sorts of creatures come to life inside her head. She had never been so happy. *Oy*, anyhow. His lips felt so *gute*. Good thing he'd thrown away his toothpick.

Titus pulled away and lifted a brow. "I hope I didn't hurt Adam's feelings."

"*Ach,* he'll be all right. I saw Martha Weaver making eyes at him at the school program last night."

"I made eyes at you at the school program last night."

Katie giggled. "I know. You gave me butterflies."

Judy *clip-clop*ped past them with strands of red, yellow, and brown yarn tangled up in her ears. Adam's parents, Katie's parents, and Adam were doing more running around than the goats and making a lot more noise. Felty sat at the table with his arm around Anna, eating his triple chocolate cake while his eyes sparkled with delight. Neither of them seemed to mind that two goats were making a mess of their house.

"Do you think we should tell them how to catch the goats?" Katie said.

Titus grinned sheepishly. "One more kiss first?"

This time she stood on her tippy toes and wrapped her arms around his neck. He sort of lifted her off the ground, and his kiss made her feel like she was floating. Better than eating three pieces of Chocolate Wonder and a whole apple pie. If she'd known how *gute* it would feel, she would have kissed Titus a lot sooner.

Oh, *sis yuscht, ach, du lieva,* and *oy,* anyhow.

"Merry Christmas, Titus."

"Merry Christmas, my dear Katie."

CHOCOLATE WONDER

INGREDIENTS

1 cup flour
½ cup butter, softened
½ cup chopped pecans
1 cup powdered sugar
8 ounces cream cheese, softened
16-ounce tub of whipped topping (like Cool Whip)
Two 4½-ounce packages of instant chocolate
    pudding
3 cups milk
¼ cup chopped pecans (optional)
2 tablespoons chocolate sprinkles (optional)

Preheat oven to 300 degrees F.

CRUST

With a pastry cutter, combine:
1 cup flour
½ cup butter, softened

Add:
½ cup chopped pecans

Mix and press into the bottom of a 9x13-inch pan.
Bake at 300 degrees F for 25 minutes. Watch closely
so it doesn't burn around the edges. Cool.

CREAM CHEESE LAYER

Mix well:
1 cup powdered sugar
8 ounces cream cheese, softened

Add:
Half of the whipped topping

Mix well and pour over the cooled crust.

PUDDING LAYER

With a hand beater or an electric beater, mix until set:

2 packages of instant chocolate pudding
3 cups milk

Spread over the cream cheese layer.

Spread the rest of the whipped topping over the top of the pudding layer. Sprinkle with chopped nuts or chocolate sprinkles (optional).

Let set in fridge for 4 to 5 hours.

THE SPECIAL
CHRISTMAS COOKIE

LISA JONES BAKER

To my greatest blessings, John and Marcia Baker,
who raised me in a Christian home filled
with unconditional love and support.

ACKNOWLEDGMENTS

I'm grateful to my Lord and Savior for publication after twenty-four years of prayers to see my work in print. Thank you to my mother, Marcia Baker, the most patient person in the world, for listening to me read my books out loud for over two decades. Thanks to computer expert and sister extraordinaire Beth Zehr for creating my Web site and for taking on my computer challenges at all times, day and night. Also thanks to niece Brittany for her huge contribution to my Web page. Thanks to my other invaluable computer assistants who help me at a moment's notice: Gary Kerr, Doug Zehr, Brooke Conlee, Bloomington Geek Squad. Thanks to writer Lisa Norato, confidante, critique partner, and true friend for riding out the entire tenure of my writing endeavors with me.

I owe tremendous thanks to numerous kind people in Arthur for patiently answering questions, having me in their homes, relating true stories during wonderful buggy rides, and allowing me special insight into a way of life that has my full respect, admiration, and fascination. Thanks to my Amish go-to girl, who prefers to remain anonymous, while faithfully reading my early copies, cover to cover, and for helping Emma to follow her heart. I owe a debt of gratitude to hundreds of writers in the RWA who reviewed my partials and offered input to hone my stories. Last but certainly not least, I'd like to give special thanks to my supportive agent, Tamela Hancock Murray, who stuck by me and rooted for me, and to my fabulous editor, Selena James, and everyone at Kensington Publishing who have been part of the production of this story.

CHAPTER 1

Emma drew a star at the top of Amos's English homework page and wrapped an affectionate arm around him. "Excellent work! You got every answer right!"

The corners of Amos's lips drew up into a huge grin that showed a row of straight teeth. The child had a kind face. And an even warmer heart. Every time Emma looked at him, the small boy's innocence tugged at her emotions.

As the first December snowfall touched the bare, frozen ground of Arthur, Illinois, the flame in the fireplace at the two-story Troyer home popped. Amos and Emma jumped at the same time. Laughter followed.

Automatically, Emma didn't waste time pulling the front of his black hand-knit sweater together. She tried to avoid mentioning Amos's unusual heart defect, but it was more important than ever to make sure he stayed warm. At the young age of six, Amos hadn't known any other way of life.

But good news had broken a year ago when he had visited a doctor at the Mayo Clinic who could fix it. Because they were Amish, they had no insurance, but thanks to the news reaching the media, there was huge support for an upcoming auction in their community to raise money for the unique procedure to take place in Rochester, Minnesota.

The smell of lemon-scented furniture polish loomed in the air. It was no secret that Amos's mother, Esther, kept the cleanest house in town when she was well. But unfortunately, she was forced to spend bouts of time in bed when the Epstein-Barr virus set her back. But even then, her sisters made sure the Troyer house stayed well kept!

As Emma regarded Amos, he turned to face her. The unexpected seriousness in his deep brown eyes took her by surprise.

When he tugged at her arm, his small white hand remained on her wrist. "Emmie, does this mean I get a cookie with icing?"

Emma broke out in laughter. For some reason, that was the last question she'd expected. He was referring to the star she'd drawn. Honored that her only student considered her Christmas cookies the best he'd ever tasted, Emma stood and proceeded to the thin red plastic platter she'd brought to his house that morning. Amos knew he had earned a cookie. And she loved making him happy. "Which one do you want?"

He quickly and eagerly joined her, pointing to the edible with peppermint icing. She plucked the chosen treat between two fingers, grabbed a napkin with her free hand, and laid both on the table.

While chewing the buttery dessert, he glanced

back at her and grinned. "I like this better than the one you drew."

Emma sat next to him. "I'll bet you do."

He lifted a skeptical brow. "In my opinion, this is my favorite."

She gave an appreciative nod. "That's good to hear." Amos was fully aware that Emma changed her recipe a tad each time for Amos to decide which batch was the tastiest. When she altered the mixture, sometimes adding more butter, or vanilla, or flour, she documented her adjustments so when Amos decided which cookie won, she would use that formula for the auction, to take place in less than two weeks.

As she put his school books in a neat pile, his soft voice made her look up. "Emmie, when I have the operation, I won't have to wear this anymore, will I?" He looked down at his heavy knit sweater, and the corners of his lips dropped.

Contemplating an answer, she shoved her chair closer to the table. The quick motion made a light squeaking sound on the tiled floor.

While he chewed the morsel, Emma pressed her lips together thoughtfully. Somehow she knew that being positive would play a very important role in the outcome of the operation.

"You won't have to wear it in the summer. But in the winter?" She lifted a brow. "It's pretty cold. You'll probably want it on."

Her answer seemed to satisfy him. After gobbling down the snack, he wrote out the answers she'd asked him to do on the paper in front of him. She watched his feet, which almost touched the floor, swing back and forth while he concentrated.

A bright beam of sunlight swept through the kitchen

window and landed on his beautiful thick mass of hair, lightening it to a softer shade of reddish-blond.

Finally, the six-year-old dropped his pencil on the table and handed the paper to Emma while displaying a proud look on his face. "That was easy, Emmie. What next?"

The adult-like way he spoke at times prompted a smile. If only every child liked homework as much as Amos did. She tried not to overreact to the high academic level he'd achieved at his age; she never wanted it to go to his head.

She quickly put another project in front of him. "Here. Read it to yourself, then see how many answers you can get." She followed the order with a wink.

Without wasting a second, he started the new project as if he was playing with a toy. Emma already knew that Amos would get every answer correct. She wasn't sure whether his reading ability was related to his inability to play outside with other children, but whatever the case, his level in English skills was heads above kids his age.

After he glanced at the page, he surprised her by dropping his pen next to the paper and looking straight ahead. Emma lifted a curious brow. Her instincts told her that some of his interest in completing his schoolwork was to please his tutor. He loved spending time with her. And vice versa.

He turned and crossed one leg under the other while getting comfortable on his chair. The serious look in his eyes hinted that he wanted to talk about something.

She hesitated. "Amos, is something wrong?"

He glanced down at the table and frowned. She

tried for a positive thought to make him smile again. "Just think, Amos, it's only a matter of time before the surgery takes place. And you'll be as good as new!"

When he looked up, his expression was uncertain. He lowered the pitch of his voice until it was barely more than a whisper. "What if there aren't enough cookies?"

"You mean donations?"

He offered a slow, sad nod.

She reached across the table and used her pointer finger to lift his chin a notch. Their gazes locked. "Amos, I have every bit of faith that God will help us get enough money."

She used her most confident voice. The last thing she wanted was for him to lose hope. "I have a list of cookie donations that would reach all the way to the North Pole!"

He laughed.

She went on to explain. "The cookies will help, that's for sure. But as I've told you, most of the revenue will come from more expensive items. Tables, chairs, and furniture that men in our community are working very hard to make."

When he didn't say anything, she proceeded in her most reassuring tone. "Other donations will help, too. From what I've heard, one of the farmers in our community will even auction off some of his land to go to your fund."

Amos pulled in a deep breath and rolled his eyes in disbelief.

"That goes to show just how special you are."

His pupils got larger.

"Because so many people across the state are

aware of this surgery . . . and of you . . . folks have committed out of the goodness of their hearts."

He frowned and scratched his nose. "You mean they're giving money without getting anything back?"

She smiled at the way he worded the question. His thoughts were so straightforward. Honest. There was never a guess where he was coming from.

The mooing noises from the cattle lightened the silence.

"You know that people all over are rooting for you to get your surgery. Even the doctor who will perform the procedure is forfeiting what he would make."

An emotional breath escaped her. She blinked when salty tears stung her eyes. She leaned closer to Amos and whispered, "Do you know just how special that makes you?"

To her surprise, he didn't grin. The expression in his large, hopeful eyes was unusually serious. "Do you know what I'm gonna do first thing after I get my heart fixed, Emmie?"

She looked at him for an answer.

"Play tag with Jake and Daniel. And nobody's gonna catch me!"

The admissions tugged at Emma's heartstrings until her chest ached. Automatically, she rested her hands below her neck and closed her eyes a moment. His wants were so simple. She knew of healthy kids with much stronger desires, but this little guy only wanted to run and play outside.

To Emma, raising sufficient funds for the operation would be one of God's greatest gifts. When Amos had asked her about it, she had stood firm that the funds would come in. But she was saying double prayers for it to actually happen.

How could any child be more precious than Amos? Emma was sure it wasn't possible, as she took in the small boy's endearing features and swallowed an emotional knot. Amos's thick mass of unruly hair fell lazily over his forehead and caressed the tops of his brows.

The child's deep brown eyes reminded her of autumn. Of pumpkin pie–colored leaves falling from tall trees. Tiny freckles on the bridge of his nose matched his pupils. And a narrow set of shoulders was the reason his suspenders continuously slipped down his arms.

Amos's wide smile was full of hope. Filled with an innocence that made Emma want to do everything she could to see him run around and have fun with kids his age.

And soon, he would get the long-awaited surgery that would allow him to have a normal life. The upcoming auction would be the ultimate blessing.

She'd been asking God for this miracle. Her faith was strong. And she knew her Lord and Savior wouldn't let her down.

The end of the school week was here. After Emma hugged Amos good-bye, she watched him tote his books to his room. That was the normal routine. Because the youngster was incredibly studious and also because she knew him so well, she didn't have to guess what he would do the rest of the evening.

As happy steps took him to his room on the ground floor, Emma took in the stairway that glistened with furniture polish. Before slipping inside of his door, he looked back at her and grinned. She offered a quick wave.

She had no doubt that he wouldn't waste time before checking out the story she'd just given him. She always took great care when selecting his material. This particular library book was about a child who had undergone surgery to correct his foot from turning inward. When she'd told Amos the theme, he'd immediately flipped open the cover.

As the fire crackled, Emma ran her hands up and down her sleeved arms. The unusually cold winds competed boldly with the gas heat, as well as the warmth from the fireplace.

As she considered the twenty-minute walk home, she pressed her lips together in a dread-filled sigh. She made her way to the dining room table to slip her teaching materials into the oversized bag her mamma had given her.

As soon as the books were tucked neatly inside the vinyl holder with extra-strong handles, Emma slipped her arms through her heavy wool coat and proceeded toward the door. As she passed the gas heater, she stopped and smiled a little, trying to savor the moment; she knew what to expect when she opened the front door.

As soon as her fingers touched the brass knob on the inside of the door, a stern voice stopped her. Automatically, she turned to face Amos's older brother, Jonathan, who regarded her with skepticism.

She forced a polite smile. "Jonathan."

His face still held a slight tan from the summer. In his coat, he looked unusually large. It was common knowledge in their community that he was easily one of the strongest men around.

"You surprised me. I thought you were out feeding the cattle."

"I finished." He hesitated, and a set of dark brows drew together into a frown. "You got a moment?"

Before she could answer, she took in the dissatisfied look on his face that told her something was awry. But she wasn't surprised. It seemed as though nothing could please Amos's older brother these days.

She offered a slight shrug. "Sure. What's up?"

He motioned to the back door. "Let's talk while I drive you home." For a moment, Emma drew in a grateful breath. At the same time, she wondered if it was proper to accept a ride from a single Amish man. She quickly decided that it was. The weather was dangerously cold, and this was common courtesy on Jonathan's part.

As if reading her mind, he smiled a little. "I don't want you to freeze to death, Emma."

"Okay."

He motioned and followed her out. The unusually high wind shear stopped her breath. She pressed her lips together to prevent the air from going down her throat. The fierce coldness stung her eyes, and she automatically lowered her lids a moment to adjust. When she opened them, she drew in a deep breath and shivered.

"You okay?"

The concerned tone of his voice prompted a comforting sensation. She parted her lips in reaction. The question showed thoughtfulness, a side of Jonathan that was endearing. She pulled in a deep breath.

"*Denki.*" She smiled a little. "What's on your mind?"

As she stepped inside of the carriage, Emma tried to stop her teeth from chattering. She knew without question that Jonathan obviously wanted to discuss something away from Amos. But the coldness quickly turned to a much-appreciated warmth as Jonathan turned on his gas heater.

Some Amish didn't use anything to make their cabins of their carriages more comfortable; she was happy he did. And the cabin in the buggy wasn't tight, so the fumes posed no danger. She relaxed a little and flexed her fingers in reaction to the change in temperature.

He cleared his throat. "It's the auction."

Emma darted him a quick glance to continue ahead.

"When you and the others voted for this fund-raiser, I never actually thought it would materialize." He turned to her and lowered his pitch to a more serious tone.

"Emma, I appreciate all you've done for Amos. Everything you do for him. Since Dad passed away, the kid hasn't been the same. It doesn't much help things that Mom is down with the virus at times. And when we found out last year about the heart defect. . . ."

He shook his head. "It's been a bad time. But since you started tutoring him . . ." He paused. "It's hard to explain. But he smiles. Laughs. And you've helped him discover his love of reading."

Emma almost choked with shock. Getting a compliment from Jonathan was rare. And what he'd said forced her heart to a happy beat. What on earth, then, was wrong?

"I'm so glad to play a role in Amos's life. And let

me tell you, he's given me much more than I've offered him."

When the wind picked up speed, the buggy rocked a bit from side to side. As she eyed the dull gray sky looming in the distance, Emma yearned for the season to change. But she knew that winter was just beginning.

They were nearly home when she glanced at Jonathan and noticed his somber expression. He looked at her, and their gazes locked. "I suppose it's no secret that I think you focus way too much on English and not enough on math. Don't numbers deserve more attention? When he's running his own business, he'll need to know figures."

She gave a firm shake of her head.

"When Amos is older and has a farm, he'll use math skills on a daily basis. Amos will compute profits and manage the budget." Jonathan threw his head back and chuckled. "Sorry we don't see eye to eye, but I hardly think English is gonna help him with that."

She gave a stronger shake of her head. "I disagree. In the long run, his English knowledge will actually be much more important than math." Before Jonathan could cut in, Emma substantiated her statement. "Just think of how important the Scriptures are. He'll read them every night. And most communication requires literacy. Amos loves books. And that's how you build vocabulary."

"That's not my main complaint, though." He cleared his throat. His voice took on a firmer, more direct tone. "Please don't take this the wrong way, Emma. But the auction's been causing me to lose sleep."

She pressed her lips together in deep deliberation.

"I've been giving this a lot of thought, and to be honest, I'm still not comfortable accepting donations for the surgery. From the get-go, you've played an important role in getting this thing going. Now I want you to stop it."

His unfair order prompted her to bite her tongue. His demand prompted her to forget the brief compliment he'd paid her. She didn't try to hide how upset she was. Trying to think of an appropriate response, she lifted a defensive hand.

"Jonathan, are you crazy?" Without thinking, she raised her chin a notch. As she looked at him for an answer, she glimpsed his deep green eyes. The shade reminded Emma of a beautiful stone she'd seen on an English girl's finger.

Wavy jet-black hair stuck out from the bottom of his hat. His jaw was square, and a dark set of thick brows hovered beneath his forehead.

To her astonishment, the expression on his face was that of amusement. She was happy she hadn't further irritated him; that was the last thing she wanted to do.

He lifted a defensive hand to stop her. "I'm well aware of the benefits. It's just that . . ." He stared straight ahead and cupped his chin with his hand. When he turned toward her, the expression in his eyes was of sadness.

Her heart pumped to an unsettling beat.

"I'm not happy taking money from people I don't know—or even those I do." He lifted a defensive hand. "I was raised to be humble and taught that pride isn't a good thing. But I'm flawed, Emma.

Something inside of me likes to be able to support my family without accepting charity. It's all about self-respect."

He offered a helpless shrug. "I'd rather earn the money myself."

"Jonathan, swallow your pride. This should be about Amos."

The emotion in her voice was so fierce, she nearly choked on her words. "As soon as this procedure's over, think of how his life will change. I know you'll see things differently."

She threw her hands up in the air. In a swift motion, she stuck her hand out to count with her fingers as she ticked off reasons. "He'll be able to do things other kids his age do. Play outside. Not wear a sweater all summer long. Or take medicine four times a day."

She continued her argument with emotion. "Do you know what your little brother wants more than anything?"

He eyed her.

"To play tag with his friends."

A hard knot in her throat made it difficult to talk. Her pulse nearly jumped out of her wrist in protest as she went on.

"Do you have any idea of the work we've put in for this auction? I've practically pulled teeth to get it. And finally, *finally*, Jonathan, momentum is on our side. People are talking about it with excitement. In fact, as soon as the press got wind of it, attention poured in from everywhere in Illinois. Don't you understand that the entire state is rooting for little Amos to get well?"

She paused to shrug. "We *will* raise enough money

for little Amos's operation. But now you're telling me to stop it? *Why?*" She lifted her chin a notch, squared her shoulders, and planted her palms against her waist.

A long, tense silence ensued. She took in Jonathan's features and pressed her lips together thoughtfully.

"I'm telling you, Emma, I won't take their money. It just doesn't feel right."

She closed her eyes and silently counted to ten. "I admire your self-respect, Jonathan. And at least, you admit it's in the way. But sometimes you've got to look at the bigger picture."

"I feel like I've failed. I mean, I'm the father figure in the boy's life. What's wrong with me that I can't take care of him like I should?"

He lowered his voice. "And how could he possibly look up to me when he sees I can't handle something like this without everyone else having to pitch in?"

Emma wasn't sure what to say. Because she realized what she was up against. How could she ever convince a man who was used to doing everything by himself, that this was a situation where he needed help?

CHAPTER 2

Emma recorded the final names of donors on the last line of her twenty-ninth page and sighed relief. She pulled a separate sheet from the notebook and began estimating the total dollars of donations so far.

While she silently added, the sweet smell of cookies baking filled the room. The timer in front of her showed ten more minutes until she would remove more desserts from the oven. Most of the batch in progress was for Amos and his family.

The little boy absolutely lived for Emma's treats! Emma knew that his mamma's bed rest was hard on him, but thank goodness, her time down wasn't forever. As Emma added, she scooted her chair closer to the table.

A soft voice prompted her to look up. "I can't believe the pace those pledges are comin' in. The Lord surely is helping us raise money."

Emma pulled her sweater tighter. The heat coming from the gas furnace struggled to compete with the unusually cold December temperatures. The first week of the year's last month ended with a record-low windchill.

"It's like everyone who has ever heard of Amos is rooting for him to have this procedure." Mamma stepped closer and wrapped an affectionate arm around Emma.

The warmth penetrated the thick navy sweater that Emma had knit last year. The comforting sensation traveled up her arms. When it settled in her shoulders, Emma pushed out a sigh of contentment. Her tension suddenly evaporated, and Emma sat back in the chair and crossed her legs at the ankles.

She turned to look up at her role model. "Mamma, I can't believe this is finally gonna happen." Her eyes filled with salty moisture, and she blinked at the sting. "I pray every night that my little Amos will get his wish to play tag with his friends. I want it more than anything."

Mamma sat down on the chair next to her and put her hand on Emma's. The low pitch of her voice cracked with emotion. "You really love that boy."

A knot formed in Emma's throat; she tried to swallow it, but couldn't. Finally, she smiled a little and offered a nod. "I'm telling you, Mamma, he stole my heart the moment I met him." She sighed. "Maybe it was that big freckled grin. Perhaps it was his unusually small build. Or his heartwarming smile." Emma threw her hands in the air. "I don't know. But I'm sure he's the most special, unique child I've ever met."

"He's a lot like you, Emma."

The statement took Emma by surprise. Her jaw dropped. "In what way?"

Mamma sat back in her chair and crossed her

arms over her waist. "For one thing, his love of books is as strong as yours. When you were his age, your papa and I couldn't read you enough stories." Mamma laughed. With her auburn hair pulled back tightly under her *kapp,* her face looked so young. Of course, she was thirty-six. "We read to you at night to make you sleepy, but instead, you wanted to keep hearing more stories."

Emma grinned. "I don't know what I would do without the library."

Emma considered her disturbing conversation with Jonathan and decided to share it. "Mamma, Jonathan doesn't want donations. He asked me to stop the auction." She hesitated to fling a set of frustrated hands in the air. "Can you believe it?"

"What?" Mamma's deep, velvety blue eyes widened as she straightened and pressed her palms on her thighs.

Emma related the conversation she'd had with Amos's older brother. When she finished, she pushed out a satisfied sigh. Sharing it with Mamma was like releasing a heavy weight off of her shoulders. In reaction, she rolled them to relax.

"Emma, maybe raising funds for such an expensive procedure makes Jonathan feel like he's not fully a man."

"But he is!" Emma threw a set of frustrated hands in the air. "Why can't he see that no one around here would be able to pay for a procedure of this nature on their own? Why can't he comprehend that stopping this would mean that little Amos will never play outside?"

"Honey, he doesn't really want to stop the fund-raiser."

"No?"

Mamma's voice softened. "Think about where he's coming from. His daddy's only been gone a couple of years, and in that time, Jonathan stepped up to be the family leader." She gave a sympathetic shake of her head.

Emma offered a quick nod of agreement. "I'm trying to understand his point of view. Although, in this situation, it would be best for him to grit his teeth and do what's right for his little brother. Either way, it's not a perfect world. But the auction's gonna happen. And nothing Jonathan does can change it."

"Too bad his daddy's not here. When he passed away, the entire community offered support to his family. Helped with chores and such. Even at that time, I recall that Jonathan wasn't happy about not being able to handle it all by himself."

Emma recalled when the senior Troyer had passed away. Still a teenager, Jonathan hadn't been given extra time to grow spiritually. Instead, he had been thrown into the difficult and unusual circumstances of taking care of his still-grieving mother and smaller, sickly brother. On top of dealing with Amos's heart defect, Jonathan still ran the family farm. And she knew that he owned over a hundred head of cattle.

Emma's heart ached for little Amos. To her dismay, it also hurt for Jonathan.

"Emma?" Mamma's voice pulled her out of her reverie. "Let's try to be a little kinder to Jonathan. He might seem gruff. But I really think you should cut him some slack. The poor man's got his own problems."

"*Jah.* I know, Mamma. It's just that with him, though . . ."

Mamma lifted a curious brow.

Emma gave a frustrated roll of her eyes. "It seems that whatever I do, I can't please him."

The corners of Mamma's lips lifted into a sudden grin. "Like I said, he's got a lot on his plate."

Emma nodded agreement. "The problem is that he's making my plate heavy, too."

The following afternoon, Jonathan rested his palms on the shovel handle and pressed the sharp edge against the floor where the wall met the concrete. As he caught his breath, he took in the scene in front of him. The barn was warmer than the outside, that was for sure. But even with the body heat from the animals, his toes still froze in his heavy socks and work shoes.

Black Angus cattle huddled around the feeding troughs that filled the far west area of the old, tall red barn. The very building that had been built years ago by his grandfather. The spot where Jonathan stood had been his dad's favorite place.

Jonathan took in a deep, emotion-filled breath. It was here that his beloved father had spent most of his time. Doing just what Jonathan was doing. Making sure there was plenty of straw for their livestock, cleaning the barn, and feeding the large herd of cattle.

Outside, freezing rain hit the ground, creating a light tapping sound that reminded Jonathan of a summer shower. Only this definitely wasn't summer. And the numb sensation in his toes told him it was time to go back in the house.

But memories of working side by side with his father compelled him to stay. His throat constricted until he could barely swallow. For a desperate moment, he yearned to have his dad back.

He nearly choked. Thank goodness no one was watching. He had to be strong for his family. His mother and little brother depended on him. He could never allow them to see how much he hurt.

For some strange reason, his thoughts turned to Amos's tutor. He took a step forward to continue tossing the hay into the cattle bed with his pitchfork. To his dismay, all he could see was the determination on Emma's face when she'd made her case for the auction.

He frowned and continued pitching straw until he stopped to get his breath. On the wall, a pair of quiet pigeons overlooked his work. A brown squirrel had grabbed one of the acorns that Jonathan had scattered on top of the cement slab behind the shed.

As his recent conversation with Emma replayed in his mind, an image of his late father appeared in his mind. Jonathan wished with all of his heart that his dad was still alive. Most definitely, the person Jonathan had respected more than anyone in the world would have figured something out. A way to get little Amos's procedure without taking donations. Now it was up to Jonathan to do the thinking.

Jonathan wasn't nearly as experienced as his role model. He swallowed a sad knot as he envisioned his dad smiling and running his fingers through his long beard. His wisdom and logic were surely missed.

He was sure that his father would come up with a way to get funds for Amos's surgery without so much notoriety. Without taking revenue from complete strangers that he couldn't pay back. Jonathan knew where he had inherited his proud nature. But he prayed constantly for God to help him be more humble and focus a little less on pride and self-respect.

But what could he do? Jonathan shrugged. Thanks to Emma and a group of women in the community, the fund-raiser had materialized before there was even an opportunity to stop it. Initially, he hadn't considered it seriously. Who would have guessed that such interest in little Amos would have exploded when the press got wind of the story? Even now, if Jonathan attempted to cease the auction, he probably wouldn't be able to. But what could he do?

He knew whom to ask. Swallowing a knot that was a combination of desperation and humiliation, he folded his hands together in front of him and knelt. Squeezing his eyes closed, he lowered his head in a quick, swift motion to pray. In a whisper, he pushed out everything he felt.

"Dear Lord, right now, I'm torn. I need guidance. I want Amos to get his heart fixed—it's not that I'm trying to stop it. I just need to know how to make that happen without accepting money from everyone around."

He shoved out a sigh. "In my heart, I know Dad would want to take another avenue. But what is it?"

He considered what he'd said and gave a shake of his head. He pressed his palms together so hard, his hands shook.

"I pray that You will help me to be a better provider. A good family leader."

When he opened his eyelids, his entire body was shaking. For long moments, he considered his prayer. An unsettling sensation filled his gut until it ached.

He folded his hands over his chest as he recalled yesterday's conversation with Emma. He hadn't neglected to notice her deep blue eyes and smiled a little. The shade was so beautiful; it reminded him of pictures of tropical waters he'd seen in travel magazines. He tapped the toe of his shoe to a beat that was a combination of uncertainty and curiosity.

Under Emma's kapp was an autumn-blond braid that had been tucked in neatly. Amos's tutor was average height and she'd worn a navy dress with sturdy black shoes. The corners of her lips had lifted up into a natural smile, and at times, when she spoke of something that enthused her, off-white flecks on her pupils danced with a childlike energy.

What intrigued him most was her fierce determination. Despite the fact that he didn't support the auction, he admired her for all she'd done to ensure it happened. He didn't expect her to understand his negative view of accepting handouts. However, he also didn't expect his position to change.

He put his pitchfork and shovel away, organized the feed bags on the south side of the barn, and closed the large, heavy doors. Inside his home, Amos's voice interrupted his thoughts.

"Johnnie, will Emmie come tomorrow?"

Jonathan smiled a little and wrapped an affectionate arm around the boy's narrow shoulders. His heartstrings pulled at him as he realized how unusually fragile his brother was compared to other kids his age.

"Not on Saturday, Amos. But she'll be back Monday."

Jonathan was quick to note the disappointed expression on his brother's face.

"She gave you a good book to read, though, *jah?*"

He nodded. "But I like it better when she reads with me."

Jonathan didn't know how to respond to the unexpected comment. While he hung his coat on a hook and enjoyed the welcome change in temperature, he raised a thoughtful brow.

He'd known for some time that his younger sibling was smitten by the blue-eyed tutor. And it didn't help that Mamma was bedridden again. However, Jonathan admitted that Emma's nurturing didn't hurt his little brother. Jonathan only wished that she would do what he wanted—and not the other way around.

Excitement edged Amos's voice. The corners of his lips turned up into a grin that spread across his freckled face. Jonathan pushed Amos's bangs off of his forehead with gentle fingers.

To Jonathan's surprise, Amos handed him one of Emma's cookies. "Johnnie, whatever's bothering you, Emmie's cookies will make it better. Here. See?"

With that, Amos bit into the treat and grinned. He rolled his eyes. "Emmie likes me to eat them. Besides, she needs me for her test run."

"What?"

"You know. A test run. Every time she makes cookies, she does something different to the recipe." He squared a narrow set of proud shoulders. "It's up to me to tell her how she's doing. She even has me score each batch from one to ten. And I have to make sure her best recipe is the one she uses for the auction."

The auction. There it is again. But the simple way Amos explained the rating system made a smile tug at the corners of Jonathan's mouth. Emma had a way of making Amos feel important, that was for sure.

And Jon could see how she'd involved his brother in the fund-raiser. She made the boy believe he was contributing. Obviously, he considered his cookie-testing role of utmost importance. And Jonathan was certain Amos didn't mind.

Jonathan strummed the tips of his fingers against the tabletop and took in the serious expression in Amos's eyes. Every time he looked at his little brother, love overwhelmed him. He wanted more than anything for the kid to be able to have a normal life. If only he didn't feel so incapable.

He wished everything was as simple as the child viewed the world. Amos was standing at his side, obviously waiting for Jonathan to take a bite of the iced cookie in the round shape of a Christmas ornament.

Obliging, Jonathan tasted the dessert and nodded satisfaction. "I'm not sure, but I think this might be the best-tasting Christmas cookie ever."

Amos was quick to nod agreement. "That's 'cause all of Emmie's cookies are practice for the auction."

Jonathan lifted an inquisitive brow. "Is that what she told you?"

He was quick to offer a proud nod. "*Jah.* She wants the cookies that get money for my surgery to be the best anyone has had. Ever."

Jonathan pressed his lips together as he considered the admission. To his dismay, it seemed as though Emma was always pushing the fund-raiser. He drew his brows together into a frown.

"Emmie would be sad."

Amos's voice was edged with disappointment. Jonathan's gaze locked with his dear little brother's. "Why?"

"Her cookies are supposed to make people smile. But they made you frown."

The little guy was way too perceptive for his age. Jonathan knew Amos wanted to be just like him. Because of that realization, Jonathan forced an optimistic tone.

"Not at all." He ordered his mouth to smile after chewing another bite of the iced dessert. He would be lying to himself if he said Emma's cookies weren't the best he'd ever eaten. He didn't know what she did to the dough, but whatever it was made the treats score high.

"You're right about what you said."

Amos looked at him to continue.

"After finishing the cookie, I'm absolutely certain, without a doubt, it wins. It's the most delicious I've ever had."

The expression on Amos's face turned more serious. He stepped closer, put a small hand in front of his mouth, and spoke in a hushed tone. Jonathan wasn't sure why. Their mother was in her room elsewhere in the house. "Even better than Auntie Elizabeth's?"

Jonathan chuckled and nudged the boy. Smiling, Jonathan pressed a pointer finger to his lips. "But that's just between us."

Amos's eyes doubled in size. "Really?"

Jonathan nodded. "No one ever has to know."

Squaring his shoulders, Amos grinned from ear to ear. With one quick motion, he clutched his fingers to his palms and raised his knuckles to meet Jonathan's. "Secret."

Jonathan met Amos's knuckles with his own. They did it when they shared something important with each other. Jonathan knew that to Amos, a secret meant he would never tell anyone.

Once, when Amos had spotted Jonathan sneaking one of their mother's sponge cakes she'd made for the neighbors, Amos had pledged confidentiality. And he hadn't told a soul.

Jonathan stood to walk him to his room. "It's time for someone to get to bed."

Amos never argued. The doctors had made it clear to Jonathan how important it was for Amos to get plenty of rest.

"Will you tell me a story?"

Jonathan wrapped an affectionate arm around the child he loved more than life itself. "Which one you wanna hear?"

As Jonathan followed the youngster to his room, Amos turned back to him and started to slip in his socked feet.

"Whoa!"

Jonathan caught him. "Watch where you're going."

Amos giggled.

Jonathan held Amos's shoulders as they made it to the child's bedroom. As Amos pulled his pajamas from the drawer, Jonathan's thoughts drifted back to Emma.

He considered her "test runs" and smiled. It certainly wasn't difficult to understand why his little brother was so fond of her. It was too bad he didn't agree with her about having the auction. Because there were plenty of things he liked about her, too.

CHAPTER 3

It had become routine for Jonathan to drive Emma home. Usually Amos came with them. She rather enjoyed talking with Amos's brother. As they approached the Yoder home, the sun came out for a moment, causing her to blink. But the moment it appeared, it went away. As usual, they discussed the fund-raiser. And they still disagreed. Again, she tried to convince him why to have it.

Those reasons by far outnumbered any reasons not to. She knew the cost of the surgery was so high, he would never be able to pay for it himself, even with the help of their close community.

After a tense, lengthy silence, she glanced at Jonathan's expression from her peripheral vision. "You know what your problem is?"

He lifted a challenging brow.

"That you've always been healthy. Neither one of us has walked in little Amos's shoes." She pushed out a deep sigh. "So we could never completely understand what it's like to stay inside all day when your friends play outdoors. Wear a sweater in the middle of summer."

Jonathan held up a defensive hand. "I think I do."

She raised her chin a notch. "How could you?"

"When I was Amos's age, I suffered from chronic asthma." Jonathan's tone was edged with regret. "Thank goodness, I grew out of it. When I was young, I would wake up in the middle of the night gasping for air."

He paused a moment and looked into the distance. "In fact, I can't count the number of times I awakened my poor parents."

"Could they help you?"

"Not really. But they tried. They did their best. To my mom, rubbing eucalyptus oil on my chest was the cure-all. It smelled good."

He chuckled. She joined in the laughter.

"The best medicine I had was a puffer."

Emma offered an eager nod. "I know what that is."

"You do?"

"*Jah.* When I visited my cousin at the hospital after her delivery, I saw a woman use one in the waiting area."

"They certainly come in handy for asthma patients. But what's bad about asthmatics, besides difficulty breathing, is that if they don't get enough rest, they catch things easier."

She frowned. "What do you mean?"

"Bugs."

She eyed him.

"They get sick with the snap of two fingers. Trust me, Emma, I was the kid who always had to bundle up. We're talking layers of clothes under my coat. I can't count the number of times I couldn't go out and play with my friends because if damp or cold air got into my lungs . . ." He shrugged. "Forget it. My mom rubbed even more eucalyptus oil onto my chest as I lay in bed." He gave a frustrated shake of his head. "And with me, it took forever to get well."

Emma offered an understanding nod. "I'm sorry, Jonathan. It's hard to believe that a big, strong guy like you was ever sick."

His shoulders straightened. The appreciative expression on his face told her that he enjoyed the compliment.

"Thanks for sharing that with me."

"You're easy to talk to, Emma. I wish I could open up to Amos and have a heart-to-heart. There are things he needs to know."

She wondered what he wanted to tell his brother that was so hard to convey. She tried to picture Jonathan in bed. It was difficult to envision. But now that she knew this about him, her opinion of him changed. His admission tugged at her emotions, and despite herself, she liked him even more.

The auction was two days away. At her dining room table, Emma held the lists of donations in front of her and carefully checked off each name that had been confirmed. She pictured how the tables would be laid out; she had assembled male volunteers in the community to set them up in the cookie tent according to plan.

As she considered the number of events that would be raising money for Amos's surgery, she strummed the bottom of her black ink pen against the lined paper to a nervous beat. She thought of all of the prayers and work that had gone into this. The dreams. Hers, in particular. The day that little Amos's doctor would fix his heart so he could play outside with other kids.

Despite the joy that last realization brought, her pulse pumped to an uneasy pace. *Why? The goal I've worked so hard for is finally going to happen. Why am I not ecstatic?*

The sound of Mamma pulling up a chair next to her prompted her to look up. The unpleasant noise of the chair legs gliding across the polished hardwood floor made Emma's brows draw together in a frown. Unable to concentrate, Emma laid her pen on the lists in front of her, crossed her hands over her lap, and looked at Mamma.

"Honey, if you don't smile, those frown lines will make a permanent home around your lips. You're too tense."

The soft faux warning made the corners of Emma's mouth lift into a half smile. As she locked gazes with her role model, Emma rolled her shoulders to release tension and blew out a deep breath. As she leaned forward, she planted her feet firmly on the floor to scoot closer to her mother.

"You want to talk about it?"

Emma noted the weariness in her own voice when she finally responded. "Oh, Mamma. If only things weren't so complicated."

"I thought you'd be excited. You've worked harder than anyone to make the auction a reality. Think of all you've accomplished! You've got volunteers. The media is involved. People are donating big items for little Amos. There's even a farmer auctioning off an acre of farmland for the charity. The momentum couldn't be stronger!"

"I know, Mamma. And it will be my dream-come-true when we add up the money and announce that we've got enough for the special surgery." Emma clutched her hands into fists and closed her eyes as she said those words. "I'm so excited about the auction, but . . ." Emma swallowed and lowered her gaze to the tabletop.

Mamma leaned forward in silence. When she spoke, her voice was so hushed, it was barely more than a whisper. It was edged with both concern and doubt. "What is it, Emma?"

"Mamma, I only wish we had Jonathan on board."

The woman Emma respected most in the world laid a reassuring hand on Emma's wrist. "Don't you worry about Jonathan. I'm sure that once this is all said and done, he'll be grateful for everything."

"I don't like going against his wishes. Now that we're so close to having the funds, I feel guilty for being so determined to do the last thing Jonathan wants."

Mamma cleared her throat. Her touch on Emma became a little firmer. "Honey, do you believe he could have come up with the money on his own?"

Emma smiled a little. "Of course not. Even with our own community helping out, I don't think the surgery could have been paid for."

"Then don't second guess what you did, honey." Mamma adjusted in her seat and crossed her legs. When she spoke, the tone of her voice turned firmer. "Emma, you and I both know what self-respect means to Jonathan."

The remark made Emma giggle.

Her mom smiled relief. "That's what I like to see! My girl's smile."

The tenseness in Emma's neck began to go away.

"But back to the older Troyer boy. Emma, I'm sure you can understand that the combination of stubbornness and such strong self-respect makes for a difficult man. Mix those traits with all of the talk and publicity surrounding the fund-raiser for his brother's heart surgery, and I imagine Jonathan's having a pretty rough go at it. I know of men like that."

Before Emma could get a word in, Mamma lifted an amused brow. "My own daddy's one of them. So you can't just look at a man and understand his position without taking in the whole picture of what he's going through. It's not a cut-and-dried situation, unfortunately."

Emma nodded agreement. "I'm starting to get why he's so hard to work with."

"I'm sure that after the money's raised, he'll be grateful for all you've done. What everyone has contributed." Emma considered her mother's optimistic philosophy and offered a half grin. How she hoped Mamma was right.

She didn't like going against Jonathan, that was for sure. At the same time, she loved Amos with all of her heart and yearned for him to be healthy like other kids his age. Every time the little boy wanted to play outside and she had to say no, her heart ached. If God granted her a wish for anything in the world, her request would be for getting her little friend well. No question.

CHAPTER 4

Emma darted an inquisitive, hopeful glance at the auction crowd. She looked down to see her shadow outside of the tent in which she stood. The dark spot disappeared immediately when two kids and an adult approached her table.

When the family pointed to the plates of iced cookies, Emma smiled a little. Selling the morsels had been even easier than she anticipated. Christmas was right around the corner, and many would use the treats they purchased for large family gatherings.

She wished she had more to offer; she was sure every cookie would sell, but at the same time, how could she hope for more? The large area of tables showed just how many donations she'd been able to raise. And the dozens of edibles were more iced cookies than she'd ever seen in her life!

A customer broke into her thoughts as he held out a twenty-dollar bill. "Which plate would you like?" she asked.

The middle-aged man shook his head. "No cookies for me. You can just add that to the pot."

"Thank you, sir."

After offering an appreciative smile, Emma slipped the bill into the large glass holder that was nearly full. Earlier, the container had been empty. But not now. The green bills of currency would barely go through the top button-like hole. She had to shove the man's donation inside.

This was the fifth container. And there were more. Emma took a couple of steps back to make room for the group of women who entered the cookie area. She smiled a little as she listened to the numerous comments. They made small talk about the surgery to hopefully come and the little boy who needed it to survive.

The plot of land being used for today's event was so packed, Emma could barely see the ground. Fortunately, it wasn't raining or snowing. The combination of a few enclosures and gas heaters kept the grounds comfortably warm.

As she took in the energy surrounding her, Emma's pulse beat to an uncertain pace as the bright sun smiled down on Arthur, Illinois. God had blessed them with an unusually calm, sunny day for the third week in December.

Everything about the fund-raiser contributed to the aura of excitement. The air smelled of grilled hamburgers, hot dogs, and a mixture of delicious-smelling foods. In the distance, she took in the old woman making saltwater taffy in a small wooden booth.

People held plastic cups of homemade lemonade.

As they sipped beverages through their straws, Emma glimpsed the auctioneer, who was testing the microphone and checking things off on the notepad in front of him.

Emma's heart skipped a beat as reality set in. Donations from her cookies looked like a lot in the clear glass jars, but she knew that the amount from her treats wouldn't make a dent in the surgery bill and the therapy to follow. She took a deep breath to calm herself and contemplated what was about to take place on the center stage.

Truly, today's success was dependent on the large donations that would come in from the expensive items under the large tent several hundred yards away. She squeezed her eyes closed to say a quick prayer. "Dear Lord, only You can help us get the money needed to fix little Amos's heart. Please bless us with what we need. Amen."

Word of mouth had it that over fifteen hundred had shown up in support of her dear little friend. Some had driven hours to offer money and support for the cause. So many different conversations took place that the voices had morphed into one solid loud sound.

A lady wearing an oversized red floppy hat asked Emma to help her package several dozen cookies. A sigh of gratitude escaped Emma's throat as the woman handed her a hundred dollars. As Emma stashed the single bill into the jar, she thanked her.

Emma motioned for one of the men nearby to help the generous donor carry the treats to her car. Emma would have loved to assist, but she had to stay at the tent. If the momentum had anything to do with the amount of revenue being brought in, they should raise enough funds for little Amos's procedure. Of course, she was a positive thinker.

She pressed her lips together and drew in a breath. Children about the age of Amos chased each other in games of tag. Mothers attempted to watch their kids at the same time they bid for furniture and other items up for grabs.

Emma smiled a little at the thought that soon, Amos would be as healthy as the little ones she watched with amazement. She wondered what it would feel like for him to chase his friends while hollering and screaming. To act like a kid instead of a cautious, restricted person.

That very realization prompted a lone tear. But as quickly as the moisture made its way down Emma's face, she caught it with her hand and focused on what made her believe little Amos would soon join a different club.

A club that couldn't care less whether he forgot to snap his coat at the neck. A new life for the special boy was about to unfold right in front of them. And it was because of the people here today. It was also due to the media attention and the Internet bids that would hopefully surpass her wildest dreams.

Emma pushed back a rebellious strand of hair that broke loose from her *kapp*. At the same time, she eyed her displays of iced stars to make sure the plastic coverings were still neatly tucked underneath the trays.

At least half of the cookies had already sold. And almost everyone who'd purchased had contributed generously. She regarded the huge number of folks who rapidly increased and prayed that the rest of the treats would bring as much revenue as the first half had.

Church friends worked in tents surrounding hers. Donations were pouring in from the Internet site set up by English friends. Emma smiled a little.

She turned her attention to the women approaching one of her tables. They were well-dressed. Because she didn't recognize them, she guessed that they were from out of town.

She glanced around the huge crowd of hundreds and wondered whether Jonathan would show up. She hoped he would—and that God would work through him to change his mind about today.

Late that afternoon, Emma pushed out a sigh that was an odd combination of high energy and sheer exhaustion. The moment she ran a clean white rag over the last table, the tent team folded the metal legs and carried it to the large stack nearby.

The cleanup phase had kicked in. As Emma caught her breath, she considered the numerous tasks going on simultaneously.

As she organized her area, crews worked in full force. A couple of guys with long metal sticks scoured the grounds, stabbing litter and eventually discarding trash into large plastic bags.

At the same time, another team carefully calculated funds to be paid by buyers who had purchased various items at the live auction.

Amish and non-Amish men from the hardworking community and surrounding areas carried furniture from the master platform to vehicles lined up in a long-winding queue close to the grounds. Others helped to disassemble tents and booths. The publicity committee took down posters and signs.

Dull sounds of running engines filled the air as drivers pulled trucks and trailers closer to the loading zone. A rush of uncertainty and anxiousness swept up Emma's spine with one swift, desperate motion and landed at the base of her neck. But she didn't try to rid herself of it. Instead, she savored the sensation of finality.

She considered all that had transpired during the past couple of months and pushed out a satisfied sigh. She had done everything within her power to raise money for the delicate and unique procedure that Amos needed to stay alive.

At this point, the outcome was out of her hands. She rested a set of satisfied palms on her hips and smiled.

Mamma's voice was a welcome interruption. Emma turned and took in her mother's immaculate appearance.

As usual, Mamma wore a long-sleeved navy-colored dress. Emma pulled in a small sigh, wishing that she was half as perfect as her role model.

"The Lord is lookin' out for us. Here, honey." Mamma waved to nearby banners draped over two metal chairs. "Let me give you a hand."

"Thanks, Mamma." As if on cue, they each folded their ends together and stepped forward to meet each other, where Emma collected Mamma's part and gave the material a final fold. Emma wasn't sure whether the signs would be used again, but so much had gone into making the large, eye-catching advertisements, it seemed a shame to throw them away.

Automatically, Emma and her mother continued what needed to be done before leaving the auction site. While she worked, Emma's thoughts traveled like the speed of light. One thing in particular nagged at her. One certain question pained her until she put it out in the open. "Mamma, I can't wait to find out how much money we raised today! What have you heard?"

"There's talk that the donations went through the roof." Mamma laughed as she waved her hands. "Or through the tents."

They giggled.

"Word has it that the Internet site brought in an astounding amount. It's amazing how much compassion people have when it comes to little Amos."

Emma's heart warmed. "It certainly was a pleasant surprise to hear of the donations that poured in at the last minute."

"Especially the one from the King family."

"*Jah.*"

Mamma shrugged. "I'm not surprised, really. Eli has always been ultra-generous. 'Course, he lost his grandson a couple years back when that driver hit their family buggy. Such a shame."

"And the boy was the same age as Amos."

Mamma gave a big nod. "*Jah.* It goes without saying that little Amos's heart condition must've hit home pretty hard."

"But what on earth will Eli do with ten dozen cookies?"

Mamma shrugged. "They've got a big clan, those Kings. Ten kids and there must be close to a thousand grandkids and great-grandchildren," she joked.

"And if rumor turns out to be true, everyone's gonna be at their house for Christmas. I'd be willing to bet that those iced stars go fast."

"They'd better build an addition. Otherwise, they're gonna be shoulder to shoulder."

"It must be every mamma's dream to have a large, happy family like that."

Mamma nodded.

To Emma's surprise, a male piped in on their conversation. Emma looked in the direction of the voice to glimpse Marvin Beiler making his way toward them. His shirtsleeves were rolled up to his elbows. Extra-wide suspenders fought to keep his dress pants up over his well-fed midsection.

He wagged a finger. "It's too much money."

Emma looked at him to clarify.

Marvin went on. "We can't raise enough green stuff for this surgery in one single auction."

Emma glanced at her mother in time to see a light brown brow raise. Emma followed suit. "Now, Marvin, you've got to admit that we couldn't have asked for a better turnout. You saw for yourself how much support little Amos has. What more can we do to convince you that this day was nothing less than a success?"

In a gruff voice, he supported his claim. "There's no way to be sure what actually materialized until we have the Internet funds that are bein' looked at as we speak."

Emma jumped in. Although she tried to keep her tone positive, she couldn't stop the harshness that edged her voice. It was common knowledge in the community that Marvin was the voice of doom. Why let him get the best of her?

Mamma had taught Emma to see the glass as half-full. It was the only way to be satisfied. And she was certain that God must like positive folks more than those without faith. To Emma's dismay, the man standing between her and Mamma was a downer.

Emma tapped the toe of her sturdy black shoe against the hard earth. At the same time, she gave a dissatisfied roll of her eyes.

From Emma's peripheral vision, she glimpsed Mamma eyeing her. The expression Emma knew all too well prompted the corners of her lips to turn upward into a smile. In reaction, Mamma grinned amusement.

In her silent code, Mamma had just warned Emma not to let Marvin get to her by a slight furrowing of her brows and by curving her lips in the way that she'd done for years.

Emma giggled.

"What's so funny?"

Emma took in Marvin's annoyed tone with a sense of humor. Mamma darted Emma a quick wink. The last thing she wanted was to appear rude.

Emma lifted her palms to the darkening sky. "I feel it. Marvin, I have faith that God will come through for us."

Marvin's jaw dropped in surprise. Emma had always been taught to respect her elders, so she lowered the pitch of her voice to a more sympathetic, understanding tone to qualm any doubt that she was disrespecting him.

"Marvin, you're a good church man."

He lifted his chin a notch.

"You surely don't think God would actually deny little Amos his heart procedure?"

Marvin reacted to the suggestion by rubbing his

fist against his chin. Several moments went by without a response. He finally shrugged. One of his suspenders had worked its way off his shoulder.

As if feeling the need to defend himself, he wagged a finger at Emma. "Don't forget that the supporters only have till midnight to come through with their promises. We have yet to get the largest donation of a hundred thousand dollars."

For a surprised moment, Emma lost her voice. She knew her eyes must have doubled in size as she digested the news. Not sure how to respond, an unexpected knot that blocked her throat stopped her from trying. Finally she got out her words. "A hundred thousand dollars?"

Marvin offered a nod. "The news came in last night. I'm surprised you didn't hear—it was a pleasant surprise. But the donor's anonymous. Hope this isn't a prank. Could be some dreamer. Or maybe someone wanted to impress everyone with his generosity. Who knows?"

Emma hesitated, touching her pointer finger to her cheek. "But if it's a real commitment, of course, the revenue will materialize."

Marvin offered a firm shake of his head. "Not necessarily. Call me the world's greatest pessimist, and they do, but I don't think it's realistic to plan for a hundred percent of the money we were promised to get."

The statement nearly stopped Emma's heart. "What do you mean?"

He gave an effortless lift of his shoulders. "Just what I said."

While Emma considered his non-reassuring words,

Mamma stepped in. "Of course everyone will contribute. The whole state is rootin' for that poor little kid to get well. How could you even doubt that each and every commitment would come through?"

He squinted at the ground before meeting Mamma's gaze. "It's hard to say. But we're human. And what I've learned over my sixty-some years is to keep my expectations low. This afternoon, I caught a conversation between a couple of young folk. One of them mentioned that he was borrowing money to contribute to the cause and he sure hoped his buddy wouldn't let him down."

Emma's heart nearly sank.

At the look on her face, the tone of Marvin's voice turned more sympathetic. "I'm just saying that there might be some who promised more than they could afford. That's all. People got good intentions, ya know. When they signed up to give money, it's only a pledge. Not a legally binding contract."

Emma's thoughts were too chaotic for her own good. She pulled in a desperate breath and wished she'd never met up with Marvin or suffered through this dismal conversation.

When Emma and her mamma remained unresponsive, Marvin went on. "Keep saying your prayers, Emma." He looked down at his black shoes. When he lifted his chin, Emma saw that his gray-blue eyes had filled with moisture.

What she glimpsed brought tears to her own eye. At that moment, she realized that stress had gotten the best of her. She had been too hard on Marvin. She realized that his gruff exterior was misleading. Looking at his sincere expression now, she was sure that he wanted the auction to be a success. For several moments, she had lost her faith. And she regretted it with all of her heart.

Marvin wasn't the cause of her stress. The issue was that the verdict still wasn't out on how much this very important charitable event had actually raised. And Emma didn't know how much longer she could stand the uncertainty of not knowing whether or not little Amos would get his lifesaving operation.

She sighed relief when Marvin finally nodded good-bye. After his departure, Emma and Mamma locked gazes. Mamma's voice was unusually soft. "Honey, God answers prayers. And I just know He'll answer ours. But the waiting . . . it's so hard."

Emma gave a frustrated shake of her head. "Mamma, do you believe what he said about people not following through with their promises?"

For a moment, Mamma looked away and pressed her lips together as if making a difficult decision. Finally, she turned back to Emma and reached for her hands. Emma closed her eyes, relishing the warmth and reassurance Mamma's touch offered.

Emma forced a calm breath and focused on the positives of the event. There were so many, she couldn't count them.

"Thank goodness, Cousin Sarah is on the revenue committee. We don't need to worry, honey. God will do His will."

"I know, Mamma. I've no doubt that she'll follow up on every single donation. So will the rest of her team." Emma glanced at the small portable clock on the one remaining chair. The ticking sound made an even beat. Above, the sun edged to the far west, and Emma realized how quickly the day had passed.

"Soon, the numbers will be out. We should have an update anytime."

Mamma nodded. "*Jah.* Good thing we've got an efficient crew on it."

When Emma looked at her to continue, Mamma waved a hand. "I mean, the money's coming in so many ways. Check. Cash. Wire transfers."

"It's a lot to keep track of. But can you believe that someone is giving a hundred thousand dollars to save little Amos?"

Mamma gave an uncertain shrug. "I wonder who it is."

CHAPTER 5

The following day, the enticing aroma of home-baked cookies floated through the Troyer home. Emma slid a new batch into the oven, closed the door, and turned at the sound of Jonathan's footsteps.

To her surprise, contentment edged his voice. "The auction was a great success, Emma. Thought you'd want to know that I've scheduled Amos's surgery for the end of December."

A huge grin lifted the corners of Emma's lips. "Great."

Jonathan lowered his pitch to a more serious tone. "Emma, there's something I'd like you to know."

As the fire in the living room popped, Emma claimed the nearest seat at the kitchen table and looked at him to go on. The room smelled of a combination of cookies and a cinnamon candle.

He took a chair a few feet away.

"I was wrong when I asked you to stop the auction. I'm sorry."

Her jaw dropped. She tapped her pointer finger to an uncertain beat against the oak tabletop while she waited for an explanation.

"Emma, I strive to be like my dad. And those are big shoes to fill. I've told you that he was proud. And he instilled in me how important it is to provide for my family."

He paused to smile a little. "I know that we Amish folk are a humble group. But I'm flawed, Emma. And like my father, I try to be self-sufficient. And the surgery?"

He pushed out a deep breath. "I felt like I wasn't doing my job as a good provider. That I needed to step it up, but I didn't know how. To be blunt, I felt like I'd failed. That Dad would be disappointed in me. And that was something I didn't know how to deal with."

His confession took Emma off guard. A short silence ensued while she processed his words.

Sympathy edged her voice when she finally found her words. "Jonathan, I'm sorry you were put in that position. And I appreciate your honesty. I'm so glad you trust me enough to confide something so personal."

Pressing his lips together, he offered a slight nod.

"But you're anything but a failure. And I know in my heart that your daddy would be proud of you."

His eyes glistened with moisture.

After a long pause, he offered an appreciative nod. "Thanks for the vote of confidence, Emma."

"I'm glad you came to me with this, because now I have a better understanding of why you tried to stop the fund-raiser." She threw her hands in the air in a helpless gesture. "When you tried to explain your pride before, I don't think I really realized how deeply you felt."

"Of course I didn't want to stop the surgery. I just felt like I wasn't much of a man, having to depend on strangers to foot the bill. And I'm a private person, Emma."

"I know you are, Jonathan."

"Finally, after some deep soul-searching, I realized my real issues. And, Emma, I owe you so much for helping me to see this opportunity as a blessing."

She swallowed an emotional knot.

He cleared his throat. "There's something else that really makes me choke up. That anonymous donor. A hundred thousand dollars." He whistled.

"It was Sam Beachy, you know. There was no way that something that big could stay a secret."

"The old widower?"

She nodded. "The famous hope chest maker himself."

Suddenly, Jonathan's demeanor changed. Smiling, he lifted his chin a notch, stood, and turned. As he left the room, he glanced back at her. "Thought I owed you that."

After he was gone, the house creaked. Whenever the wind picked up speed, the old boards reacted. The sound reminded Emma of a squeaky buggy wheel.

But Emma's mind returned to the auction. And to Old Sam. Emma's heart warmed at the thought of him. He was kind to everyone whom he came into contact with.

As she opened the gas oven, she stepped back to allow the strong surge of heat to dissipate. Little Amos rushed to the warm spot and wrapped his arms around his tiny chest. "That feels good, Emmie."

Pulling the metal sheet from the oven, she glanced at him and removed her baking mitt. In his stocking feet, his trousers were rolled up a notch. As usual, his beautiful mass of hair needed to be combed. She smiled a little, seriously doubting that the temperature change was the reason for Amos's sudden appearance. It was no secret that he liked being close to the cookies.

"*Jah.* It certainly does."

He moved to where she'd laid the hot treats and shrugged. "You know why this is my favorite room?" Before she could guess, he answered his own question. "'Cause it smells like cookies. Emmie, I have a question."

As she eyed him, his brows drew together in an uncertain frown. "Can we have these all year round? Even in the summer?"

While she considered his innocent question, she slid the hot desserts onto a plate. As she transferred the very last star, she offered him a nod.

"I don't see why not."

Without wasting time, she scooped tablespoons of raw dough onto the sheets. When she'd filled the tray, she reopened the oven to slide the new batches inside. Amos closed his eyes in delight. After closing the door, she stepped away and took him by the arm.

"Let's chat."

Obediently, he sat next to her at the table. Automatically, she shoved aside a pile of unopened mail. "Besides, I'm ready for a break."

She rested her hands on her hips and sat up straighter. "Did you finish your English homework?"

He pressed his lips together and gave a proud nod.

"Good. Now . . . you were asking about Christmas cookies in the summer?"

He offered a quick nod.

She shrugged and contemplated his question. "I don't see why not."

"Yeah, 'cause cookies are good all year round."

She smiled at his logic, fully aware of how much Amos appreciated the treats. And no doubt, the sweet child would do whatever he could to convince her to bake them every single day of the year. She hadn't neglected noticing that he'd put on a few pounds since she'd started tutoring him.

She reasoned the best she could. "Cookies aren't seasonal."

He gave a strong shake of his head while she paused to rest her hands on her thighs. Then she snapped her fingers.

"Tell you what. I have an idea. I'll bake them in the summer. But we won't cut them into ornaments. Maybe we can do other shapes."

To her surprise, Amos gave another shake of his head. He crossed his arms over his chest; the expression in his eyes was that of sheer determination. "I want them to look just like the ones you sold to raise money for me." He wrinkled his nose. "They won't taste the same if they don't."

The honest confession pulled at Emma's heartstrings. Amos was tenacious, that was for sure. He tugged at Emma's long sleeves. "Emmie, please?"

Before she could respond, Jonathan's deep voice interrupted them. Emma and Amos turned at the same time.

The worry crease on Jonathan's forehead was much less noticeable. His cheeks were flushed from being outside. But it was his eyes that offered the most change.

She lifted an inquisitive brow, noticing that they were filled with a newfound acceptance. Should she dare to believe it? Satisfaction edged his voice. She contemplated his change in demeanor and smiled relief. Emma liked him better like this.

For some reason, today he seemed taller. Jonathan lifted a set of calloused palms to the ceiling. As he started to speak, she took in his features. Muscles tried to push their way out of his shirt. And his everyday denim pants fit him as if they'd been custommade.

His nose wasn't perfect; he certainly wasn't pretty. But it showed character. A light scar on his chin only added to his tough, take-charge nature. All in all, his rugged features cried out that what Jonathan Troyer attempted, he accomplished—and that he preferred to do it on his own.

"We've got to celebrate."

The corners of Emma's mouth lifted another notch.

Before offering the boy a gentle pat on his shoulder, Jonathan shrugged acceptance.

"I can't stop thinking about the surgery. To be honest, I find it hard to believe."

Without wasting time, Amos bounded up from his sitting position and threw his arms around the older Troyer in a tight, warm hug.

Emma swallowed an emotional knot. Her chest ached with happiness whenever she glimpsed such a strong bond between family. As Amos released his hold, he looked up at Jonathan.

Amos's voice bubbled with excitement. "In that last book Emmie gave me, there's a party after the doctor fixes the little boy's feet." Amos added, "There's balloons and lots of treats!"

Jonathan's lips curved in amusement. The green flecks on his pupils danced.

Emma grinned at both brothers. Amos took the books she gave him to heart, that was for sure. She loved making him happy. And Jonathan? She was relieved that he'd changed his mind about the donations. And she was happy to have played a role in helping him to see the auction as a blessing.

Emma eyed Jonathan with curiosity. "You're right, Amos. We should do something," she offered with enthusiasm. "God has given us good plenty of reasons to be grateful. And I've been thanking Him."

She crossed her legs at the ankles and leaned forward. "It's hard to believe, but the money came in." Excitement edged her voice. "The fund-raiser couldn't have gone better. Now, we should enjoy the fruits of our work! But how?"

She glanced at the Troyer men. "What would you like to do?"

Jonathan eyed the oven before turning his attention to Emma. "I take it you've got another round of cookies in there?"

"*Jah.*"

Jonathan stepped closer to the oven and nodded satisfaction. "And we know they'll taste good. Right, Amos?"

Amos clapped his hands.

Jonathan cupped his chin and turned to Amos. "I have an idea."

Amos stood perfectly still. Emma wasn't sure, but she thought she could hear his jubilant heart pound with anticipation. The boy's eyes doubled in size as he looked up eagerly at Jon. At the same time, Emma glanced at him to continue. What did he have in mind?

As the fireplace continued putting out heat several arm lengths' away, a loud *pop* made them startle. They looked in the direction of the noise before returning their attention to the party idea.

Jonathan wagged his hands in the air. "How 'bout we go for a buggy ride and take the cookies?"

Emma giggled. The fun-sounding plan surprised her. Especially hearing it from the gruff character who'd thought of it.

Without wasting time, Amos jumped up and down. Jonathan nodded approval. "I'll take that as a yes." He turned to Emma. But when he spoke, he lowered his voice with uncertainty. "Will you come with us? The celebration wouldn't be complete without you."

To her surprise, the question was posed without conviction. Since when did Jonathan Troyer lack confidence? Suddenly, she realized that he was waiting for her to respond.

With enthusiasm, she offered a small lift of her shoulders. "Of course! How could I refuse a buggy ride?"

The midafternoon late December sun played hide-and-seek. Visible or invisible, the chilly temperature stayed the same. At times, Emma was amazed how homes could withstand such winds. It surprised her that they didn't blow over. At times, the sun appeared proudly in the sky.

But as quickly as it shone, it slipped behind marshmallow-looking clouds that floated like boats on a lake. Amos sat between Jonathan and Emma. While the horse's hooves clomped at an uneven beat, Emma sighed contentment and rested her hands on her lap.

She'd always loved horse-drawn carriage rides. She especially enjoyed the homey, familiar ambience inside of the buggy. The homemade knit blanket on the bench . . . the smell of horses. The sound and pace of clopping.

But today, the mode of transportation smelled unusually good. The sweet scent of iced cookies filled the small cabin. In the distance, Emma glimpsed another buggy headed for town.

Cold weather didn't keep her Amish community inside. There were too many chores. Feeding livestock. Milking cows. Amos removed three cookies from the plastic container. The lid made a popping noise as it came off.

With a quick flash of his hand, he gave one to Emma. Then to Jonathan.

Jonathan chuckled. "This is the first time I've celebrated by eating in the buggy."

"Don't you think it's fun?" Amos's small voice bubbled with contentment as he downed a bite.

Jonathan lifted a brow and glanced at his brother. He talked in a silly voice. "I'd be crazy if I didn't like it, wouldn't I?"

Amos giggled. Emma joined him. Still pleasantly

surprised by Jonathan's change in attitude, it was hard not to laugh when this tall, strong, gruff man with so much responsibility on his shoulders acted like a kid. And she enjoyed it.

Emma took a bite of her iced star and nodded satisfaction as Amos pointed to the house down the street. "That's where Jake lives."

Emma straightened with interest. "Jake? The boy you're always talking about?"

Amos gave a big nod. With one swift motion, he shifted in his seat. His feet didn't quite touch the floor, and he swung them back and forth. "After my heart gets fixed, we're gonna play together. And he said that I can be 'it' first."

Emma's heart melted as she imagined the small child next to her running and laughing as he played. Things kids did and took for granted. But little Amos had never experienced such privileges before. And that was about to change.

It amused her the way he talked about "fixing" his heart, like it was getting a new wheel for a buggy. Or replacing a part in Mamma's gas oven.

No doubt, correcting a heart defect took much more expertise and prayer than repairing something man-made. Besides, material things could always be replaced if the "fixing" didn't work. Little Amos couldn't.

He was a human being and one who was very dear to her heart. She pressed her lips together thoughtfully and considered the coming steps to take to get to Minnesota and have the surgery. The corners of her lips dropped into a frown.

Numerous phone calls were required. Thanks goodness, her family and the Troyers shared an outside

phone. There would be a number of pre-op appoint-
ments, as well as hotel reservations. They would need
to hire a driver to get them to the Mayo Clinic.

Jonathan's low voice pulled Emma from her
thoughts. "Hey. That's not a frown, is it?"

He looked at Emma for a response.

Automatically, she forced a smile. Why was she
doubting the surgery? She had fought tooth and nail
to get it. And it was the only hope for a normal life
for the precious kid beside her.

"Of course not!" Ashamed of allowing herself to
focus on worry when joy was all she should feel, she
leaned forward and faced the driver. "God has blessed
us in every way. Despite what we went through to raise
the money, we did it!"

She closed her eyes a moment and pushed out a
sigh of relief. "How could I have anything but positive thoughts?"

She stuck out her fingers one at a time and ticked
off obvious reasons. "We've got the funds. The appointment is scheduled. The doctor is optimistic of
the outcome. The whole state of Illinois knows about
Amos and his surgery and is praying for him."

Jonathan chuckled. "You've got that right."

Emma smiled, but her thoughts didn't linger on
Amos and his procedure. They were on his older
brother. She appreciated his honesty. She was happy
that he trusted her enough to confide in her. And to
her dismay . . . she liked him.

Jonathan said good-bye to Emma and waved as she
walked in to the side entrance of her home. As he

stepped back into the buggy, the sweet, pleasant aroma of homemade butter filled his nostrils.

It was common knowledge that Emma's mother made the best around. The bright sun slipped behind a haven of fluffy clouds. He blinked to adjust to the difference in light. By the looks of it, they were finished seeing the sun for the rest of the day.

Inside of the black buggy, he reached over to pull the covering his mother had knit over Amos's legs. Even with the gas heat, he made sure to keep the sickly boy warm at all times. It was exciting to imagine that soon, Amos wouldn't be so fragile.

As the two made their way home, Jonathan's mind drifted to Emma and the huge role she had played in the auction. Because of her big heart, he couldn't deny that he was starting to feel a bond with her. Of course, Amos was the glue between them. Yet, even without Amos in the picture, he liked her.

And Amos? Jonathan pressed his lips together as he came to a decision. It was time to have a talk with his sibling. He didn't feel like it today. But it had to be tomorrow.

CHAPTER 6

As the Troyer home grew closer, Jonathan glanced at Amos's solemn expression and frowned. "What's wrong?"

A lengthy silence ensued while Amos lowered his gaze to the floor. He did this when he was embarrassed or sad about something. Jon's instincts told him the latter was the case this time.

Jon pushed out a decisive sigh and laid a gentle hand on the boy's wrist. "You wanna talk about it?"

While Jon awaited a response, he tightened the reins to head up their drive. Loose rocks made for a bumpy ride to where the buggy and horse were kept. Gravel crunched under the wheels.

But he barely heard it as he focused on Amos. Jonathan's heart pumped to an unsteady, frightened beat as he waited for the boy to open up. Jonathan had learned not to push too hard. When the kid was ready to talk, Jonathan would patiently listen.

But right now, Amos said nothing. Jonathan swallowed an emotional knot. He forced himself to stay calm, but it was difficult. He'd made a commitment to God to do his best for his sibling.

This promise had to do with the tremendous guilt Jonathan had over Amos losing his role model. Jonathan's dad had been everything that Amos aspired to be. And Jonathan, too. Jonathan would never forget the moment he'd been forced to explain to the young child that his favorite person in the world had passed away.

The devastated expression on Amos's face still broke Jonathan's heart. To his dismay, salty dampness stung his pupils. He blinked to rid himself of the uncomfortable sensation. But to his chagrin, a lone tear slid down his cheek. With a quick, frustrated motion, he wiped it away and regarded Amos to make sure he hadn't seen.

Jonathan never forgot that his role in life was to compensate for the huge loss of their larger-than-life father. It was nothing less than his dad would have expected, and it was the Lord's purpose for Jonathan.

Jonathan knew it with every God-given breath he took. But was he living up to those high expectations? Lifting an undecided brow, he drew in an uncertain breath.

Trying not to show too much emotion, Jonathan wrapped a gentle, reassuring arm around Amos's fragile, narrow shoulders. "Amos, I know I'm not Dad. But I'm here for you. And you've got to tell me what's naggin' you so I can help."

Amos crossed one leg over another and lowered his gaze to his shoes. Jonathan was quick to note moisture glistening on the boy's long, thick lashes.

Finally Amos lifted his chin and darted a sideways glance at Jonathan. "I miss Emmie." His voice cracked with emotion. "I wish she lived with us."

The following afternoon, Emma left the Troyer home early to help Mamma make extra batches of cheese for the holiday. She chose to walk home, since the temperature had warmed several degrees.

A few minutes after her departure, though, she stopped and pushed out a sigh. She'd left her small hand mixer in the kitchen. She needed it this evening to make a dish for a family in town with a newborn. Without hesitation, quick steps took her back to the Troyer home, where she entered, as usual, through the back porch.

The moment she turned the brass knob on the door to the kitchen, she glimpsed Amos on Jonathan's lap. The expressions on their faces told her they were having a serious conversation.

Her hand froze on the knob. The last thing Emma wanted to do was to interrupt. Whatever Jonathan wanted to tell Amos must be important.

Pulling in an uncertain sigh, Emma definitely didn't intend to eavesdrop, but there was nowhere to go. She tried to close her ears. She didn't want to be guilty of listening in on a private discussion. At the same time, she couldn't go home without her hand mixer. But what could she do?

She considered her options. There were two choices. To go in and interrupt something important or to hang tight. She decided on the latter. Besides, how long could the talk last?

Jonathan's deep, low voice was calm and steady.

"We've scheduled your appointment for after Christmas. The doctor wants us to follow his complete instructions. You're so diligent, Amos, and this is important."

"Don't worry, Johnnie. I'll do everything right so the operation will work."

There was a lengthy pause. Emma pressed her lips together thoughtfully as she listened to Jonathan's convincing tone. "It will—I have no doubt. But following the doc's instructions will give you the best results. This is a once-in-a-lifetime opportunity, little brother."

"I've been asking in my prayers for Emmie to come with us. Can she come, Johnnie? *Please?*"

Emma grinned at how the last word was emphasized and drawn out for best effect. Amos was nearly a perfect child. Obedient. Polite. Studious. Thoughtful. But because of his special condition, he was used to having his way.

And despite Jonathan's gruff attitude, Emma had taken note that when it came to his little brother, Jonathan sweetened. She gave an amused roll of her eyes.

For whatever reason, big, tough Jonathan was extra-sensitive to the boy's wants. It was obvious that Jonathan would make Amos happy any way he could. But this time, she was sure he wouldn't give in. Taking her would add more expense. And it wouldn't be proper, either.

Amos's pitch changed to a matter-of-fact tone. "I think we should take Emmie. If we leave her here, I'll really miss her. Besides, who will I read to in Minnesota? Mommy might not be able to go. And who will bake the cookies?"

Another long silence ensued. Emma stood perfectly still. Her palm never left the knob. Her shoulders tensed, and her heart picked up speed to an uncertain beat while she wondered what Jonathan's response would be.

To her surprise, none came. But Amos persisted. "Johnnie, don't you like Emmie?"

The question seemed to take Jonathan off guard. Emma could tell by the surprised edge of his response. "Of course, Amos. Why would you think I don't?"

"I dunno. Maybe 'cause you didn't want the auction to happen." Amos lifted the pitch of his small voice. "Once, I heard you tell her to stop it. I think you hurt her feelings. Johnnie, don't you want my heart to get fixed?"

Emma stepped as far away as she could from the entrance. She definitely didn't want to infringe on such a private conversation. It was wrong. But it was too cold to stand outside for long. And there was no way Emma could shut out the talk.

Even from some several yardsticks away, Emma was quick to catch the older Troyer's deep intake of breath. Little Amos wasn't shy. And she was certain Jonathan would do anything he could to put Amos's creative mind at ease. The love for his small, sickly brother was strong. That she was sure of.

In the meantime, the speed of Emma's heart ticked to a crazy beat. She hoped that Jonathan would take his time and make Amos understand whatever it was that he wanted to explain. At the same time, Emma was becoming quite uncomfortable in her small space. She was sure it was the most awkward position she'd ever been in. Despite the cold temperature, she wanted to fan her face. Taking a deep breath, she ordered the fast pace of her pulse to slow.

"Amos . . ." Jon finally proceeded. "I never want you to be unsure of anything. To doubt. Never be afraid to ask me anything you want. You understand?"

Emma didn't hear a reply.

Several heartbeats later, Amos spoke. "Is this about Emmie?"

Jon cleared his throat. "It's about our daddy."

The pitch of Amos's voice lowered to a melancholy tone that was barely more than a hush. "I miss him, Johnnie."

Emma squeezed her lids closed in pain.

"Me, too. But when he was alive, he taught me all the time."

"Oh, I get it. Like Emmie teaches me."

"This . . . was a little bit different. It wasn't really learning from books. I guess you could say that he taught me his beliefs. Values he'd inherited from his own father. He tried to instill in me all that he thought I should know."

Jonathan hesitated. When he started again, his serious tone was edged with a newfound emotion. "Daddy was my best friend, Amos. My role model. And I miss him every day."

"Me, too."

A long pause ensued while Jonathan blew his nose. Emma lowered her lids in sympathy. Uncomfortable moisture formed in her eyes. Automatically, she blinked to clear her foggy vision. A knot tightened in her stomach. Her chest ached. The gray walls of the small space in which she stood seemed to close in.

It took a few moments to digest what she'd just heard. She'd never been this privy to the older Troyer brother's emotional side. But she'd already learned that there was much more to Jonathan than met the eye. And she might be the only person who knew it. The newfound knowledge pulled at her heart.

"And what I learned from him, well, it wasn't stuff you get from books. It was about how to live my life."

He paused.

"Daddy taught me to be honest. To finish the job. To have a good work ethic."

"What?"

"In other words, a man has to put out his best every day. You hang in there and do what needs to be done, kid, even if you're sick or tired. You take care of your family. To him, that came first."

There was a slight hesitation before he continued. "And he instilled in me to do things on my own. You know," he added, "that being a man means supporting your family. To buy only what you can afford."

"What if there's not enough money?"

"Then you don't buy it."

There was a slight pause. "Ya see, Amos, I strive to be like Dad."

"Me, too."

"But I'm glad I accepted help in this case. Otherwise, we wouldn't be getting your heart fixed."

"Daddy would want me to play outside—I know it, Johnnie."

"There's no doubt in my mind that he would."

Emma closed her lids. *It's wrong to listen in on this. But what choice do I have? Please, God. Close my ears.*

"It took me a while to admit that sometimes we've got to accept help. That in the end, swallowing my pride was worth you having this procedure that will change the rest of your life. But while the auction was taking place, I remembered something Dad told me out in the barn."

"What was it?"

Jonathan cleared his throat. "We were talking about our family. Of a man's huge responsibility to put their needs before his. I realized that taking care of you, little guy, is what that means. And if that requires using donations from all over the state of Illinois, so be it."

"I understand. One day, when I have a bunch of kids, I'll try to be as good as you, Johnnie. But I'll never be as good as Daddy."

The last statement prompted a laugh out of Jonathan. Emma held her hand over her mouth to stop a giggle that struggled to come out.

Amos was incredibly honest and open. He didn't consider holding anything in. Maybe it was good; perhaps it wasn't! At any rate, Emma wasn't happy she had caught the private conversation intended for only little Amos.

On the surface, Jonathan appeared tough. But that was a façade. Because inside . . . Emma drew her hands over her chest and took in a deep breath of understanding. He was a teddy bear.

Emma straightened when she heard what she guessed was Amos jumping off of Jonathan's lap.

"Let's go have one of Emmie's cookies."

"*Jah!*"

When she heard both pairs of shoes leave the room, she opened the door and went in. Jonathan had spoken heart-to-heart with Amos. But somehow Emma felt that the talk had also been meant for her.

CHAPTER 7

Spurts of chilly wind slipped in between the cracks of the old red barn. Jonathan stopped a moment to pull his hat down over his ears. While he carried a bale of hay from the storage unit to the cow troughs, he considered his recent brother-to-brother conversation and sighed in relief.

For a moment, he stopped and gently set two pails on the floor on both sides of him. From where he stood, he took in the herd of milking cows outside in the bare pasture. He smiled in satisfaction.

He wished his dad was here to talk to while they did chores together. But his father had trained him well. Jonathan had now been given a mission and that was to step into his dad's place.

Jonathan cupped his chin with his hand and recalled Amos's honest comment about when he became a daddy. "*I'll try to be as good as you, Johnnie. But I'll never be as good as Daddy.*"

Jonathan laughed so hard, he coughed. He finally collected his thoughts and picked up his pails, continuing toward the troughs. The flock of pigeons on the upper windowsill had increased in number. They eyed the grain that he dumped into the food troughs.

He knew their purpose. As soon as Jonathan stepped away, the flock swooped down to steal tiny kernels of grain. As he returned, they scattered and flew back to their perch.

Cattle sounds filtered in through the wood. Bales of straw loomed on the west side up to the ceiling. He began carrying them, one at a time, to the stable area. The smell of livestock floated through the barn.

It wasn't a pretty building; it needed a new coat of paint. Sturdy metal pails hung from hooks. So did other work paraphernalia, like pitchforks. Shovels.

Most people probably wouldn't be fond of the strong odor that was a mixture of livestock, dried seed, and hay. But to Jonathan, this was his comfort zone.

He smiled a little. Within these four strong walls, he could think clearly. And right now, something bugged him. Nervously, he stepped back and forth, piling loads of filthy straw and replacing it with fresh.

As he contemplated what bothered him, he worked faster, finally becoming numb to the cold while he considered his heart-to-heart with his little brother. And it was then that he realized the crux of his problem and frowned.

Not because he wasn't happy with how their talk had gone. He was. And he was fairly sure that, even at Amos's young age, the boy understood Jonathan's responsibility to family and why he'd been torn about accepting donations.

For a six-year-old, Amos was exceptionally bright.

He quickly read everything Emma gave him. He also absorbed it.

Because Emma didn't focus on math, Jonathan attempted to make it up, teaching Amos what he needed to know. Something in his conversation with Amos made Jonathan's pulse on his wrist pick up to a disturbed pace.

As he grasped the top of his pitchfork and rested the spikes on the cement, he nodded when he realized what ate at him. To his surprise, it wasn't Amos's perception that Jonathan couldn't compete with their dad. It was something asked at the get-go of their talk.

"Can Emmie go with us to Minnesota?"

Jonathan swallowed as he envisioned the hopeful expression in Amos's eyes when he'd posed the question. It was asked with innocence, but it was obvious to Jonathan that the more times Emma baked cookies for the boy and helped him with school, the more Amos had bonded with her.

Is that something to be concerned about? Why would his strong love for Emma bother me? That's ridiculous. With Mom down, he's craving affection. Besides, I don't have to worry about Emma disappointing him. She's so dependable.

Finally, he lifted his shoulders in a shrug. He continued cleaning the grazing area and dreamed of spring. In a few months, he would be working inside of the barn with wide open doors. The pasture would be a deep shade of green, not the pale brown it was today. The fresh smell of clover and sweet scent of wildflowers would fill the air.

And Amos would be healthy, wouldn't he? Jonathan stopped what he was doing and pulled in a deep, frightened breath. At this moment, he knew what troubled him most. It was Amos's procedure.

He was grateful that the surgery would take place. Jonathan closed his eyes and tried to think only positive thoughts, like Emma claimed to do.

He rested an elbow on his pitchfork and squeezed his eyes closed in a desperate prayer. "Dear Lord, You know my thoughts and fears. Right now I'm afraid. Scared of losing my dear brother."

He caught an emotional breath. "Help me to be brave and to rest assured that You will protect Amos during his procedure. I know that only You can work miracles, Lord, and I ask You with all of my heart to get Amos through the surgery safely. Protect him. And I pray with everything I have that You would be with his surgeon and help Amos recover quickly."

He opened his eyes and blinked away salty moisture stinging his pupils. Then he smiled relief. He would rely on his holy Father to protect Amos. The situation was out of Jonathan's control.

He continued clearing dirty straw, only this time, he whistled while he did it. He wanted to shout with happiness. The heavy weight of fear had been lifted off of his shoulders. He knew his Lord and Savior would watch over his little brother and heal him.

And as far as Amos's request to take Emma to Minnesota? Jonathan's lips curved in amusement. He couldn't blame Amos. How could he hold loving Emma against him?

Jonathan rolled his eyes. He couldn't. Because he was fond of her, too.

Two days before Christmas, Jonathan put on his coat to drive Emma home in the buggy. As Emma slipped her arms into her coat sleeves, Amos's small voice prompted her to look down.

"Aren't you going to put on your coat, Amos?"

He shook his head. "Mom asked me to stay here." He bubbled with excitement. "I'm going to show her how good I can read the story about Daniel and the den of lions." Amos raised the pitch of his voice to a more excited tone.

He clutched his fingers over his waist as his eyes grew larger. Holding the small picture book with his right hand, he lifted it and exclaimed with a combination of energy and enthusiasm. "It's my favorite, Emmie. I can't believe God saved him from the lions! If God did that, He will fix my heart. I know it!"

Before Emma could reply, Amos bounded out of the room. Jonathan's voice interrupted her thoughts.

"You've got him addicted to stories, Emma." He grinned. "And that's a good thing. I'm relieved that Mom's starting to feel well enough to get up and about. Amos needs her." He chuckled. "The kid's got an imagination bigger than the state of Texas. Have you seen all the pictures he's drawn of Daniel in the lions' den?"

Emma missed Amos. She enjoyed the threesome in the buggy. Everything about the little boy inspired her. His attitude. His faith. The way he loved everything he read and imagined what would happen after the denouements.

As they stepped outside, she eyed Jonathan from her peripheral vision and smiled a little. She must tell him she had overheard his conversation and why. Before they reached her home. At first, she'd been certain she shouldn't interrupt his talk with Amos.

Now, she wasn't sure. She didn't feel good about being in on such a private, emotional conversation.

"Ready?"

Jonathan's eager voice pulled her from her thoughts, and she turned and tightened her neck scarf. "Sure."

He motioned her in front of him. When he opened the back door, bitter cold wind hit her in the face, and she stopped to catch her breath.

"Are you okay?"

"*Jah.* I wasn't prepared for this."

"It's supposed to be another record-breaking low tonight," he said. As he spoke, she half heard his words because the fierce wind absorbed part of what he said.

He opened the carriage door and offered a hand as she stepped inside. She gasped as she looked at his hand on her coat sleeve. It wasn't proper for a single Amish man to touch a single girl. But she knew he'd only meant to help her. Still, her heart skipped an uncertain beat at what had just happened.

He joined her and closed the door. As the horse pulled the carriage forward, Emma rubbed the palms of her hands together before crossing them over her chest.

She turned to him and grinned.

"Thanks for the lift."

"As always, my pleasure."

For long moments, she couldn't think of what to say. She was even more embarrassed now that she'd listened in on a private conversation. The decision had been made in a split second. She hoped he'd understand.

If it wasn't for that, she'd enjoy the ride. She eyed him from her peripheral vision and drew in a sigh.

She admitted that after his talk with Amos, she knew him better than she'd ever dreamed she would.

Her heart had actually softened to him. She gave a frustrated roll of her eyes, unsure whether she liked this or not. She had gotten used to their friendly sparring. Could she adapt to the Jonathan who wanted to be as good as the father he still loved more than life itself?

"You're awfully quiet over there."

She pulled in a breath and darted him a glance.

"Jonathan, I have to tell you something." She cleared her throat. "I think I shouldn't have done it, but I was caught and I wasn't sure what to do."

He pressed his lips together in uncertainty and raised an inquisitive brow. "What?"

"I hope you won't be angry with me." She paused before continuing. "Yesterday, I overheard your conversation with Amos."

Without offering him an opportunity to respond, she explained what happened. Afterward, they sat in tense silence. Emma's heart pumped to a nervous, uncertain, fearful beat. How she wished she hadn't happened upon that discussion. What if Jonathan resented her actions? Her throat was dry. Despite the cold, moisture made her dress cling to her torso.

Outside, the cloudy, dismal-looking sky mimicked her sentiment. Right now, she just wanted to talk to Mamma. *Was I wrong? I'm not sure, but right now, I just wish Jonathan would say something. Please.*

When he finally spoke, amusement edged his voice. "So you were behind the kitchen door when I had my talk with little Amos."

She offered a nervous nod. "I'd left my hand mixer

in your kitchen. I needed it that evening. Otherwise, I wouldn't have come back for it."

"Emma, you must have frozen to death."

"Yeah!"

He chuckled. "It's okay. In fact, I respect you for what you did. For some time, I've tried to sit down and talk with my little brother. Finally the opportunity presented itself, and I'm actually grateful you didn't interrupt it."

She exhaled relief. "I was so worried."

He gave an understanding nod of his head and reached over to nudge her elbow. "You were caught between a rock and a hard place." He lowered the pitch of his voice to a more emotional tone. "Besides, how could I ever be mad at you?"

Suddenly, the sun came out from behind the clouds. Emma blinked to adjust to the unexpected brightness. His question left her surprised and comforted. Relief swept up her arms and landed on her shoulders. She sighed.

"So you forgive me?"

He offered a strong nod. "I'm convinced that you would do anything in your power to protect Amos. At the same time, you were looking out for me. I had my say. To be honest, I feel like a weight has been lifted from my shoulders."

"Jonathan, I wasn't sure I did the right thing. At the same time, I didn't want to eavesdrop."

"When you think about it, you were in a no-win situation. But now it's out in the open . . . You were honest with me, and I appreciate that, Emma. You didn't have to tell me."

"I did." She lifted her palms in the air and shrugged

uncertainty. "I was going crazy. It bothered me that I listened in on something so private. Yet now it's over, and I can't undo what happened."

"And I'm glad you didn't." He rubbed the back of his neck. When he continued, he looked straight ahead. She was happy that he had the horse to focus on; it made their discussion feel less intimate. And less personal was definitely easier for her. Jonathan was slowly carving a place in her heart.

She hadn't figured out what kind of spot it was, but for some strange reason, warming up to him made her a bit uncomfortable. She fidgeted with her hands in her lap.

When he pursued the subject, her jaw dropped in surprise at his uneasy tone. "Emma, I have something to ask you."

She looked at him to continue.

"I'm not a good communicator. Never have been. But it's important that Amos understands why I opposed the surgery. Now that I think about it, I can't believe I ever tried to stop something that would change my little brother's life for the better."

Emma's voice was soft and unsure. "I understand why you did it, Jonathan. You felt you should be able to be the sole provider for your family. And I respect you for that."

"You do?"

"Uh-huh."

As she considered their conversation, the *clomp-clomp* of the horse's hooves serenaded the thoughtful silence that floated through the small carriage. The knit blanket over Emma's thighs slid to the right, so Emma moved to adjust it.

Finally, she knew what to say to Jonathan. "Ya

know, all the while, Jonathan, you've been trying to take responsibility for everything. Amos's heart defect, how to get money to pay for the surgery without accepting help, but at the same time, you've been taking care of your mamma and brother." Emma pushed out a sigh and turned toward him. "Don't misunderstand. There's nothing wrong with that." She lowered the pitch of her voice for emphasis. "I admire you."

"You do?" Doubt edged his voice. She realized how very vulnerable Amos's older brother really was.

"*Jah*. You work so hard." Emma contemplated how to word her thoughts to best help him understand where she was coming from. "What a wonderful world we would have if everyone cared about their families the way you do." She hesitated. "But you've got to realize that Amos's situation is different from most."

He gave a firm nod. "That it is."

"It was as if God placed the hardest conflict at your doorstep. He knows you have a lot of self-respect, yet He handed you a situation too big for you to handle by yourself. I think He was testing you, Jonathan. And in the end, you came through with flying colors."

His voice held a combination of doubt and acceptance. "Ya don't know what it means to hear you say that, Emma. But since you overheard our conversation, I can ask you something else."

She allowed him to continue.

"I wonder if Amos actually understood why I opposed the auction. I love my little brother."

"I know you do, Jon."

"And it's important to me that he get why I opposed the fund-raiser. The last thing in the world I want is for him to think that I didn't want his heart fixed." Jonathan harrumphed. "And I admit that, looking back, I didn't make it clear why I felt the way I did. All the while, Amos thought I didn't want him to have the procedure. That wasn't it at all."

He cleared his throat. "I guess I was naïve to believe that funding the procedure was something I could do alone. Or even with the help of the community. But now my eyes are wide open, and I'm not going to argue that paying for this surgery took every donation we got."

He hesitated as the horse slowed its trot to enter Emma's long drive. As he tightened his grip on the reins, he turned to her and smiled. "I suppose you'll be cookin' a big dinner for Christmas."

Emma grinned. "You're welcome to come, Jon. All three of you."

She hesitated, realizing what she'd just said. She softened her voice. "Do you mind if I call you that?"

He grinned. "I suppose we don't have to keep things so formal."

Excitement bubbled in Emma's voice as she thought of her neighbors joining them in celebration. "There will be lots of food—that you can be sure of."

Emma considered her new relationship with Amos's brother. She sat up straighter and lifted her chin a notch. Jonathan had actually confided in her again. And for the first time, she'd called him Jon.

For several moments, she allowed that very realization to sink in. This hardworking man whom she had once believed had no heart, actually had one. And it was the size of the good ol' U.S. of A.

As he helped her out of the carriage, she held on

to his arm for support. Inside, they said good-bye. But while she waved to him from the window, her thoughts lingered on Jon Troyer. As she breathed in the enticing aroma of homemade sponge cakes, she strummed nervous fingers against her thigh.

Emma hung her coat on a hook and removed her sturdy black shoes. Mamma's voice made her turn. "Time to get ready for dinner, honey."

"I'll be right there, Mamma."

As Emma washed her hands, her recent talk with Jonathan replayed in her thoughts. She'd called him Jon. She wasn't sure why. For some reason, it had felt right. And he had approved.

On the outside, he offered a tough façade. There was no doubt that he was difficult to read. But now that she knew him, she was keen to what he was feeling. She still had a strong calling to be with Amos and help him recover physically and emotionally from his upcoming surgery.

But Amos wasn't the only one who needed her attention. It was obvious to her that Jon also needed her. And she was committed to being there for him, too.

Emma proudly displayed the cream-colored platter of iced Christmas cookies in the middle of the Troyer kitchen table. As Jon thanked her, Amos removed the end of the plastic covering and grabbed a morsel, grinning from ear to ear as he skipped out of the room, treat in hand.

He briefly turned back to address Emma. "Thanks, Emmie."

Emma smiled at Jon. "I'll be on my way."

With one swift motion, Jon grabbed his coat from a hook and motioned to the door. His voice was firm. "Not so fast, there. I'm not letting you walk home in this cold weather. It's too dangerous. I can't believe you came all the way over here by foot."

Emma sighed in relief. "A lift home would be appreciated. I'll take you up on the ride."

Inside of the buggy, the warmth from the gas heater caressed her hands and she rubbed them together in delight.

"I hope your mamma feels well for Christmas, Jon."

"Me, too. And I believe she will. She's overjoyed about the surgery. The news definitely lifted her spirits. And good news definitely won't hurt her recovery. At least, with Mom, she doesn't stay sick forever. I'm grateful for that. The virus comes in spurts."

He cleared his throat. "There's something I need to say, Emma."

As the wind rocked the buggy, she waited for him to continue. The air coming in through the door made a light whistling sound.

"The last thing I want to do is to burden you with my problems."

"You're never a burden, Jon."

"I've talked to you a little bit about my relationship with my dad. Since I lost him . . ." He cleared an emotional knot from his throat. "Getting through Christmas hasn't been easy. I try to stay upbeat for Amos. He's just a kid. And I want to make him as happy as I can." He hesitated. "I miss my dad so much, it hurts. He was my best friend in the world. The person I most admired and respected."

He breathed in and gave a shake of his head. "There's no one to talk with about it. Except you."

Emma caught the raw emotion in his voice. Her chest ached for the man next to her. How she wished his daddy were alive. She imagined what a different world it would be for the Troyer family.

"You've helped make this holiday season bearable, Emma."

She breathed in and drew her hand over her chest in surprise. "Oh, Jon, l know how hard it must be. And I'm grateful I can help in a small way. But I know talking about your dad doesn't bring him back. I wish it did. I can't imagine life without my daddy."

A tear slipped down her cheek, and she wiped away the moisture. "God must have a reason for taking your father when He did."

Jon shrugged. "I sure wonder what it is. But I know that only our Lord knows the end result of our lives. There's so much we aren't aware of, we just have to continue to trust Him to guide and protect us. But, Emma . . ." She eyed him with curiosity as he went on. "Sometimes that's not easy. Especially when you hurt inside."

Emma's heartstrings pulled at her with such strong ferocity, her chest ached. "Jon, I'm going to pray every night that that God will continue to give you strength."

He smiled a little. "That's one thing I like about you, Emma."

Her voice was edged with a combination of uncertainty and happiness when she responded. "What's that?"

"You never give up. And your determined spirit

helps me to keep my faith. You inspire me, Emma. I understand why Amos likes having you around."

The thought of the cookie lover prompted a giggle.

"You've brightened his life in a way that only you can do. You've been his sounding board. You've nurtured him in every way imaginable." From her peripheral vision, she caught the roll of his eyes. "And there's no doubt in my mind, Emma, that the kid's been privy to more treats than anyone around, I'm sure."

He laughed, and she joined him.

"Emma, Mom wants to do something special for you once she starts feeling better."

Emma waved a hand and shook her head. "That's not necessary."

"We're both grateful for everything you've done. And there's one thing that we both agree on." He paused. As the horse trotted into her drive, Emma waited for him to go on.

Long moments later, he turned to her and lowered the pitch of his voice. "You'll make a great mother."

CHAPTER 8

Christmas dinner was delicious. The extended family had left. As Emma washed the last dish and ran a towel over the glass, a knock on the door made her stop.

"Mamma, are you expectin' anyone?"

"Not today." The expression on Mamma's face was a combination of amusement and secretiveness.

Emma stepped to the door. As she opened it, a rush of cold air swept in, lifting the arm of her coat on the hook. She locked gazes with Jon.

As she turned to glance at her family, the room had mysteriously emptied.

Emma pressed her lips together thoughtfully.

Jon eyed her. "Aren't you going to ask me in?" He lifted an amused brow. "You did extend an invite."

"I didn't think you were coming. How nice!" Emma put her palms over her mouth and drew in an embarrassed breath. "I'm sorry." An excited giggle escaped her. "It's just that you took me by surprise."

She waved a hand toward the dining room table.

As she glanced back, the room was empty. Where had everyone gone?

"Here." He pulled a beautifully wrapped gift from his oversized pocket. "This is for you."

After she closed the door, he handed her the present. Deep blue ribbon circled bright red foil wrapping and fell apart in circles to form a bow.

He sat down next to her and turned to face her.

For an awkward moment, she glimpsed the gorgeous box. "I . . . I didn't get anything for you."

The corners of his lips seemed to be turned up in a permanent smile.

"Aren't you going to unwrap it?"

She was still happily stunned by Jon's changed disposition. Curious, she lowered her chin to look at the small gift box. The color of the oversized bow took her breath away. She'd never seen such a gorgeous deep shade of blue. It was the hue of pictures she'd seen of the Caribbean.

The pitch of his voice was unusually hesitant. "I hope you like it."

"This is so thoughtful of you, Jonathan. I wonder what it is!"

Heartened by her enthusiasm, he said, "You can guess all day, but you'll never know unless you open it."

She grinned. But her hands stopped as she began to undo the bow. Breathlessness edged her voice as she rolled her eyes with uncertainty. "It's too pretty to touch!"

"Ah, but then you won't know what I made just for you. Aren't you curious?"

Her jaw dropped, and she leaned forward. "You *made* this?"

He offered a proud nod. "I wanted to show my appreciation for everything you've done for my little brother. So I came up with something I knew you would appreciate."

She slid her fingers under the top of the package to take in the deep wood grain of the beautiful cherrywood recipe box. On the very top was a hand-carved letter *E*.

She drew in a surprised breath and eyed the man who obviously waited for a response.

"Emma, you've worked so hard. And I'm thankful."

When their gazes locked, she was quick to note the brisk, nervous tapping of the toe of his black shoe against the shiny oak floor that shone with polish.

She turned the gift and looked it over. "Jonathan, this is absolutely precious. I can't believe you did this especially for me."

He pointed a shaky finger to the hand-engraved *E* in the middle. I wanted to personalize it." He smiled a little. "And I have no doubt that your famous Christmas cookie recipe will be on the very first card."

When she opened the lid, her jaw dropped in pleasant surprise as she glimpsed the star he'd carved into the wood. "Since the stars with blue icing were my little brother's favorites, I thought it only fitting to replicate one."

She laid a gentle hand on the gift and lowered the pitch of her voice to emphasize her gratefulness. "Thank you so much, Jon. I will treasure this and every time I use it, I will think of you, Amos, and the auction. It represents a dream come true."

"Emma, you've helped Amos. And my family." He gave a quick roll of his eyes while he shook his head and grinned mischievously. "I admit I've been a pain throughout the entire process, and I regret it. Now that the fund-raiser's over, I'm grateful Amos will have his procedure."

He tried to clear an emotional knot from his throat, but when he continued, his voice cracked with emotion. "Now that the operation's scheduled and all, I've realized I need to swallow my pride to make sure Amos gets the treatment he desperately needs."

Still absorbing the gift and the change in his demeanor, she eyed him to continue.

"Though I've tried every resource I could get my hands on, I wasn't able to find a way to pay for the surgery on my own. Believe me, I asked God over and over to help so I wouldn't have to accept it. But while I listened to the auctioneer push for ever higher bids, I thought of my father. And I recalled a particular conversation we'd had before he passed away."

"You were at the auction?"

He nodded.

Emma sat very still. She lifted a curious brow as Jonathan shifted in his chair.

Jonathan went on. "I remember it like it happened yesterday. We were talking in the barn. It was while we loaded the stable with fresh straw for the cattle." Jonathan chuckled as his gaze drifted off in space. She knew how close he'd been to his father.

"He was giving me advice for when I became a dad. There were certain things he instilled in us.

One of them was to be a good provider. To do things on our own and never depend on others."

Emma offered an understanding nod. She fully got why he'd been so intent on coming through with the money on his own. She knew Jon had loved his dad more than anything in the world, and Emma was sure that he had attentively heeded his role model's advice.

"We were discussing how a man should lead his family. But something else came up in the dialogue. Something I had forgotten."

Emma curled her fingers around her precious gift. "What was it?"

Jonathan uncrossed his legs. "That family comes first. And nothing's more important than protecting them and making sure they're okay."

He bent his head a notch and looked directly into her eyes. The flecks in his own eyes danced with passion. Mesmerized, she found it hard to look away.

"I've given this a lot of thought, and now I'm sure that this fund-raiser was meant to protect Amos." He closed his lids and pushed out a deep breath. "If I had stopped the auction that was intended solely to benefit my family, how could I ever have forgiven myself? And after a lot of thought and prayers, I'm sure Dad would approve of accepting the donations."

Emma didn't blink. Had she heard him correctly?

"Every moment that my brother is in surgery, I'll thank God for you and everyone who worked so hard to protect the person I love more than anyone in the world." He paused and lowered his gaze. "I'm sorry I didn't show appreciation sooner."

She smiled a little as she considered his change of

heart. Finally, she offered a slow, thoughtful nod of acceptance. "You're forgiven."

He sighed relief. The tenseness in his shoulders seemed to go away.

"I'm glad it worked out the way it did."

He blew out a deep breath and offered an agonizing shake of his head. "I was headstrong, Emma. And I truly regret my stubbornness."

She spoke in a soft, reassuring voice. "It's okay, Jon. The story had a happy ending. And you're only human. And to be honest . . ." She paused, then waved a hand. "Oh, it's nothing."

"Tell me. I've just bared my soul to you."

She decided on a straightforward approach. "I like that about you. I mean, that you're such a fierce protector. Because you stepped right in and led your family when your dad passed away."

He smiled a little and lifted an inquisitive brow.

"It certainly took me by surprise. Although it's not uncommon for an Amish boy my age to take care of a family. But my circumstances weren't exactly by choice—Dad taught me well. It's difficult, though, 'cause I don't have him to lean on now." He gave a quick roll of his eyes to change the subject. "Now I have a question for you."

"Go ahead."

He hesitated and squinted in doubt. "I need your honest answer."

She offered a quick nod. "Sure."

She clutched her hands together, wondering what on earth he could ask that would cause him so much uncertainty.

He tapped the toe of his shoe against the floor again. This time, the pace was much faster. The light coming in from the window made her foiled paper sparkle. "I've asked your parents' permission to court you."

She swallowed. Suddenly she found herself without a response. Was this really happening? Gruff, difficult-to-get-along-with Jon Troyer wanted to *date* her? She tried hard to control her emotions, which were a combination of happiness and great surprise.

He studied her with intense curiosity before looking down, as if trying to decide what to say next. When he lifted his chin, his eyes sparkled with moisture. She was touched.

"You're the kindest, hardest-working woman I've ever met. When I look at you, I see everything that God would like us all to be. You won my brother's heart from the get-go." He softened the pitch of his voice. "And mine."

Emma stood absolutely still. Could she believe what he was telling her?

His voice softened to a hushed whisper. "Would you give me the honor to court you?"

Several long moments passed before the potent, unexpected question completely sank in. When it did, she grinned and a small, excited giggle escaped her throat. "I would love that, Jon."

That evening, the light from the candle on Emma's bed stand flickered as the pleasant scent of vanilla floated through her bedroom. As soon as she opened her lids, Emma propped her pillows against the headboard of her oak bed and sat back into the cushions.

The softness prompted her to relax. As she stretched her legs on top of the quilt that had been made by her mother, she clasped her hands together under her neck and gazed out of the window that overlooked their pasture.

The darkness made it impossible to see what she knew was there—cattle, the huge red barn—but her front-row view of the Milky Way was crystal clear. As the bright moon hovered amidst the constellation of bright stars, a sigh of amazement escaped Emma's lips.

If God could design such a complex pattern in the sky, surely He could fix Amos's heart. While she contemplated the soon-to-be procedure, she scooted down toward the foot of the bed a notch and wiggled her bare toes against the soft, comfy fabric.

Pressing her lips together, she considered God's role in the surgery. It hadn't been mere coincidence that they had raised more than enough money to pay for Amos's surgery, transportation, and lodging. She knew that it was her Lord at His best. Thousands of prayers had made it to the Creator, and He had responded with great enthusiasm.

While Emma mentally prepared herself for all of the steps leading up to the operation, she thought of Amos's recovery. Immediately, her shoulders tensed. The tempo of her pulse stepped up a couple of notches. She moved her hands to her lap, where she interlaced her fingers.

As she considered the fast-approaching operation, she closed her eyes and pushed out a stressful sigh. As soon as she did, she remembered her faith and knew that God would continue to bless them.

A few moments later, she opened her lids, which clung to her pupils. Moisture clouded her vision. But the tears weren't a bad thing; instead, she found them to be a combination of happiness and relief.

She turned onto her left side to take in the beautiful view looming on the other side of her window. The stars and the moon were miles away—she couldn't even begin to imagine the great distance—yet they had been made by the same Creator as she.

That realization caused her jaw to drop. She went on to prop her head with her hand and attempted to make sense of what was so unbelievable, but real.

She recalled her sixteen years, which had been filled with love, Scripture, and blessings, and she silently praised God that she had been brought up in a Christian home. As she took in the perfection and complexity of the constellation above her, she smiled.

How on earth could anyone look up at the sky and not believe in God?

With great care not to burn her arms, Emma pulled a batch of Christmas cookies from the gas oven and smiled in satisfaction. As she set the baking sheet filled with star-shaped desserts on hot pads on the cream-stone countertop, she pushed out a sigh of delight. From the window above the sink, she took in the Troyer home in the distance while her dad cleared the new batch of snow from their front sidewalk.

Icicles hung from the sides of the roof. The family buggy was parked beneath the covered area next to the house.

She eyed the recipe box that Jon had given her yesterday and grinned. She traced her pointer finger over the star that he had so beautifully carved into the polished wooden lid.

Jon wants to court me. As she slid the delicious-smelling morsels onto the paper tray, the unexpected compliments he'd given her replayed in her mind until she gave a shake of her head in happy disbelief.

All the while she had fought to keep the auction alive, he had really wanted it, too. Deep down inside. It was just that accepting money from others had made him feel as though he wasn't following through with his duties as head of the household.

Between Jon's conversation with Amos and their buggy rides, she had gotten to know the man better. And she liked him. In fact . . . She pushed out a happy sigh. She loved the way he made sure she got home safely. She appreciated that he toted her book bag for her.

And now, he had designed this beautiful recipe box especially for her. Her heart warmed as she thought of the time he must have put into it and how he'd personalized it with the letter *E*.

Mamma's voice pulled her from her reverie. Emma startled.

"Didn't mean to scare you."

"It's okay, Mamma."

The expression in her role model's eyes was a combination of amusement and joy. "He seems fond of you. He'll make a good husband, that Troyer boy."

"Mamma!"

"Don't deny that you like him, Emma. And when he asked your father permission to court you . . ."

"What, Mamma?"

Mamma offered a cute roll of her eyes. "It must

have been the sweetest request I've ever heard. He explained how much he respected you and how he'd take good care of you."

Emma lifted a brow. "You and Dad never said a word to me."

Mamma grinned. "That would have spoiled the surprise."

"How long have you known?"

Mamma pressed her lips together before pointing a finger in the air. "The day after the auction. Your dad was outside feeding the livestock, and Jonathan pitched right in to help. They started talkin' about the fund-raiser, and before he left, he came up to the house and approached your father and me about courtin' you."

Emma hadn't seen him there. Of course, she'd most likely been at the Troyers teaching little Amos.

Emma drew her hands over her heart and turned to the soft-spoken woman next to her. "Little Amos has his surgery next week, Mamma." Emma pulled in a satisfied breath. "I can't believe I'm finally getting my wish."

Mamma paused. "Your wish?"

Emma giggled. "*Jah.* I can't wait to see my little boy healthy and running around outside with the other kids. In fact, I want it more than anything."

"You really love him."

Emma nodded. "I'll do everything I can to help him, his mother, and Jonathan prepare for the surgery. I've even offered to do Jon's chores while they are in Minnesota."

Mamma put an affectionate hand on Emma's. A long silence followed while their gazes locked in a mutual respect. "I'm so proud of you, Emma. When I watch you taking care of that little boy, my heart feels good. And someday, when you have your own children, you'll be so warm and loving to them." Mamma lifted her palms and dropped them. "What more could I expect from you?" She paused. "I'm a happy mamma. I've watched you work so hard for all of these donations, and I'm proud you're my girl."

Emma's breath caught in her throat while she considered the meaningful words she'd just heard. Finally, a response came to her. "Mamma, I'm a little embarrassed. I don't need praise for helping with the auction. A lot of people donated their time and money. I just did my part."

Mamma smiled a little. Suddenly, Emma remembered her project and she finished scooping the cookie dough onto the baking sheet.

As she gazed out the kitchen window, she glimpsed Jon feeding his cattle. It was still difficult to digest all that had happened in such a short amount of time. The fund-raiser. Getting enough donations to pay for little Amos's surgery. Jon asking permission to court her.

Emma put the cookie sheet into the oven, closed the door, and removed the protective mitt from her hand. She turned to Mamma and shrugged. "I have everything I could ever want, Mamma. I'm so lucky. I wonder what I've done to deserve such blessings from God."

Mamma began to step away. She turned to wink at Emma. "God rewards the faithful, Emma. And He'll continue to bless you."

LISA JONES BAKER'S
CHRISTMAS COOKIES

When I took my first bite of these cookies, over four decades ago, I knew they were, without a doubt, the best I had ever eaten. The recipe came from my aunt. At the time, I was in 4H and loved to cook. I still do! Over the years, when I visited my sister's family, I would take the ingredients with me and make the cookies at their house. The batch would quickly disappear. Now the cookies are a Christmas tradition. My niece bakes the treats for her boys, and I'm sure this recipe will stay in our family forever.

INGREDIENTS

2¾ cups all-purpose flour
1 teaspoon baking powder
½ teaspoon salt
¾ cup butter
1 cup sugar
2 eggs
1 teaspoon vanilla extract

Preheat oven to 375 degrees F. In a medium bowl, sift together and put aside flour, baking powder, and salt.

In a separate bowl, let the butter soften naturally. Mix in sugar, eggs, and vanilla extract. Once blended, add flour mixture.

After the cookie dough is made, bunch it into a ball, wrap it tightly in waxed paper, and refrigerate for two to three hours. Then, take half the batch, roll it out, and sprinkle lightly with flour so the dough won't stick. Cut into ornament shapes.

Bake on a cookie sheet at 375 F for eight minutes or so. Enjoy!

For icing, I let a stick of butter get to room temperature. When it's soft, stir in enough powdered sugar and milk to make the icing smooth and creamy.

If you enjoyed *The Amish Christmas Kitchen*, be sure to look for the newest collection by the same authors, *An Amish Christmas Candle*, available now!

At the heart of winter's darkness is the joyous glow of the Christmas season. In this love-filled holiday collection, warm yourself with the peaceful light of Plain gifts.

SNOW SHINE ON ICE MOUNTAIN
Kelly Long

When staid Naomi Gish's mischievous father hires strapping Gray Fisher at their candle shop for the season, she's positive the old man has an ulterior motive. She doesn't need help—but as Gray learns the craft of candle making, Naomi learns that love is not only possible, but God's most precious gift.

A HONEYBEE CHRISTMAS
Jennifer Beckstrand

Of all the sacrifices Bitsy Kiem made to raise her three nieces Amish, giving up her Englisch life was the only thing she missed. With the girls married now, she has a chance to kick up her heels this Christmas—unless widowed Yost Weaver can convince her that Plain love is a flame that will never go out.

THE CHRISTMAS CANDLE
Lisa Jones Baker

Blessing those in need at Christmastime is one of Lydia's favorite traditions. But without her newly married sister's help this year, the task seems daunting—until handsome Mennonite John King shows her that hands joined to do good may unite hearts, as well.

Connect with Us

Visit us online at
KensingtonBooks.com
to read more from your favorite authors, see books
by series, view reading group guides, and more.

for sneak peeks, chances to win books and prize packs,
and to share your thoughts with other readers.

facebook.com/kensingtonpublishing
twitter.com/kensingtonbooks

Tell us what you think!

To share your thoughts, submit a review,
or sign up for our eNewsletters, please visit:
KensingtonBooks.com/TellUs.